Eden tried not to panic

Someone was trying to scare her. Was this another carnival initiation? Well, it wasn't going to work. She took a deep breath, threw the latch and jerked the handle. The door didn't budge. She kept trying until the truth hit her. Whoever was out there had jammed the handle.

The walls seemed to be closing in on her as she yelled, "Unlock this door. You're not funny."

The person didn't answer, merely moved about, making sounds Eden couldn't identify. She began banging on the door and yelling.

"Someone help me! I'm locked in the donicker!"

She only heard the weird sound behind her because she stopped to take a deep breath. The sound of liquid dripping from above.

She couldn't see a thing in the dark. She could smell it, though. Sharp. Toxic.

This was no rite of initiation.

Someone meant to kill her.

ABOUT THE AUTHOR

Patricia Rosemoor likes to think just about anyone has the potential to be a hero. That's why she uses ordinary people in her Intrigues. She places them in impossible situations to see how they figure their way out. She also enjoys playing characters against unfamiliar backgrounds, as she does with Eden in *Ticket to Nowhere*. Besides, there's a certain mystique about carny men.... Pat also writes with Linda Sweeney as Lynn Patrick for Harlequin Superromance.

Books by Patricia Rosemoor

HARLEQUIN INTRIGUE

38–DOUBLE IMAGES
55–DANGEROUS ILLUSIONS
74–DEATH SPIRAL
81–CRIMSON HOLIDAY
95–AMBUSHED
113–DO UNTO OTHERS

HARLEQUIN SUPERROMANCE

301–AGAINST ALL ODDS
334–WORKING IT OUT

Books by Lynn Patrick

HARLEQUIN SUPERROMANCE

343–GOOD VIBRATIONS

Ticket to Nowhere

Patricia Rosemoor

Harlequin Books

TORONTO • NEW YORK • LONDON
AMSTERDAM • PARIS • SYDNEY • HAMBURG
STOCKHOLM • ATHENS • TOKYO • MILAN

To the members of the Chicago North Chapter
of Romance Writers of America,
who never fail to challenge my weaknesses
and always complement my strengths.

Harlequin Intrigue edition published September 1989

ISBN 0-373-22121-5

Printed in U.S.A.

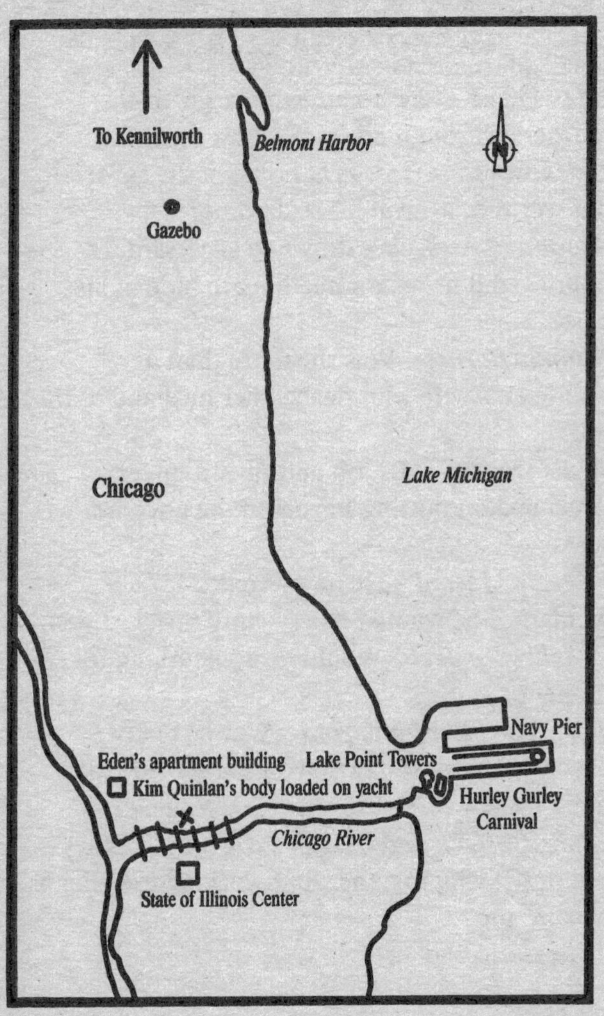
To Kennilworth
Belmont Harbor
Gazebo
Chicago
Lake Michigan
Navy Pier
Eden's apartment building
Lake Point Towers
Kim Quinlan's body loaded on yacht
Hurley Gurley
Carnival
Chicago River
State of Illinois Center

CAST OF CHARACTERS

Eden Payne—She became the target of a murderer through no fault of her own.

Chick Lovett—He was at home in the carnival, but was the carnival his real home?

Stanton Barnes—Wealthy and successful in politics, did he have something to hide in his past?

Rhonda Barnes—Was she more than a politician's wife who pushed her husband to the top?

Wylie Decker—His job and future career depended on putting Barnes in the governor's seat.

"Sheets" Iaconi—He never lacked for a woman, if he wanted one . . . until he met Eden.

"Nickels" Vogel—Would he do anything for money?

Jud "The Stud" Nystrom—Was he really a peacemaker, or did he have a darker side to him?

Giner Tresnick and "Gator" Yost—Were they not only living together, but working together as a team, too?

Chapter One

Numb with exhaustion, Eden Payne slipped her wallet into her jacket pocket, swung her briefcase strap over her shoulder, and traded the Tourism Office for a glass-walled elevator of The State of Illinois Center. Her eyelids drooping wearily over her blue eyes, she stared out at the glass-ceilinged atrium and open floors, and gazed over the partitions into the outer offices. All empty. Not that she expected to find anyone but a maintenance person or security guard around at half past nine on a Friday night.

Eden left the elevator and crossed the lobby, the click of her heels echoing through the building. If she hadn't done this innumerable times, the situation might have given her the creeps. But at this point, even that feeling would have been welcome. Eden was in an odd mood. Mere discontent had regressed to serious boredom. The routine was killing her spirit.

Working late, stuffing reports into her leather case, signing out at the security station—she could tolerate it all, if only her job included a creative outlet to compensate for all the paperwork and responsibility. Somehow her career hadn't gone the way she'd envisioned when she'd chosen to make her own way, rather than accept a life of privilege.

If things didn't change soon, she would go out of her mind.

Outside, the moisture-laden air made her flip up her jacket collar to protect her slick shoulder-length black hair. The September night was miserable, and the rain-washed downtown Loop streets were almost as deserted as the building. A city-smart woman, Eden was always aware of her surroundings. Several vehicles sped by—a couple of cars, a bus going south rather than in her direction. For once damning the high heels she wore out of vanity, Eden hurried toward the River North apartment that she rented with her best friend. On nights like these, taxis were nonexistent, as if swallowed by some perverse god.

Metal screeched overhead as a train moved along the elevated tracks of the city's rapid transit system. Eden cringed when a spray of greasy black water rained down upon her new designer suit. To make things worse, she missed seeing the puddle at the curb that engulfed her Italian leather shoes. The curse that passed her lips would have scandalized her proper mother.

Dampness turned into a steady drizzle, chilling her, haloing the streetlights ahead. As she approached the next intersection, the traffic signal was in her favor. A siren wailed, coming closer. Not about to wait on a corner for the ambulance to pass, she sprinted across Wacker Drive and onto the bridge spanning the Chicago River. As always, rain intensified the smell of fish. She plunged forward and was three-quarters to the other side before she chanced to look over the rail.

Fog rose from the water. To the south, occasional headlights flashed eerily as vehicles swept through the open-sided lower level street that ran under Wacker Drive. And almost directly below her on the north bank, a lanky man in evening clothes furtively waved to someone she couldn't see.

Instinct slowed Eden's stride and made her step closer to the rail. She heard the thrum of a motor. As she stretched for a better look, water dribbled down her back, making her shiver. A yacht bobbed on the river near the retaining wall. She could barely make out the name: *Ambition*.

What was a private boat doing out in this weather?

Frenzied activity from the bank caught her attention. Two hulking men were supporting a young woman in a black evening dress. Her head rolled to one side, her long, curly red hair a flame in the night. She seemed to be unconscious. Drunk? The two men took her aboard the lighted yacht. The fair-haired one removed a padded cover from a long bench seat. The larger, dark-haired man hefted the woman into his arms and threw her into the storage area, as he might a sack of potatoes.

Eden's eyes widened as the padding was replaced and the larger man sat down; the woman's hand stuck out of the box like a broken part on a doll.

"Oh, my God, she must be dead."

Eden had spoken softly, yet a fourth man, who had just joined the others, looked up directly at her, and she knew he had heard. Their eyes locked, and her heart fluttered like a bird beating against its cage. Taking in the middle-aged man's smooth good looks and dark hair winged with silver on both temples, Eden was sure she recognized him.

Impossible.

It couldn't be.

"Hey, Lou... Jack!" the man yelled.

She tried to back away from the railing, but her briefcase had swung through the intricate iron grille and had caught. Eden fumbled with it, but to no avail. Exhaustion was making her clumsy, playing tricks on her, creating illusions. Or so she tried to tell herself. But the man who was pointing up at her and shouting to the others was no figment of her imagination. She'd seen him too many times to be mistaken—not only on television, but in person in the State of Illinois Center. He was Stanton Barnes, current attorney general of Illinois, and the Democratic candidate favored to become the next governor.

By the time his identity had registered with her, so had the danger to herself. Stomach churning, Eden slipped the strap off her shoulder and tugged at her briefcase, but a wrought-iron flower held it fast. Below, the two burly men were bounding off the yacht, their expressions menacing.

"The steps!" Barnes yelled. "Get her and bring her down here!"

The concrete staircase would bring them up to street level mere yards from where she stood. Her palms damp with rain and sweat, she tugged sharply at the leather strap. It broke in her hand. The men were at the foot of the steps now. Valuing herself more than a briefcase, Eden ran. She didn't think the attorney general was extending an invitation to tea. The drama she'd seen hadn't been meant for her eyes.

A quick glance over her shoulder assured her that the men had reached street level. The fair-haired one went to his knees at the rail, while the other hesitated only a second before coming after her in earnest. Good God, what was she to do? This section of the city was practically deserted at night.

Except for a few bars...

That was it. That bar on Kinzie next to the adult book store. What was it called? The guys in there looked like motorcycle gang members or something. Surely she'd be safe there.

Eden flew off the sidewalk and onto the street, dodging a car whose driver blared his horn at her. Without breaking her stride, she looked behind her once more. The dark-haired man was so large that he was slower than she was, even in high heels. She had put some distance between them. But farther back, the second thug was after her now, as well. Fear put speed she didn't know she possessed into her long legs.

Turning west on Kinzie, she headed for a blinking, hot pink neon sign. *Chains*. That was the place.

A couple of men stood in front under the canopy. Despite the chill of the night, neither wore a shirt under his leather vest. Eden whipped past them and their motorcycles and entered the bar. The place was dimly lighted, but not so dark that she didn't realize she was the only woman in the crowded room. Most of the men were dressed in chain-decorated leather, wearing heavy boots and billed motorcycle caps. The bizarre scene might normally have intimidated her, but now wasn't the time to be fainthearted.

Eden elbowed her way to a spot at the bar, and, breathing heavily, told the young man behind it, "I'm in trouble."

He arched a perfect blond brow. "No, you aren't, darling, you've just wandered into the wrong establishment."

"You don't understand!" Eden gasped, suddenly wondering if she'd made a very serious error. "Two men are following me. Two very *dangerous* men."

The customer next to her moved closer, displaying obvious interest. "Hmm. Sounds like they might liven up a dull night."

Blinking at him through wet lashes, she noted the nasty little smile twisting his cruel-looking mouth. *Uh-oh*. She *had* made a mistake. She backed away from the bar.

"Look. I'm desperate," she said, bringing the flat of her hand down onto the bar in a show of bravado. "Where's the telephone?"

"Over there." The bartender nodded to his right.

She was already moving. "Good. I've got to call the police before he finds me."

Another man reached out and clamped a hand over the wall phone. Belligerently he stuck his face into hers. "We don't want police here, so why don't you get lost?"

Eden swallowed hard. "You don't understand. He'll get me for sure, maybe kill me." Her pleas weren't getting her anywhere, so she asked, "Do you have a backdoor?"

"The bathroom," the bartender told her, pointing to a doorway farther along the wall. "A window opens onto the alley."

"Thanks." She couldn't get out of there soon enough.

"And we'll be happy to stall those dangerous men for you," the customer at the bar added. "This place has been pretty dull lately. Right, boys?"

Hearing their snickers, feeling their eyes on her, Eden ran into the bathroom and rushed right through, focusing only on the window—and escape. Luckily the window opened easily.

"Hey, what's going on?" a deep voice queried from a stall, as Eden hitched her skirt practically to her waist and threw a leg over the sill.

Eden didn't answer. She was too busy leaning out and surveying the steep drop to the cobblestone alley. Her stomach took a tumble. Why wasn't she sensible enough to wear sneakers to work like other women? At least the rain had stopped for the moment.

"Hey, you—"

"You never saw me!" she hissed, keeping her back to the man. "And I didn't see you. Okay?" she asked desperately.

"Okay, okay."

Both legs dangling from the ledge, she took a deep breath, slid forward and jumped. On contact, one heel twisted under her and she went down hard, her thigh and derriere smarting as they hit the wet bricks, some of which were broken. The sound of material ripping made her want to scream in frustration, but she didn't have time to indulge herself. If she didn't get the hell out of there, she might never have to worry about anything as mundane as clothing again.

She had to reach her apartment and call the police; only then would she be safe from the murderers.

Murder. The very word made her skin crawl, and she wanted to deny what she had seen. But if the red-haired woman hadn't been the object of foul play, why was she herself a fugitive?

Eden limped out of the alley and zigzagged toward home, ducking into doorways every few minutes to catch her breath and to see if anyone followed. Cars and trucks splashed fine sprays of water from the street as they passed, a bagman made himself comfortable for the evening on the curb, and a few couples entered a local eatery. She saw no one on foot who looked menacing. As she neared her place, three women in sweats got out of a car and headed for the East Bank Club, the ritzy health spa on the next block. No threat there.

Still she remained cautious, fortunately so, for when she came within sight of her apartment house, she spotted the faint glow of a cigarette in the doorway of the building on the other side of the street.

Fear made her heart pound, her throat close, and her feet freeze.

He was waiting for her. Eden was certain she recognized his bulk. She backed into the shadows, never taking her eyes off the doorway. How had he known where...

The briefcase!

It was the fair-haired man who had lingered behind to search her leather case. Good Lord, the identification tag would have given him her name and address, the reports her place of business. All the information had been laid out for him. Ducking around a corner, she ran two blocks to a pay phone on the street. Broken. She took off again. The second time she had more luck. A dial tone. She punched out the emergency number. *9-1-1.*

The police department operator had barely made the connection when Eden demanded, "You've got to help me."

"Are you reporting a crime in progress?"

"Not exactly." Shivering, she looked around uneasily. "It's already been done. These guys are following me. They're going to kill me, too."

"Do these alleged assailants have weapons?"

"How should I know? It's dark. I'm not about to walk up to one of them and ask."

"Then how do you know they want to kill you?"

This conversation wasn't going as Eden had expected. She told herself not to get hysterical. "I saw them carrying a woman's body through the fog. Stanton Barnes was with them." The silence on the other end flustered her. Wasn't she making sense? "I guess Barnes knew I recognized him, because he sent these two men after me. I thought I lost them in the leather bar—"

"Whoa, wait a minute. Is this a crank call?"

"No!"

"Okay, lady, you're at a pay phone at the southwest corner of Grand and Wells. Why don't you identify yourself and give us your address and phone number? Then you can go on home, and I'll send a squad car to your place to take a report."

A chill of apprehension shot through her. The fact that he knew where she was calling from was unnerving. These new computer systems made her feel as though Big Brother was sitting on her shoulder. The receiver slipped in her sweaty palm.

"You don't believe me."

"Your name and address, ma'am," he repeated impatiently.

Concluding that he thought she was nuts, knowing she couldn't go home, and wondering whether Barnes might not have the police in his pocket anyway, Eden hung up.

Now what? She stood on the street, feeling lost and vulnerable. Her roommate Taffy was off on a weekend jaunt with her newest boyfriend, her parents had retired and moved to North Carolina the year before, and her brother was spending a few months working overseas at the London branch of his company. But involving them, or anyone else, might not be a good idea. She was in big trouble. She couldn't put anyone else in danger. So what could she do to help herself? All she'd done so far was react. She needed time to think.

Eden checked her pocket and breathed a sigh of relief. Her wallet was still where she'd put it. Maybe she could get a hotel room for the night. Oh, for a glass of brandy, she thought, and to be able to slip into a tub of hot water....

The sense of relief that poured through her as she stepped away from the phone was short-lived. A man was walking toward her. She checked him out as he passed under a streetlight. Dark-haired, olive-skinned and oddly light-eyed. He had the musculature of a bodybuilder. A bodyguard? Nervously backing away from him, she spotted what she hoped might assist her escape. A bus heading east had just pulled up to a nearby stop. She sprinted to the vehicle, fumbling with her wallet for a dollar bill.

The man ran, too.

Eden clambered on board. The doors closed in the man's face and the bus took off. She blessed the driver, who was clearly determined to keep to his schedule. Eden squeezed through the crowd to the back, never letting her pursuer out of sight. He jogged a ways, as if he thought he might catch the vehicle at the next stop, then gave up and futilely signaled a taxi that sped by. But another bus was only a few blocks behind, Eden noticed. He saw it, too. *Damn!* Either there wasn't a bus to be had, or they were lined up as if part of a parade!

There was nothing she could do other than hang on to the overhead metal bar. A couple of teenage girls stared at her as if she were an oddity, although they were the bizarre ones; dressed in black, wearing colorful makeup and jewelry and sporting wildly gelled hair.

It occurred to her that there was safety in numbers, and she didn't think her pursuer would do anything desperate with a lot of witnesses around. Despite her disheveled appearance, Eden remained poised, as she'd been taught in her youth. "Going to a party?" she asked the teens, who continued to stare.

"The pier," the girl with purple hair said.

"Navy Pier," the other clarified. Her hair was crayon red, with a couple of white streaks around her face. "Septemberfest started yesterday. Black Fungus is playing at midnight," she added. "The music stage is set up in a tent, but I still hope it doesn't start raining again."

"Black Fungus, huh? Well, I'm sure it'll be fun. Maybe I can join you."

As Eden's idea blossomed, the girls gave each other horrified looks. The festival meant music stages, booths selling food and crafts and a carnival. Best of all, it meant people. Hundreds of thousands of people, if the weather hadn't wet their spirits. She looked back at the second bus, which was barely a block behind them. If she got off anywhere along the route, the man would be sure to spot her and get off also. But if she rode to the end of the line, which was less than a mile away, she could lose herself in that crowd.

For the first time since she'd left her office, Eden allowed herself to relax. She was soaked to the skin, covered with filth and her clothes were ruined, but she was going to be all right. She would lose her pursuer and figure a way out of this mess.

And never—*never*—would she again be dissatisfied with her life. Boredom was looking just as inviting as the brightly lighted carnival ahead.

ENJOYING THE SOUNDS that filled him with nostalgia—food vendors hawking their wares, jointees working their marks, music and screams coming from the rides—Chick Lovett leaned forward over the counter and grinned at the teenage couple about to pass him. The guy was a jock, his broad shoulders encased in a letter man's jacket that identified him as a high school student from a ritzy suburb. The petite girl at his side might be a cheerleader. Chick tossed a softball into the air and winked at her as he caught it.

"Hey, blondie, want to win a stuffed animal for your boyfriend? All you have to do is knock down three milk bottles." He indicated the shelf behind him, where four stacks of bottles stood evenly spaced—each with two on the bottom and a third on top.

The girl giggled. "I've never been very good at sports." But she stopped and watched him with interest.

"Wouldn't you like to have one of these?" Chick grabbed a plush cat from the display shelf in front of the game and held it out toward her.

"Ooh! A snow leopard." The girl pulled her date toward the booth and inspected the potential prize. "What about it, Brian? Do you think you can win this for me?"

The boyfriend showed off a little by flexing his throwing arm. "No sweat, Sheila." He looked at Chick. "How much?"

"A buck a throw."

"That's kind of expensive."

"But the cat is worth fifteen." And from Brian's clothes, Chick judged the kid could easily afford to pay double that—if he hadn't already blown all his money. "You look like a sports freak, so this should be a cinch. No sweat, right?" He got into the patter that every carny worth his salt could mouth in his sleep. "Besides, what's a couple of bucks to make your girl smile?"

"Please, Brian?" the blonde asked hopefully.

"All right."

The guy pulled out a five-dollar bill. Chick exchanged it for a softball. The kid got five tries, but each time he succeeded in knocking down one of the bottom bottles as well as the top, while leaving the third wobbling. And each time Chick carefully reset the trio.

"Not quite as easy as it looks, is it, pal?" he asked. "Better luck next time."

"Wait a minute." Brian was already searching his pockets. "I know I've got a few more dollars somewhere."

Chick frowned. He didn't really want to take the kid to the cleaners, but if he refused the money, Brian would make a stink, someone would hear and get suspicious. So despite his reservations he took another four dollars—two bills, the rest in quarters and dimes. He set the bottles even more carefully, this time hoping to give the kid an edge.

But Brian's first throw popped only two bottles onto their sides.

"C'mon, kid, I can't do you better," Chick muttered to himself as he reset them. To Brian he said, "I get the feeling your luck's about to change. Try again."

"Yeah, c'mon, Brian," Sheila added encouragingly. "I know you can do it."

The next shot was a winner. All three bottles fell. Sheila squealed and threw her arms around her boyfriend's neck before looking to claim her prize. Chick handed her the cat and held out two dollars to Brian.

"What's that for?" the kid asked. "I've got two more throws. Maybe I can win another stuffed animal."

"You've got your prize. Be satisfied." Chick offered the money once more. "Take the refund, pal, but keep this to yourself. I don't want anyone around here to think I'm soft."

Brian grinned and took the money. "Thanks." Then he put his arm around the blonde and waltzed her across the carnival grounds.

Chick was scanning the crowd for another promising mark, when Maisie Washington surprised him by appearing and leaning on the counter. She shook her head so hard that her shiny black ringlets danced around her dark face.

"Mmm-hmm. I overheard that conversation. It's already a slow night, baby. Between the prize and the refund, you just gave away every cent of your profit and then some. Keep that up and you'll be broke in no time."

If he had been the typical jointee, she would be right. Chick appreciated the good-hearted woman's concern, especially since she'd only known him for a few days. Maisie and her husband, Felix, ran the game booth next to Chick's. Theirs was a hanky-pank, the kind of joint that catered to Mom and the kids.

"I'll make the money up tomorrow," Chick assured her. "I've always had a soft spot for little blondes."

His attention wandered as he noticed a bedraggled woman who stood out from the small crowd of teenagers opposite him. The lady was tall, dark-haired, had elegant lines—and looked as if she'd been mud wrestling.

Maisie poked him to get his attention. "I'm getting a couple of dogs for me and Felix. You hungry?"

"Not right now, Maisie."

"You sure? You can owe me."

"Thanks for the offer, but I had a late supper."

"If you say so."

Maisie took off for the hot dog stand, her full hips swinging and straining the straight, hot pink skirt she wore with a purple knit top. Wolf whistles from the crowd followed her. Maisie tossed her head and smiled, as if acknowledging her due. Carnies were just as much a colorful bunch of characters as ever, Chick thought.

Not to mention the customers.

He searched the crowd for the lady mud wrestler. She had disappeared. No—she was waiting in line for a ticket to the Tilt-a-Whirl. She appeared out of place. And frightened. Her stance was self-protective, and she was looking around almost furtively.

Then her attention focused on something that made her frown. Chick saw she was staring at a small, carrot-topped boy of five or six who stood alone in the midway, his face puckered, tears rolling down his chubby freckled cheeks. With seeming reluctance, the woman stepped out of line and approached the child. She stooped and spoke to him for a moment, then helped him dry his tears. The next thing Chick knew, they were hand in hand, walking straight toward him. He stuck a toothpick between his teeth.

"Excuse me," the woman said, quickly glancing over her shoulder before stopping at the counter. "But Jimmy here lost his older sister and her friends."

The blue eyes meeting his were shadowed, so Chick couldn't read the woman's thoughts. Her voice was low, her speech precise. Cultured. And despite her disheveled appearance, he realized that the lady was wearing expensive clothes. He rolled the toothpick to one corner of his mouth. "Are *you* all right?"

"Yes." She answered too quickly, glancing behind and all around them. "I'm fine. Jimmy's the one with the problem. Can you help him find his sister?"

"There are a half dozen policemen wandering around—"

"No police!"

Her eyes widened, and in them Chick now recognized fear. His brow furrowed, and he was about to demand an explanation, but she didn't give him the chance to question her.

"I mean, you must have a loudspeaker system or something, right?" she asked.

"We have a Lost and Found by the front gate."

"This is a child we're talking about, not an article of clothing."

"I wan' Laura!" Jimmy shouted, then burst into sobs that racked his little chest. "I wanna go home."

The woman dropped to her knees and tried to comfort the boy. She stroked his carrot top and lifted his chin. "Shh. You're going to be fine. We'll find your sister, and she'll take you home." She glared up at Chick, anger burning away the other emotions he'd seen reflected in her finely boned face. "Well?"

Startled, Chick looked away from her and was lucky enough to spot Abe's shock of white hair and mustache. He and Zelda had been making their rounds down the midway together. They'd stopped to talk to the ride jock at the Tilt-a-Whirl. Chick waved the older couple over.

"Abe and Zelda Hurley own the Hurley-Gurley Carnival," he explained. "We couldn't put the kid in better hands."

Rising to her feet, the woman sighed, sounding relieved. "Thank goodness."

As the couple approached the booth, Zelda let go of her husband's arm. Her odd, almost translucent gray eyes went straight to the child. "What have we here? You wouldn't be lost, would you?"

"How'd you know?"

Jimmy stared up at her in awe and looked as though he was thinking about crying again. With her white-streaked black hair, overly made-up face and gaudy costume bagging around a short, plump body, Zelda did appear a little weird. But as Chick knew from personal experience, she was the soul of kindness.

"This is Madam Zelda," he told the boy. "She's a real fortune-teller. Maybe she can tell yours, while you're waiting for your sister at the Lost and Found. What do you say?"

"Why, he'll say yes, won't you, Jimmy?" Zelda held out a wrinkled hand. Her fingers were covered with jeweled rings, her wrist with dangling bracelets that made a delightful sound when they jingled. "All little boys like to have their fortunes told."

"Go with her," Abe urged. "You don't have to be afraid."

Jimmy trustingly slipped his hand into that of the elderly woman. "Okay."

"You'll have to tell me what your sister looks like and what she's wearing," Zelda said. "Then we can send some people to look for her."

Together they made their way toward the booth near the entrance. Chick watched for a moment, then turned to speak to the younger woman. "She's gone." He searched the surrounding area, even checked the line at the Tilt-a-Whirl, but this time she'd disappeared for real.

Abe looked around as well. "She who?" he asked Chick.

"The woman who found the lost kid."

The older man shrugged. "Maybe someone was waiting for her."

"Yeah, maybe."

Or maybe she'd had a reason to do her disappearing act, Chick thought. Something had definitely been awry with her.

"So how's it going?" Abe asked.

"Huh? Oh, great."

The owner of the Hurley-Gurley lowered his voice. "Anyone suspect you're not a regular on the circuit?"

"I don't think so. Our secret's safe."

Abe smiled. "Good." He clapped Chick on the shoulder. "It's just like old times."

Not quite, Chick thought, but he didn't want to spoil the old man's illusions. Abe left him to business, just as three guys stopped at the booth. Each one took a half-dozen turns, while his companions made smart remarks to unnerve the thrower. Though they'd had a little too much to drink, the guys were good-natured about losing and went on without a problem. An older couple was next. And then a bunch of teenage girls, who seemed more interested in Chick himself than in winning a game. He bantered with them for a while, but turned down their invitation to party when the carnival closed for the night.

All the while he worked, he was distracted and kept searching the crowd for the stranger. Instinct told him she was in trouble—not that it was any of his business. A carny saw all kinds of crazy goings-on.

But for some inexplicable reason, Chick couldn't help wanting to know what was going on with his mystery woman.

SHE'D SPOTTED the man in the crowd....

Taking a shaky breath, Eden leaned against one of the carnival trucks at the end of the lot opposite the front gate. She told herself the dark-haired thug hadn't seen her before she had slipped away from the game booth, but that self-assurance neither stopped her pulse from racing nor made her stomach settle down.

The carnival itself was situated on dry land, but she was facing the rest of the festival, which was set up on the south side of Navy Pier, the twin buildings that stretched for a mile over the lake. Above, the sky was clearing and the moon played hide-and-seek among the banks of clouds. Waves washed around the pilings under the pier and brushed the nearby shore. Their rhythmic sound was blotted out by the noise of the carnival that mixed with music from the nearest sound stage.

Black Fungus?

Eden laughed softly, feeling safe in her temporary refuge. She had no desire to return to the carnival before she was sure her pursuer was gone. No energy. Now that her adrenaline was crashing, she was ready to drop. If only she could find a comfortable place to rest until the festival closed down for the night.

The truck's cab, she thought. Maybe it was unlocked.

Eden tried the handle. The door opened. *Thank God.* She could rest, just for a while. When the grounds quieted, she would leave. Climbing in, she curled up on the passenger seat and listened to the odd sounds around her. Every set of footsteps that came too near made her heart lurch. She slid to the floor of the cab and rested her head on the cushioned seat. After what seemed like hours, the sounds blurred and her eyes closed....

SHE WAS RUNNING AGAIN. Terrified. Her heart thumped so hard that she felt as if the organ would burst through her chest. They were following her. All of them. Stanton Barnes. The two thugs. The lanky man who had directed them onto the boat. Her feet ached. Legs burned. She could hardly breathe. A door loomed ahead. Escape. A hiding place. She grabbed the handle and turned. From the opening, a spill of red hair fell and draped over her hand. And then a woman's lifeless body fell against her. She screamed—

"A-A-H!"

Eden sat up fast and hit her head against something hard. She was confused. Disoriented. Trying to focus on her surroundings. A large dashboard and steering wheel. Pale skies. Daylight. A face. Chestnut hair mussed over hazel eyes.

The man from the game booth was leaning over her. His startled expression mirrored her own sense of shock.

"Well, if it isn't the lady mud wrestler," he said. "I wondered where you'd disappeared to. Now how about answering another question before I call the cops—what the hell are you doing in here, anyway?"

Chapter Two

"I must have fallen asleep."

The woman scrambled up into the passenger seat and made as if to leave immediately. Chick stood in the open doorway as she pressed futilely against his raised arm.

"Whoa. Not so fast, Toots. Why did you climb into the cab in the first place?"

Between the smudges of dirt, pink shone from her cheeks. She backed off as if embarrassed, yet her steady gaze and tone were not in the least conciliatory.

"I was tired and needed a place to rest," she said in that low, cultured voice that he'd taken note of the night before. "I didn't mean any harm, and I didn't steal anything."

He could see the pulse throb in her long neck above what had once been a clean, feminine white blouse. Now the delicate material was soiled and torn, ripped apart like the very fabric of her life, if his instincts were on target. But why? What had happened to her before she'd sought refuge on the carnival grounds?

He didn't think she was going to be open about her problems, so he probed in a roundabout manner. "Most people go home when they're tired."

"I can't!" She shifted her eyes away from his. "I mean I don't have a home to go to."

More than likely the first was the case. For whatever reason, she was in trouble and *couldn't* go home.

Chick took a better look at her. Her hair was a mess, but it was thick and shiny, obviously well taken care of. Though her clothes were ripped and as dirt-streaked as her face, they whispered money. The pale blue suit wasn't exactly conservative, yet the outfit gave him the impression that she was a career woman. The impractical high heels told him that she was also a bit vain.

"So, you're a bag lady?" he asked, forcing himself not to smile. Her situation was obviously serious, and he was certain that she wouldn't appreciate being the object of his amusement.

"Not exactly... but, uh... something like that."

"You can't have it both ways," Chick told her. "What did you say your name was?"

Ignoring the question, she tried again to leave and jostled Chick's arm. When he continued to restrain her, she tried to slip below the barrier. He shifted his body so that he blocked her way, and she backed off once more. A feeling he couldn't quite explain made him refuse to give way. His stubbornness had nothing to do with her looks, which were quite ordinary except for her height and elegance of line. Despite her bravura, she was frightened, and her rising anxiety stirred a protective instinct he hadn't known he possessed.

"Please..."

The word was both demand and appeal, but he didn't budge.

"What's the hurry?"

"I'm in your way," she said, wrapping her arms around her chest in a defensive manner. "And I'm sure you have work to do."

"Not really. It's too early." Not wanting her to leave yet and prompted by impulse, Chick said, "Speaking of work, you wouldn't be in the market, would you?"

"Pardon me?"

"For a job. You seem down on your luck, fallen on hard times."

"How perceptive of you." Sarcasm laced her words. "You're offering me a job?"

"I could use an assistant."

She frowned. "I don't know anything about carnivals."

"You could learn. One-Ball's an easy game. And the nice thing about working with other carnies is that they don't care about your past. Most of them have things they don't care to talk about."

He watched her face. She was thinking about it. But why? What had happened the day before to make this woman so desperate that she might agree to a job that paid peanuts?

"I was about to get some breakfast," Chick said when she didn't answer. "You wouldn't want to join me?" He could tell she was hungry, that both offers—food and the job—tempted her, yet she didn't jump to agree to either. He gave her his most convincing smile and went on in a coaxing manner. "I haven't tried Maisie's cooking yet, but she assures me her husband's never gotten sick on it."

"She didn't invite me."

"You're my new assistant. That makes you family, so to speak."

She raised her chin defiantly. "And I didn't agree to work for you."

"Then agree, and you'll have food to eat and a place to sleep tonight. I don't get the feeling you have too many options at the moment." He moved out of the door opening, giving her the chance to escape, if she still chose to do so. "Or am I wrong?"

The defiance visibly drained away, and she shook her head. "I could use a place to... to stay."

He was sure she'd been about to say hide. "The name's Chick Lovett." He held out his hand. Warily she took it. Hers was not a weak clasp. He liked the solid feel of her handshake. Still, she didn't offer her name. "Am I going to have to call you Toots?"

"Eden."

"Is that your first name or your last?"

Ignoring the question, she stepped down out of the truck cab. "So where do we get breakfast?"

Chick closed the door and threw out one arm toward the small, old-fashioned silver trailer that Maisie and Felix called home. "This way, Eden Eden."

She gave him a swift look, and he could have sworn he caught the beginnings of a smile curving her full mouth. But before he could be certain, she marched off in front of him, giving him a clear view of her long legs, which were exposed almost to the thigh by her ripped skirt seam. He restrained himself from whistling. Eden would probably appreciate that even less than his attempt at humor. She was a real class act.

As he followed her, Chick wondered why he was bothering with the woman. He could have let her go as she'd asked, but she'd aroused his curiosity—as well as other instincts. Eden might be good at evasion, but Chick figured he could go her one better—and worm the truth out of her at the same time.

EDEN WASN'T SURE why she'd allowed herself to be talked into taking a job as Chick Lovett's assistant. After all, she wasn't exactly down-and-out, even if she was in hiding. But where would she go? At least working at the carnival would give her a cover until she could figure out what to do.

Now all she had to do was keep her new boss at a distance. Although he hadn't pressed her too closely for the truth, she sensed Chick was biding his time. He had a way about him . . . that she couldn't deny. And right now he was sitting so close that he might as well be in her pocket. She would have protested if there had been room to move, but there wasn't, so she sat in uncomfortable silence.

"Here ya go, baby." Maisie set a plate stacked high with pancakes in front of her. "This'll get rid of that hollow feeling."

Eden inhaled and her mouth watered. "Thanks. These smell delicious."

Felix winked at her from across the table. "Wait till you taste those. My woman knows how to keep her man happy with her cooking . . . among other things."

Maisie waved a spatula at him. "You hush now."

Eden smiled at these kind people, who were so gladly sharing their breakfast table with a complete stranger. They left no doubt in her mind that they were madly in love with each other and happy, despite their less than ideal circumstances. While the place was homey and cheerful inside—due, no doubt, to Maisie's colorful touch, if her chartreuse knit dress was any indication—the rooms were tiny. The trailer itself was probably older than Eden herself. And although Felix looked dapper in his neatly pressed three-piece suit and with a fresh flower in his lapel, the clothes had seen better days—long, *long* ago.

"The first thing we have to do, before I show you around the midway," Chick said, reminding her of her own situation as he paused to take another full plate from Maisie, "is get you cleaned up."

Eden felt herself cringe at the reminder of her appearance. She'd already washed her hands and face and smoothed her hair as best she could. His assessing gaze embarrassed her, and she felt herself flush.

"Eden can take a shower here," Maisie said, slipping into the seat next to her husband. "And I've got a few things I don't wear anymore."

"No, I couldn't." Despite her full mouth, Eden felt obliged to protest. "If you have a needle and thread—"

"Now don't be silly," Felix interrupted. "My Maisie is still an extraordinarily beautiful woman, but she has filled out in all the right places over the past few years. She has some things that don't fit her, and they're just taking up precious storage room."

"Someone might as well make use of them." The other woman reached over the table and patted Eden's arm. "I'm always saying I'm going to lose weight and fit into all my old clothes again, but I might as well stop trying to fool myself."

"Well, if you're sure... all right. Thank you again."

Eden frowned down at her plate as she cut into the stack of pancakes. She should offer to pay for the clothes. She had some cash in her wallet, and the couple could certainly use it. But then they would really wonder why she was willing to work at a carnival. So far they hadn't asked. As Chick had intimated earlier, other carnies didn't ask too many questions. She'd make it up to the Washingtons when she was free to leave, which she hoped would be soon. Maybe even that evening, if she could figure out whom to approach with her story.

A knock at the door startled her, and she jumped.

"Easy, baby," Maisie said, giving her a curious look. "Door's open!" she shouted. "Come on in."

A tall, broad-shouldered man in his early thirties entered, carrying a stack of newspapers. With golden-blond hair and green eyes that accentuated the handsomeness of his face, he was a real hunk. He gave Eden a thorough once-over, saying, "Here's your paper, Felix."

The dapper man took his copy of the Chicago *Tribune*. "Eden, this is Jud Nystrom. Jud, Eden is going to be Chick's new assistant."

"Lucky Chick."

"Have any room for my pancakes?" Maisie asked.

"No, ma'am. I just had breakfast. But I'll take a rain check on that offer." His eyes filled with curiosity, they swept over Eden again as he backed out of the trailer. "See you all later."

For some reason, though his scrutiny had been every bit as thorough as Chick's, Jud hadn't made her as uncomfortable, Eden reflected. "Another jointee?" she asked.

"Jud's a patch," Chick said. "Some of the jointees pay him to patch up disputes with customers to keep the police from being involved. From what I've seen, he's good at what he does."

"The best." Felix swallowed a mouthful of food. "He's a born peacemaker."

"Are there a lot of problems that need to be settled?" Eden inquired.

Felix shook his head. "Not too many. Abe runs a clean operation. That's why the carnies call him Honest Abe." When Eden laughed, he added, "Most of the men who've been around the circuit have nicknames."

"Like what?"

"I'm known as Felix the Black Cat."

"Then there's Nickles Vogel," Maisie added. "Short for Nicholas. Gator Yost from Florida got an alligator tattooed on his arm. The guy you just met—he's Jud the Stud," she said in a deep, sexy tone. "Another ladies' man is Sheets Iaconi. I'll leave that explanation to your imagination."

SWEET PROMISE

Erica was starved for love. Daughter of a Texas millionaire who had time only for business, she'd thought up a desperate scheme to get her father's attention.

Unfortunately her plan backfired and she found herself seriously involved with Rafael de la Torres, a man she believed to be a worthless fortune hunter.

That had been a year ago; the affair had almost ruined her life. Now she was in love with a wonderful man. But she wasn't free to marry him. First of all she must find Rafael . . .!

Printed in U.S.A.

Amused, Eden turned to Chick. "What about you? Is Chick your nickname?"

He grinned. "Short for Chickie-Loves-It."

"Loves what?" The words were out of her mouth before she could stop them. Her breakfast companions' laughter made her flush. "Oh." She decided to concentrate on her pancakes.

No doubt Chick Lovett had all the women he could handle. He really was good-looking, if in a less ostentatious way than Jud the Stud. Shorter than the golden-haired giant, he was nonetheless lean and well muscled. And he exuded both masculine charm and a blatant sexuality that a less perceptive woman might easily fall prey to. Even the tiny scar on his chin was attractive.

Across the table, Felix unfolded the paper and scanned the front page. "Think this Stanton Barnes guy has a shot at the governor's seat?"

In the middle of swallowing a mouthful of food, Eden almost choked.

"You okay, baby?"

All eyes were on her. She took a sip of coffee. "I'm fine. Just swallowed wrong." She knew she should leave it at that, but she had to ask. "Barnes is in the news again?"

"Right here on the front page." Felix was mumbling to himself. "The Republicans have run this state for too many years. Barnes seems like a man who could do anything—even pull off a statewide victory for the Democrats."

Maybe he could even commit murder.

The thought had just popped into her mind—and stayed there. Eden told herself she didn't know that he was responsible for whatever had happened to the redhead. She couldn't even be sure the woman was dead. Her own exhaustion could have amplified everything she'd experienced the night before. Maybe she wasn't in danger at all.

But remembering the dark-haired thug who'd chased her, Eden realized that she was guilty of wishful thinking. Suddenly her appetite was gone; she let her fork fall.

"Something wrong?" Chick asked, glancing at her plate, which was only half empty.

"I'm full. Maybe I can take that shower, while the rest of you finish eating."

"You go ahead." Maisie indicated the back of the trailer with her fork. "The bathroom's right off the bedroom. Soap and shampoo's already in the shower. I'll get you clean clothes, soon as I finish here."

"I'm sorry. I didn't mean to hurry you. I can wait."

"Don't make no nevermind. Go on."

In the narrow confines of the eating area, Eden had to brush against Chick when he rose to let her out. They were so close that they might have been dancing. She freed herself and noted that he followed her every movement with unconcealed interest. Self-conscious again, she made her way to the tiny bathroom, which was on the same scale as the rest of the trailer. She didn't mind. The secluded area offered her a hiding place, an escape from the questions no one was asking—at least not outright.

While undressing, she bumped her head for the second time that morning. Her vision blurred for a moment, and her clothes hit the floor. She managed to pick them up without opening the door for more room, then hung the ruined suit and blouse on a hook and stepped into the shower. The hot water felt wonderful as it beat upon her neck and back. She worked shampoo into her hair and carefully massaged first her scalp, then her neck to rid herself of rising tension. Her plight wasn't hopeless. The police would help her. The night before, fear had made her panic.

Rather than calling a general emergency number, she would contact someone in authority and calmly explain what had happened. But whom? Maybe Dennis would know. She was still friendly with her ex-fiancé, a lawyer who had recently entered the political arena himself. Surely he would help her out of this mess. She would call him as soon as she could...after she checked out the story on Stanton Barnes in the morning newspaper. Knowing her adversary was of prime importance—of that Eden was sure.

She had just stepped out of the shower when a knock came at the door.

"You ready for those clothes?" Maisie asked.

"Perfect timing." She opened the door a crack and took the offering. "I'll be out in a minute."

"No hurry. Chick went to tell Abe and Zelda about you. Felix and I are gonna take a walk down by the lake. We'll be back in half an hour. If you leave before then, just close the door behind you."

"Thanks, Maisie. You've been so kind."

"Just one of God's children, baby. The good Lord tells us to help each other when we can. By the way, clean towels are under the sink, and you'll find a comb, blow-dryer and makeup in the drawer."

With that, Maisie left. Eden found the towel and dried herself. The short purple skirt and a long-sleeved, low-necked yellow satin blouse fitted her almost perfectly, though she wasn't altogether comfortable in the skimpy garments. Not that she had a choice. She used the dryer, which made her hair fluff out wildly, and then applied purple liner and purple and gold eye shadow.

Having been in the drama club both in high school and college, Eden felt as if she were getting ready for another opening night. The figure staring back at her from the mirror looked only vaguely familiar. A character in a play. The only problem was, she didn't know her lines. She would have to improvise....

Ready or not, she went in search of the newspaper that Felix had left on the table. She found and unfolded the lead section. The front page made her stomach turn. Side by side were two stories with pictures—one about Barnes, the other about a dead woman.

Eden had no trouble recognizing the person who'd been found floating in the Chicago River in the small hours of the morning. The redhead she'd seen carried onto the boat was identified as Kim Quinlan, model. A thin abrasion marked her neck. The cause of death was as yet undetermined.

She studied the larger photo, taken the night before at a fund-raiser for Barnes's campaign, held at the Hotel River View. That was barely a block from where she'd seen the man. Barnes and his wife Rhonda were flanked by three other Democrats, one of whom was the man who'd been standing on the bank. The caption identified him as Wylie Decker, Barnes's campaign manager. The other two were staunch supporters—the mayor and the police commissioner.

Trembling, feeling as if she'd taken a blow in the solar plexus, Eden fell into a chair. The logical plans she'd made in the shower had just gone up in smoke. Not only did Barnes have an airtight alibi—hundreds of people had been present at the event—but he had a solid connection with the city police as well as with the state attorney's office which, as attorney general, was under his direct jurisdiction.

The implications were frightening. No one would believe her story.

What was she going to do?

She couldn't go home and resume her life as if nothing had happened, yet she couldn't take the chance of going to the police. Maybe she could go to one of the newspapers with the story. No, she couldn't do that, either, at least not without some kind of proof that she wasn't a lunatic. The need to gather such evidence was overwhelming.

Not only would she have to find a connection between the young woman and Barnes; she would have to find a motive for murder, as well.

HIS WIFE and campaign manager keeping vigil with him, Stanton Barnes paced the length of his living room as though his Gold Coast town house were a prison. The analogy made him shudder.

"Will you sit down!" Rhonda demanded through clenched teeth. "You're making me crazy."

He sank onto the couch next to his wife, who was diving into a box of Godiva chocolates. His stomach turned as she popped a truffle into her mouth. It was only nine in the morning, for God's sake. They'd been up all night, and hadn't had more than a cup of coffee for breakfast.

"*You're* going crazy? How the hell do you think *I* feel?" he asked her.

"I'm sure you'll tell me. Again." She selected another piece and studied the candy intently, while her canary diamond ring winked at him. "You do go on and on, my pet. But what else can I expect from a bloody politician?"

"Don't give me all the credit for—"

"Calm down, both of you." Wylie Decker uncrossed his legs and adjusted his lanky body in the wing chair. He picked up his cup of coffee, took a sip and smacked his lips contentedly.

His campaign manager's seeming nonchalance irritated Barnes almost as much as his wife's shrewishness. "My future is at stake here," he growled.

"*All* our futures are," Decker stated as the front door opened. "Since we're all in this together."

Before his manager finished, Barnes was out of his seat. He met Jack Tanner at the entrance to the living room. "Well, did you get her?"

The bodyguard shook his blond head. "The Payne woman didn't show at her place. Lou relieved me."

Barnes already knew that the other man had chased the witness down to the pier and had lost her in the crowd. "Damn! What kind of incompetents have I hired? Two supposed professionals against one inexperienced woman, and she gives you both the slip. Who knows where she could be...or who she could have blabbed to?"

"My God, if she went to the police, we're finished!" Rhonda shrieked, a dribble of chocolate trickling from one corner of her mouth.

Revolted, Barnes turned away from her. "Not necessarily."

Despite her excesses involving gourmet food, expensive jewelry and secret excursions into the seamier parts of the city, his wife had always been a great asset to him. But lately he'd been thinking of her more and more as a potential liability. He liked his life neat and tidy, with no loose ends. If only she weren't so important to his campaign...

"I am not without influential friends who could be convinced that hers are the ravings of a lunatic," he went on, facing Rhonda once more. "Besides, who is to say the Payne woman recognized me?"

"Your very recognizable face is plastered on the front page of both newspapers, my pet. We can't even take the chance of little Miss Payne starting a scandal, no matter if anyone believes her."

Barnes was afraid it might already be too late to stop the only witness from talking, but he didn't say so. He didn't need to start his volatile wife on a harangue.

Decker rose from the wing chair. "Why don't the two of you get some rest? We have a press conference this afternoon. I'll take care of this . . . unpleasantness."

"Good idea," Barnes said.

Unpleasantness. Yes, that was all this was, Barnes assured himself as he headed into the hall and up the circular staircase that led to the master bedroom. He didn't look back to see if Rhonda was following. The problem would soon be taken care of in the most expedient way. Decker could handle whatever she could dish out. Decker could handle anything. He'd proven that the night before.

Barnes reached the landing and turned toward his private sanctuary, reminding himself that he was still on his way up. What had happened with Kim Quinlan had been an inconvenience. Nothing and no one would stop him from reaching the top.

WANTING some fresh air, and growing tired of waiting for Chick to come and get her, Eden left the trailer to find him. She wandered about the carnival grounds, which were hushed compared to the night before. The area was just awakening, employees wandering around and socializing or getting ready for the new workday. Some were setting up their wares, while others checked the mechanics of their rides. Happy laughter floated toward her, making her feel better than she had since she'd left her own work the night before.

Mixed feelings warred within her. She hated being a fugitive, yet she was looking forward to learning more about carnival life.

"How much did the thief get?"

Startled, Eden stopped for a moment. The voice belonged to Chick. She circled to her left as another man's voice answered.

"Five, maybe six hundred. Frankie's upset. Now he won't have enough to pay his rent this week or next."

"Abe'll let him ride," a woman said. "He knows Frankie's good for it. Right, Gator?"

"Yeah," the man agreed, "but that kind of money isn't exactly peanuts. C'mon, Ginger, you know what that means at this time of the year. Poor Frankie. This is the second time he's been hit. I only hope he can find a sucker job real quick when the carnival goes into winter quarters."

Eden frowned. The fact that several hundred dollars meant so much to one of these people was depressing, when she compared their financial state to her own. She thought nothing of spending that much money on a single shopping spree, though she couldn't afford to indulge herself as often as she used to, when she'd lived on an allowance from her father.

"Have there been a lot of robberies?" Chick asked.

"One maybe every few weeks since the season started," Gator was saying as Eden turned the corner of the game booth.

"I only hope the creep doesn't hit us." The woman named Ginger hugged her thin arms around her near-emaciated body. A cigarette in her hand burned, its lighted tip carrying an inch of ash. "We can hardly afford to feed the kids, as it is."

Eden got the feeling that Chick was about to question them further when he spotted her. He did a double take, and his brows rose. Then he inspected her slowly from the roots of her flyaway hair to her long, exposed legs. She felt self-conscious—and at the same time flattered by his lazy grin. It made him appear downright irresistible. A man hadn't looked at her in quite that way in some time. Maybe she'd have to get out of business suits and into creative wear more often.

"Who's the babe?" Gator asked.

The man was staring rudely at Eden. Almost as thin as Ginger, he was unshaven, and his light brown hair hung around his face in greasy strings.

"Get your eyes back in your head," Ginger muttered. Her words were followed by a hacking cough, but the orange-haired woman took another drag on the cigarette. "Don't mind him," she told Eden. "Gator's harmless. I should know."

"Shrew!"

"Oh, shut your trap, before I use it as an ashtray!"

At a loss for words, Eden was grateful when Chick came to her side and intervened.

"My new assistant, Eden." He took her arm and began steering her away from the other couple, who were glaring at each other, their faces filled with mutual hatred.

"Uh, hi."

"This is Ginger Tresnick and Gator Yost." Chick didn't wait for any more pleasantries. "We'll see you two later."

"What a weird couple," Eden whispered. "They act like they hate each other."

"Maybe they do."

"Then why do they stay together? They're not married, are they?"

"Not that I know of." Chick gave her a searching look. "You're awfully curious for someone who's so reluctant to talk about herself."

That made Eden hold her tongue until they arrived at his booth, which was closed and padlocked. Her surroundings made her think about the circumstances that had brought them together in the first place.

"Chick, that kid Jimmy—"

"Was reunited with his sister, shortly after you did your disappearing act. Zelda had barely gotten him to the Lost and Found when she showed."

"Thank goodness."

His eyes were on her again, this time looking beyond the disguise. He was trying to read her, and Eden was growing uncomfortable. She felt the muscles in her neck tightening. Starting to turn away, she stopped when Chick put a hand on her shoulder.

"What are you running from?"

Her pulse jumped under his fingers, and fear blossomed anew. She had a difficult time controlling her response. "I thought carnies didn't care about those things."

"Maybe I'm not the typical carny."

Eden's heart fell. She should have known that this was coming. She couldn't just keep evading Chick's questions. And with him watching her too closely, she'd never be able to find the evidence she needed to resume her own life. Maybe she should just get out of there. But she had nowhere to go, unless she left town. The thought of having to leave her home—her city—because of some criminal with political aspirations, made her dig in her heels and glare at the man who was studying her thoughtfully. She shrugged away from him.

"Either you want me to work for you or you don't," she said belligerently. "My personal life is none of your business."

He had the grace to look sheepish. "All right. Putting you on the spot wasn't fair. I realize something terrible must have happened to bring you here." She was about to object, when he pressed a fingertip against her lips. "I know what it's like to be on the run, not to have a cent to your name and to be dependent on the kindness of strangers. So I'll back off. But if you need someone to talk to, I'm willing to listen. Maybe I can help. I'm a pretty resourceful guy."

"Sure. Thanks."

Eden tried to relax while she waited for Chick to open the booth. She appreciated his pretty speech. Undoubtedly he meant every word. But he was a carny, and carnies didn't move in the same circles as did men like Stanton Barnes.

Eden knew she had only herself to depend upon.

A FEW MINUTES LATER, Chick was on his way to the office to talk to Abe about the latest robbery. He'd left Eden at the booth doing busywork—sweeping, washing down the sticky counters, dusting the milk bottles. Surprisingly she hadn't objected, but had gotten right into the swing of things. He wondered how long those manicured nails of hers would last.

And more than ever he wondered what had put her on the run.

"Hey, Chick, wait up."

Turning to see Maisie coming toward him from her trailer, he met her halfway.

"Something wrong?"

"No. Eden dropped her wallet in the bathroom when she was changing." She held it out to show him. "I thought you might know where I can find her."

Chick stared at the fine leather in her hand and knew that it held some tempting answers. "I'll be seeing Eden in a minute. I can save you the walk."

"Good." Maisie handed him the wallet and backed off. "Eden'll be frantic if she thinks she's lost it. I gotta change for work. Later, baby."

"See you in a while."

Chick waited only until Maisie had gone back inside the trailer before he satisfied his curiosity. Without so much as a qualm of conscience, he flipped the wallet open. The driver's license identified his new assistant as Eden Payne. He checked the address—a little more than a mile from where he stood. High-rent district. The wallet was loaded with credit cards. Marshall Fields, Bloomingdale's, Neiman Marcus and American Express, among others. And inside lay neatly placed bills totaling more than a hundred dollars.

So Eden wasn't busted. He'd been feeling sorry for her, thinking that for some reason she had no assets. He'd even imagined she might have been fleeing a sadistic husband and had gotten into more than she could handle. And she had strung him along. All the while she'd had both money and credit cards at her disposal. What kind of a game was she playing? Remembering his heartfelt speech, Chick flushed with anger.

She didn't need the kindness of strangers.

And he didn't appreciate feeling like a fool.

Deciding he could talk to Abe about the robbery later, Chick stalked back toward his booth. He would have the truth out of Eden Payne, if he had to wring her elegant neck to get it.

Chapter Three

Eden's wallet clutched in his fist, Chick got within yards of the One-Ball booth before his righteous anger began to leak away like air from a pricked balloon. She wasn't visible behind the counter.

"Eden, if you're within hearing distance, I suggest you get your pretty behind over here right now!" he yelled. "We have something to discuss."

She rose from behind the counter and plopped a wet rag onto its horizontal surface. Her expression conveyed her annoyance. "Like what?"

His own ire rekindled, Chick strode toward her and practically shoved the expensive piece of leather into her face. "Like this, Toots."

"Where did you get my wallet?" she asked, making a grab for it.

He snatched his hand away and raised his arm. "Maisie found this in her bathroom."

"Well, it's mine, so give it to me."

Eden rose onto tiptoe and reached for his hand. Chick merely stepped back out of her way.

"First we talk. I ask the questions and you give the answers."

"You said—"

"I said a lot of things, because I felt sorry for you." Remembering tightened his voice. "That was before I looked in here."

"You went through my personal possession!"

"Don't sound so shocked. It's not like I went through your underwear drawer."

Eden was looking around nervously. "Can you keep your voice down?"

"Why?" he whispered. "So Maisie and Felix don't know what a little cheat you are?"

"I am not." Her face reflected outrage at the accusation. "I've never cheated anyone!"

"What would you call someone who takes food and clothing from people who can barely exist on what little money they make? All the while you thanked them for their charity, you could have afforded to buy your own breakfast and your own clothes."

"I intend to repay them."

"When?"

Frustration marred her features, which he decided were a bit above average, after all. Or perhaps the wild hair and makeup made her seem a little more glamorous.

"I'll repay them now, if it'll make you happy." She held out her hand. "But I'll need my wallet to do so."

Chick shook his head and slipped the article in question into a jeans pocket. "Not until I get those answers."

"You won't believe them."

"Try me."

Eden sputtered ineffectually, and the color in her face deepened. Chick sensed she would like to pummel him. But, like the lady he figured her to be, she straightened her spine and took a deep breath, instead.

"All right, but not here." She spoke softly. "Too many ears."

Chick gave her a piercing look and wondered if she was trying to con him. "All right. I'll lock the place up and we can take a walk."

A few minutes later they were crossing Navy Pier's deserted north side. Later the walkway would fill with people trying to get away from the congestion of the festival that lined the south pier, but for now they were alone, except for the pigeons.

Chick waited until they'd gone a quarter of the way along the promenade, then stopped and leaned over the railing. "Is this private enough for you?"

"I hope so, or..."

Her voice trailed away, and Chick wondered if she had done that for effect. Then common sense tempered his anger. From the first he'd known she was running and afraid. His pride had merely been pricked because he'd mistakenly assumed she was penniless. He had been blindly solicitous, when she could easily have afforded to take care of herself, and now he was feeling foolish. That didn't mean Eden wasn't in trouble. Still, he was too stubborn to back down.

"You can knock off the dramatics and give it to me straight. I'm a big boy. I can take the truth."

"*If* you believe what I say." She leaned against the railing and laughed softly. "This is going to sound like something right out of a B movie. Even I don't want to believe it."

"I can't make a judgment until you tell me, can I?"

"For what it's worth, here goes," Eden mumbled to herself. She didn't look at him, but stared straight out at the shoreline. "I worked late last night and couldn't get a taxi because of the weather, so I was forced to walk home. I don't live too far from here."

"I know."

Her eyes met his. "Yes. You're privy to quite a bit of information about me."

"Go on with the story."

"I was crossing the river and looking around, the way I always do when I'm alone. There was a man on the bank below, and a yacht with its motor running nearby."

"A private boat was out in that weather?"

She nodded. "That's why I stopped to get a better look. What I saw was a dead woman being carried on board."

"Whoa. A murder?" She'd been correct in wondering if he would believe her. And yet she seemed so convinced of what she was saying.... "How did you know this woman was dead?"

"Why else would they have dumped her body into the river?" When Chick narrowed his eyes, she added, "Photo and story on page 1 of this morning's newspaper."

"So why did you think I wouldn't believe you?"

"What if I told you there was another man down there I recognized—one who realized he'd been seen, and sent two thugs racing after me?"

No wonder she'd been in such a state when she'd first appeared. His lady mud wrestler had been a terrified woman fleeing for her life.

"I believe a murderer wouldn't want witnesses."

Eden took a deep breath and stared at him, her expression at once intent and vulnerable. "But could you believe the murderer was Stanton Barnes?"

Chick swore. "The gubernatorial candidate? Are you sure?"

"One and the same—and I'm positive. Of course, according to the morning paper, he was occupied all night by a fund-raiser for his campaign. I'm sure someone will vouch for every moment of his time at the Hotel River View."

"Which is how far from where you saw the body being brought onto the yacht?"

"About a block."

"Then it's possible he could have slipped away from the function for a short while, and no one would miss him."

"You believe me?"

Her body rigid, Eden wrapped her hands around the metal railing. He could see she was afraid to hope for too much. If she wasn't telling the truth, she had to be an escapee from a nuthouse. Only Chick didn't think Eden was crazy. And he knew for a fact that all politicians weren't honest and altruistic human beings.

"I believe you," he said finally. His words made her sag with relief, and she clung to the railing for support. "Why haven't you gone to the police?"

"I called the police, but the guy on the other end thought I was a crank."

"That's not a reason for you to go underground."

"I also tried to go home, but one of those thugs was waiting for me. They got my briefcase, so they know everything—my identity and address, and that I'm an assistant director in the Illinois Tourism Office. I've got to hide out until I can prove there was a connection between Barnes and the dead woman. Until I can find a motive for murder."

"Now that's a tall order. How were you planning to get that kind of information?"

"I wish to God I knew." Her voice trembled as she said, "If I don't try, I might as well leave town and adopt a new identity. Even then I may not be safe."

"Running away never solved anything," Chick said, remembering how he'd done just that. "You can put your problems on hold for a while, but they'll be there waiting for you."

Eden swallowed hard and seemed to be talking more to herself than to him when she said, "I have no intention of letting Stanton Barnes drive me away. I'm not going to be his next victim. And I refuse to let him get away with murder. Somehow I'm going to see that justice is served." Her blue eyes were brimming with tears when they met Chick's. "Please help me. *Please.* All you have to do is say nothing. If anyone asks any questions about me, plead ignorance."

"I'll go one better."

"What do you mean?"

He was the crazy one, Chick told himself. But he couldn't get a picture out of his mind: Eden, running for her own life, looking over her shoulder in fear, and yet taking the chance of bringing attention to herself to help a lost little boy find his sister.

"I'm going to help you nail Stanton Barnes."

RHONDA BARNES put the finishing touches to her makeup, smoothed back a lock of dark blond hair and admired herself in the mirrored closet doors. At forty-five she was still a very attractive woman. Though she could stand to lose some weight, as her husband was always reminding her in his nasty little ways, her taste was impeccable. Stylish outfits and accessories that complemented her outgoing personality camouflaged her faults well. She was Stanton's greatest asset, and she never let him forget it.

Checking her watch, Rhonda realized they were running late. The reporters would already be waiting downstairs, bloodhounds on the scent, whenever a press conference was called. Today Stanton would announce his new plans to enforce penalties on perpetrators of violent crimes. Ironic, really, in light of what had gone on the evening before.

If the press ever got wind of their connection to Kim Quinlan... The very thought made Rhonda shiver.

"Stanton, are you ready?" she called.

"Almost."

She walked through the bath that linked their bedrooms. He was standing in front of a mirror and seemed to be taking his time.

"Well, hurry. The press does not like to be kept waiting."

"Do you have to nag me at every moment?"

"My nagging hasn't hurt your career."

If it weren't for *her*, she reflected, Stanton would still be in some law firm, instead of heading for the governorship. His political career would not end at the state level, either. Someday... Rhonda had always wanted to live in the White House. Power was an aphrodisiac, and she had never been able to get enough to satisfy her. She deserved to be satisfied. After all, the desire had gone out of her marriage years ago. Stanton's appetites had become quite distasteful to her.

"I'm ready."

He turned from the mirror, and her eyes opened wide in outrage.

"You're not wearing that tie."

"I beg to differ with you."

"I distinctly remember telling Maggie to lay out the blue and silver paisley."

"I hate that one."

"Why? Because I picked it out?"

A knock at the door stopped the argument from continuing. Glaring at her husband, Rhonda opened it to admit Wylie Decker.

The campaign manager stepped inside and closed the door behind him. "I could hear you down the hall," he said, speaking to them as if they were children. "Are you crazy, arguing at a time like this?"

"My wife can't seem to control her mouth, when it comes to words . . . or food."

Rhonda ignored the slur. She turned to Decker. "Before we go downstairs, I have to know. Has Lou called in yet?"

Decker shook his head. "No, and it's worrying me. As much as I would like to get this thing all settled now, Eden Payne isn't cooperating. We'll discuss the situation later. Let's not keep those reporters waiting any longer."

The Payne woman could cost them everything, but Decker was right. They had to meet their obligations as though nothing had happened. Hiding her growing agitation behind a practiced smile, Rhonda took her husband's arm, and they left the room to face the press.

"STEP RIGHT UP for a shot at one of these cute stuffed animals. One dollar, one throw." Eden beckoned to a man wandering the midway by himself. "Take a chance. C'mon, mister, you look like you have a good pitching arm."

The man looked away and moved on. Disappointed, Eden flashed a look at Chick, who appeared amused.

"I would ask how I was doing," she said, a bit chagrined, "but that's obvious."

"Oh, lighten up. That wasn't so bad for your first try."

"But he wasn't interested."

"Not everyone will be. You have to psych out a potential mark, even one who voluntarily comes up to the booth. You want the person to keep trying. All you have to do is calculate how to get to him or her."

"Maybe I'd be doing better if I had majored in psychology."

"Or if you studied human nature." He took a toothpick out of his shirt pocket and placed it at the corner of his mouth. "Some people like to show off for friends and family. A few want to prove to themselves that they can do it.

Others just want to have fun, whether they win or lose. Your job is to figure out what they need and then let them have it."

The subject matter animated Chick. He was in his element. But Eden had some doubts about what she'd committed herself to doing. "Don't you ever feel... weird... taking their money?"

"Why?" He seemed truly puzzled that she'd even ask. "This is a form of entertainment. The price of a first-run movie with popcorn and soda is more than ten bucks, and getting into one of the better clubs in town is fifteen. Folks can do those things anytime. Carnivals are special treats, and while the carnies do vie with each other to make the most money, this is a clean operation. Abe and Zelda don't go in for anything underhanded. So we entertain people and give them the chance to take home great prizes like these," he said, indicating the row of stuffed animals.

"Fat chance."

If anyone went home with a prize, it was just short of a miracle. Though she knew the carnies had to make a profit to survive, and though this operation might be clean, there were still a few shady aspects of the business that bothered Eden. Calling customers "marks." Setting the pyramid of milk bottles in a way that made them nearly impossible to knock down. That it *was* possible soothed her conscience, but she wasn't cut out for this kind of endeavor. She wondered what kind of a background and personality made one a con man.

"Listen," Chick said. "Before it gets busy, I'm going to find Abe. I want to talk to him about that robbery Ginger and Gator told me about. You'll be all right on your own for a few minutes, won't you?"

"As long as you don't actually expect me to make money."

Chick laughed. "Give it your best shot."

"I'll pass along that advice to anyone who pays to play," she mumbled as he left.

Eden spent the next quarter of an hour trying to lure customers to the booth. She had two, neither of whom came close to knocking down all three bottles, and who, therefore, had no interest in repeating the experience.

That gave her a lot of time to think about Chick's offer to help her nail Barnes. She still wondered about his motives. He'd met her query as to whether he had something against the attorney general with a quelling look, and she hadn't been about to challenge him. She needed Chick's help.

Just as she was thinking that a con man might come in handy in her search for the truth, two carnies stopped at her booth. One man was scrawny, unkempt and had shifty eyes. The other was about her height, well muscled and darkly handsome in a smooth, oily way. One of the short sleeves of his white T-shirt was rolled up to hold his cigarettes. He removed the pack and offered her one.

"No, thanks. I don't smoke."

"You're new," he said, lighting a cigarette for himself. "Did Chick quit already?"

"No. I'm his assistant."

"Really?" He gave Eden a smile that was probably supposed to be seductive but didn't do a thing for her. "What do you assist him with?"

The shifty-eyed man snickered and elbowed his companion in the ribs. "Wha'd'ya think, Sheets?"

Eden didn't like the insinuation. She leveled her gaze at the unkempt man. "I beg your pardon."

"Now, Nickles, behave," Sheets told him between drags. "We have a real lady here." He gave her a look hot enough to melt butter. "Don't we, sweetheart?"

She didn't know whether to be annoyed or amused. "The name's Eden."

"You tellin' us you and Chickie-Loves-It ain't gettin' it on?" Nickles asked.

"I wouldn't think of discussing my personal life with you."

He snickered again and wiped his nose on his plaid shirt sleeve. "Don't have to. We got imaginations."

"The lady doesn't appreciate your imagination." Sheets turned his back on the other man and leaned closer to her. "Ignore Nickles. His middle name is 'crude.'" He reached out and ran his fingers along the back of her hand, then looked teed off himself when she pulled away. "Listen, if Chick really isn't your old man, why don't we get together later tonight... for a drink?"

"The lady isn't interested."

Chick opened the gate that let him in behind the counter. Eden was relieved to see him, until he put a possessive arm around her. She gave him a warning glare. He merely smiled in that lazy way of his and stared into her eyes, as if smitten. Her breath caught in her throat.

"Say, don't you two have something to do?" he asked, never looking in the carnies' direction.

"I can take a hint," Sheets said, backing off. "I'm history."

"Yeah, the marks are gettin' thick as thieves." Nickles snorted to himself as he followed the other man. "I feel my palm itchin' for that money already."

Eden waited until they were a few yards from the booth, then told Chick, "Let me go." When he didn't do so instantly, she elbowed him in the side and ducked under his arm. "Don't ever do that again."

"Are you kidding? You're ticked at me, when I just came to your rescue? You have no idea of what royal pains those guys can be to a single woman on the circuit."

"I can take care of myself," she insisted.

"That's why you're here, right?"

"That's not fair."

The argument was nipped in the bud by customers stopping at the booth. Chick stepped back and let her handle the play. The two kids—a boy about ten and a girl about twelve—both took turns at the bottles. Eden could tell the parents had money and could afford to indulge the kids, so she continued to encourage them, each time setting the bottom bottles exactly even with each other.

Whether or not Chick liked it, she was going to give the kids the best possible chance at winning. On her eighth try, the girl knocked over all three bottles and chose a giraffe as her reward. The boy, miffed that his sister had beaten him, refused to throw again.

Eden watched the family leave, sure that Chick would admonish her about giving away prizes.

"Good job," he said, surprising her. "Now back to this taking care of yourself. If you don't want any hassles, you'll pretend to be my old lady. . . and make it convincing."

Eden wasn't sure she liked that idea. "Maybe you'd better spell it out."

"Be sweet to me." He grinned lazily. "Don't try to break my arm if I put it around you. Give me some lovesick looks when the other carnies are around—"

"Oh, please."

"You don't have to make it sound so distasteful."

Chick appeared indignant, but then so was she.

"I'm sure there are plenty of women around here willing to give you lovesick looks."

"But how many of them need protection?"

He had a point.

"All right. Lovesick looks. What else?"

"You sleep in the back of my truck with me."

"You're pushing this a bit. There must be other single women working for the carnival."

"Yes, and they all have old men of their own. Ever heard of the saying, 'Three's a crowd'?"

Eden was appalled. She wasn't about to check into a hotel in her borrowed finery—she could imagine the stir that would create. The carnival it was. She might not be able to bunk with anyone else, but that didn't mean she couldn't come up with an alternative.

"I'll sleep here in the booth," she told him with a smile. "I can make the prize counter into a bed."

Chick shrugged. "That's your decision. Sheets and every other unattached male will have his eyes on you. Who's going to protect you if you have an unexpected visitor?"

Who was going to protect her from a man the others called Chickie-Loves-It? Eden stared at the sexy little scar on his chin. Though she knew he was right, that she had to depend on his goodwill, she hated to back down.

"How about catching the interest of that couple over there?" Chick suggested, giving her a reprieve. He pointed to a man and woman who were obviously trying to decide which game to play.

Relieved, Eden lured them over. The couple played One-Ball without the same advantage she had given the kids—she doubted Chick would be happy if she bankrupted him—and they left empty-handed. Not wanting to give him a chance to discuss sleeping arrangements again, she brought up the subject that had been bothering her earlier.

"I was thinking about your offer to help me, and wondering why you're willing to do so for someone you don't know."

"Why are you so suspicious?"

"I'm not." At least she hadn't thought of it that way, but perhaps he was right. "It's just that I can't help thinking maybe you or your friends had some kind of a run-in with the guy or his office, and you're looking for a way to even the score."

"Yeah, I was arrested for littering, and Barnes made sure I served time," he said, his expression disgusted.

"Be serious."

"Look, if you don't want my help, just say so."

"I *do* want your help."

"Then what's the problem?"

"It's just hard to believe that someone like you . . ." She faltered. He was taking this all wrong.

"That a con man would want to get mixed up with the law, is that it?" When she didn't answer, his hazel eyes darkened. "You really do need to study human nature. Maybe you wouldn't jump to so many conclusions."

"I'm sorry, and I appreciate your offer to help. I was just trying to figure you out, like you told me to do with the customers." Realizing that her admission hadn't exactly mollified him, she changed the subject. "I'm going to need some clothes before we do anything."

"Maisie probably has others you can use."

"*My* clothes. We're not going to find out anything about Barnes here, and I'm not about to walk around the city in an outfit like this. Too conspicuous," she added quickly, lest he decide to take offense at that also. "My roommate will be back in town tomorrow. She can bring me some things."

"And let her lead them right to you?"

"You think Barnes's men would know about Taffy?" Why hadn't that occurred to her? Barnes had a whole network of information open to him. "Great. She could be in hot water right along with me. I'll have to warn her. And then we can pick a meeting place where I can get my stuff and make sure she's safe, too."

"Do you know where she is?"

"Not really. Taffy and Hank drove up to Wisconsin to camp. No telephones. But we have a machine. I can leave a message. I'll tell her I'm in trouble and to please stay put once she gets home, and that I'll keep calling all day Sunday until I get hold of her."

"Sounds like a reasonable plan."

"Maybe I should make that call now, just in case they decide to come home early." And she wouldn't mind a break from Chick Lovett. Something about the man was getting to her. Opening the gate, Eden couldn't help herself. "You'll be all right alone for a few minutes, won't you?"

"As long as you don't expect me to make money," he said, parroting the smart remark she'd made earlier.

Then Chick grinned—and Eden left the booth in a cloud of confusion.

"THE TWO OF YOU were impressive," Wylie Decker said as he closed the door behind the last reporter.

"I'm just glad it's over." Barnes sank onto a couch and absently rubbed his temples. "I've got a migraine."

"So take some aspirin," Rhonda told him.

"You could get them for me."

"Like a good little wifey?"

"Stop it, both of you." Their taking shots at each other in private made Decker nervous. Someday their true natures would surface in public. He'd worked too hard to get where he was to let anyone bring him back down. "We're all tense—"

"And you're not doing a damned thing about it!" Barnes grumbled.

"But I'm about to."

"To what?" Rhonda demanded. "Have you figured out a way to find the Payne woman?"

"Lou's a whiz with locks. While Jack keeps watch, Lou's going to search the Payne woman's apartment."

And when Lou found what they needed, they could all breathe easier. Decker had known Kim Quinlan had been bad news, the first time he'd set eyes on her. He'd never guessed she would be a threat, even from the grave.

Chapter Four

The carnival settled down in the small hours of the morning. Exhausted, still unsure that she'd be safe with Chickie-Loves-It, Eden reluctantly followed him to the back of his truck. Though she might not have a choice about her accommodations, she wasn't going to sleep *with* the man. As a matter of fact, she intended on staying as far away from him as possible.

"Let me help you," he offered after hopping up into the back of the vehicle.

Ignoring his outstretched hand, she found the small metal shelf that had provided him meager footing. "I can get up there myself."

Eden placed her foot on the makeshift step and tried to find a secure handhold. She bobbed and shifted her weight forward, but couldn't steady herself there. Chick watched her fall back without attempting to conceal his amusement. He made a noise that sounded suspiciously like a snort. Irritated, she tried again. Succeeding this time, she threw her upper body onto the floor of the truck and awkwardly clambered in.

"What a hero," Chick said.

He stooped to turn on a battery-generated lamp, which glowed softly, lighting the immediate area and leaving the rest of the cavernous interior in deep gloom. Eden looked around. Nearby, piled to one side, were several layers of foam, obviously Chick's makeshift bed. But three-quarters of the floor was taken up with shelving and packing crates. There was hardly leeway to move. Where in the world was she going to sleep?

"This isn't as much room as I thought." She wouldn't be able to remove herself from Chick, after all.

"You don't need much room to stretch out. Do you have a problem?" he asked.

"I hope not."

She thought she heard another muffled snort, as Chick separated the layers of foam and set them next to each other.

"Just pretend you're camping."

"That would be difficult, since I've never tried that particular activity."

"You've never roughed it? What *do* you do for fun?"

He was challenging her, making her feel like a curiosity, when she was quite normal. He was the one who lived a vagabond and somewhat questionable life-style. Ignoring the grin that made him too attractive by far, she crawled forward and moved her foam as far away from his as she could manage—all of two and a half feet.

"You're going to get cold." When she looked up at him questioningly, he added, "I only have one blanket. It won't stretch that far."

"If you were a gentleman..." She left the conclusion to his imagination.

"Go on."

"Never mind." Eden was once again regretting the skimpiness of her borrowed skirt; her legs were exposed to the cold metal of the vehicle's floor. She scanned the interior of the truck more closely and spotted a small pile of familiar dirty blue material. "My clothes." The suit and blouse were piled on a shelf.

"Maisie wanted to know what to do with them. I thought you might want to keep them for sentimental reasons."

Already on her feet and climbing over some boxes to get at the garments, she stretched until her fingers snagged the cloth. "This'll come in handy to keep me warm, until I can get a blanket."

"Are you sure there's enough material to cover your legs?"

She shot him a look over her shoulder and realized he was staring at the legs in question, which were exposed almost to the hip. Since he wasn't looking at her face, her scowl had been wasted. Grabbing the old clothes, she adjusted both her stance and her skirt. When Chick's hazel eyes met hers, the appreciative gleam made her pulse skitter nervously through her system. But just when she thought she was going to have to castigate the man—as if he could be intimidated by anything—he turned away and began removing his own clothing.

Now it was her turn to stare—until she realized what she was doing.

Eden lunged for her makeshift bed, but not before she got a good look at a tanned muscular torso—and buttocks barely covered by a pair of leopard print bikinis. She'd never known a man who wore something so... so decadent. But then she'd never known a man even vaguely like Chick before, and Eden wasn't sure she wanted to now.

She turned her attention to her suit, completing the destruction of the skirt by splitting it where the seam had ripped the night before. Spread out, the material concealed her legs to the ankle. Kicking off her shoes, she pulled up her knees so that her feet were covered, and adjusted the jacket over her chest and shoulders.

"Have you given any thought to how you can prove Barnes and the Quinlan woman even knew each other?" Chick asked.

A quick look assured her that he was stretched out on his bed and decently covered by the blanket. All the same, she wasn't altogether comfortable.

"Making the connection is all that I've been thinking about this evening. Barnes's home is probably out of the question, though I might be able to get the address. His office is another story. I work in the State of Illinois Center," she explained. "The security in the place isn't what it could be. We can go there Monday morning, when I have something more appropriate to wear," she suggested, having learned that the carnival was closed that day. "I'm sure we can get into Barnes's office."

"That's Monday. What about tomorrow?"

"I thought I would check with the local harbor offices and find out where the *Ambition* is docked." It was sheer luck that she'd noticed the name of the yacht. "I'll pretend to have a delivery for Barnes and say that he forgot to include the slip number. Hopefully, when I hit on the right harbor, the person on the phone will fill in the missing information. Since the carnival closes down early Sunday night, that might be a good time to check out the yacht."

"If you can find it, and if it's in its slip, and if it's deserted."

"If," Eden echoed, frowning at the negative sound of the word. She couldn't let herself get down or she would lose hope and give up. Her brightly burning anger and her intrinsic belief in justice triumphing over wrong were the only things that were keeping her from turning tail and disappearing for good. "I'm going to find the yacht, and we're going to search it."

She glared at Chick, challenging him to disagree with her. He merely stared at her and nodded. "All right. What do you hope to find?"

"Proof that the Quinlan woman's body was dumped into the river from that boat."

If Barnes hasn't had every inch of the yacht scoured, she thought. Now she was the one being negative. Surely they would find some evidence... or at least some other information that would be useful. She had to believe that.

Chick doused the light and Eden tensed.

But all he said was, "Get some sleep. We have a long day ahead of us tomorrow."

"Good night."

Eden didn't know how she was going to sleep, not with Chick less than a yard away, not with all that was going through her head about the dead woman. She couldn't close her eyes without seeing the body being chucked into the coffinlike bench seat. Who was Kim Quinlan, and why did she have to die? Eden shifted position and tried to make herself more comfortable. The suit material slipped off her legs, and she sat up to fuss with it.

"Something wrong?" Chick whispered.

"No."

"Too bad. I thought you were planning on joining me over here."

"Think again."

"Don't be so proud, Toots. If you get cold, I'll be glad to share my blanket."

She'd freeze before she took him up on that offer. Eden wasn't stupid. Chickie-Loves-It was extending a carefully worded invitation to do more than share a blanket, but he couldn't even be honest about it. Another woman might be delighted by this opportunity. Nonetheless, thinking about it made her fidgety. She turned yet again, seeking a more comfortable position, then had to readjust the material over her legs.

For a brief respite, images of a dead woman gave way to visions of Chick in his leopard print bikini.

"THE WASHINGTONS were hit last night," Abe Hurley told Chick first thing Sunday morning.

Having awakened with the dawn, Chick had left Eden sleeping in the back of the truck, her long legs enticingly tangled in her makeshift blanket. He'd sought out the owners of the Hurley-Gurley for the express purpose of discussing the robberies. That was why he was there, after all. One of the reasons. He'd found the elderly couple in their trailer, awake and dressed as he'd known they would be. They always had been early risers.

"What happened this time?"

Sprawled in his favorite chair, one of the few pieces of furniture not built into the trailer, Abe shook his white head. "Damnedest thing. Felix was locking up, when Ginger went by, carrying a box load of prizes. She lost her footing and everything went flying. Being the gentleman he is, Felix ran to help her. He swears his back was to the booth for no more than a minute."

"But long enough for his cash box to disappear."

Chick frowned at the note of anguish in Zelda's voice. She'd been like a mother to him once, and he responded to her pain as any real son would do. The Hurleys' world was collapsing around them. Half the size it had been twenty years before, their carnival had been reduced to a forty-miler, with winter quarters across the border in Wisconsin, where land and taxes were cheaper.

The robberies had begun earlier this spring. Now as the season drew to a close, the thefts were becoming more frequent, threatening to end what little business the Hurleys had left. Once a carnival got a bad reputation, local police didn't want the trouble it could bring in their district. If the Hurleys couldn't get bookings, they would be forced to retire. Then they would surely give in to old age, their hearts broken, just as they'd told Chick when they'd asked for his help.

"Two robberies in a row," Chick said gruffly. "Sounds like someone is determined to get a good enough stake to last the winter. You think Gator and Ginger set up Felix?"

"I don't know." Abe's hands trembled, and he gripped both arms of his chair to stop the motion, as if it implied weakness. "I hate to think those two are so greedy that they'd rip off their own. They've been with me for a couple of years now. Not the pleasantest of folks, but they grow on you."

"More like you get used to them." Zelda rose from the couch to join her husband. "I don't think they ever grew on each other, and they've got two kids. But that doesn't make them guilty. Neither one has been directly involved in a robbery like this before."

"Maybe they're getting careless," Chick suggested.

"Or desperate," Abe added.

Zelda stood behind her husband's chair and patted his shoulder. "Gator's a desperate man, all right. I've seen his aura... but Ginger is less readable."

Chick didn't have the least inclination to smile at Zelda's pronouncement. If, for the most part, her fortune-telling act was show, there were times when she truly sensed things that others couldn't. Having experienced her natural talent firsthand, he would trust her instincts over his own, if she felt strongly about something.

"Is Felix going to make out a police report?"

"No, of course not. He's one of us," Abe said. "He wouldn't be caught dead in a cop shop."

The word "dead" reminded Chick of the other mystery he'd allowed himself to become embroiled in. Hell, he'd volunteered. He was a regular hero, Chick thought wryly. He wondered how eager he would have been to prove that a leading politician was involved in murder, if Eden Payne hadn't almost been the second victim. He hated to think of her in those terms, yet she was almost as much a casualty as Kim Quinlan. Though Eden was still alive, she couldn't go home, couldn't resume a normal life until the other woman's murder was resolved.

Realizing the elderly couple was staring at him expectantly, Chick felt a rush of guilt. *They* should be uppermost in his thoughts right now.

"I'll keep my eyes and ears open," he promised as he rose to leave. "You know I'll do whatever I can to find your thief."

"You've always been a good boy." Zelda stepped away from her husband to hug Chick. "And whether or not you succeed, we'll always be grateful to you for trying."

He had to stoop to receive her embrace, which was not as vigorous as it had once been. She felt fragile in his arms. His determination to stop the robberies and give the Hurley-Gurley a renewed lease on life strengthened. He couldn't let Zelda and Abe down.

He straightened, but kept one arm around the plump little woman. "This person has to be pretty desperate for money to stage two robberies so close together, one right under the jointee's nose. Whoever they are, they'll slip up." He only hoped that that would happen within the week, before the carnival moved on.

"Like Zelda said, we know you'll do what you can," Abe declared.

Chick took his leave of the Hurleys and headed for the truck, wondering if Eden was awake. If not, he could stare at her legs until she did, then amuse himself by teasing her. Something about the woman brought out the old carny instincts that he'd never quite been able to suppress completely in all these years. He might work at what the carnies considered a sucker job, but it was one that allowed him to take advantage of what he'd learned about human nature during his time with the Hurley-Gurley.

He had to admit that he'd gotten soft in other ways, too. He had to recapture that lost edge, and he had to do it fast, not only for Abe and Zelda's sake, but for Eden's. They might lose a business, but she could very well lose her life.

EDEN WAS PACKING AWAY prizes for the night when Jud Nystrom stopped by the booth.

"Need some help?"

She flashed the hunk a smile. "Thanks. That would be great. I'm almost done here, but I could use a pair of strong arms to help me get these cartons to the truck. I can't imagine where Chick is. Are you sure you don't have something better to do?"

"Not at the moment. Some of the jointees and ride jocks are planning to visit one of the local bars in a half hour or so. Want to join us?"

"Sounds tempting. But I'm not used to these long hours on my feet. I'm bushed." She really was, though exhaustion would not stop her from going through with her plans for the evening. She would run on adrenaline, if necessary. But she didn't want to tell Jud she had plans, in case he wanted to know what they were. Lying didn't come easy to her. Evasion she could handle. "Maybe some other time."

Jud didn't argue, but good-naturedly shrugged his broad shoulders and leaned on the counter to watch her pack the last carton. Setting the milk bottles inside, Eden wondered where Chick had disappeared to this time.

All day long he'd taken every opportunity to leave the booth in her hands and had strolled off and visited with the other carnies. She hadn't minded, since that had left her plenty of time to make her phone calls. She was still jubilant that she'd struck pay dirt. Getting the information on the *Ambition* had been easier than she'd imagined. The yacht was docked at Belmont Harbor, a ten-minute stroll from the Lincoln Park gazebo, where she and Chick would meet Taffy at midnight. She'd warned her roommate to be careful and had asked her to bring some clothes. Eden couldn't wait to change into a pair of jeans.

Now if only Chick would appear, so that they could keep to schedule.

"Done?" Jud asked as she dropped in the softballs with the bottles.

"As soon as I get the cash box."

"You'd better be careful with that."

"I know. Maisie told me about the robbery last night. I feel just awful. She and Felix are such nice people. They didn't deserve to lose money they couldn't afford."

"Scum don't distinguish between nice folks and those less deserving."

"I guess not."

Eden turned away from Jud and lifted the curtain that ran around the prize shelf. Chick hid the cash box there, leaving only enough money out front to make change. When she'd questioned him about keeping so much cash around—a natural target for a thief—he'd insisted that it was the way of things in a carnival, because the business moved around so much. Besides, rent and other expenses had to be paid on a weekly basis. After payouts, not much was left over to bank, anyway.

She pulled the metal box from its hiding place, set it on the counter next to Jud, then retrieved and positioned the change drawer beside it.

"Looks like you did pretty well today," Jud said.

"Not bad. What about you?" Eden counted the contents of the drawer and added the money to the box. "Break up any potential fights?"

"Only one. Sunday's usually a slow day for me, maybe because going to church puts customers in a better mood than they're in the rest of the week. I guess they feel guilty if they start trouble after communing with God."

"Interesting theory." She locked the cash box. "Well, I'm done. All that's left is securing the booth."

"Hand me the cartons. I'll stack them out here."

Eden did so, all the time keeping an eye on the money. Her caution almost made her feel guilty, as if she were pinning the thefts on Jud. He was just a nice guy who'd stopped by to ask her out for a friendly drink. She had no reason to be suspicious of him. All the same, she kept the cash box with her, tucked under one arm as she locked up the booth for the night. Losing the money of the man who'd vowed to help her would make her feel even guiltier.

As she joined Jud, set the metal box on top of one of the lighter cartons and picked up both, Eden looked around for Chick. Not a sign of the man. A swell of impatience washed through her, but she told herself to settle down. He wouldn't forget their plans for the evening. Something had held him up, or he would have been there by now.

"Ready?" Jud asked as he easily lifted the remaining two cartons.

"Sure."

Side by side they walked toward the back of the lot. Other jointees were also in various stages of closing up for the night. Some ride jocks had gathered in a little knot close to the Ferris wheel, Sheets Iaconi among them. She felt his dark gaze follow her as she and her companion cut behind the ride that separated the carnival from the trucks and trailers. Eden quickly grew uncomfortable.

Was Sheets staring at her or at the cash box?

"So what did you do before you joined the Hurley-Gurley?"

Jud's question startled her, and Eden almost dropped her load. "Oh, lots of paperwork," she hedged as they drew closer to the truck, which was deserted.

"Secretary?"

"Something like that." So he wouldn't badger her for a more direct answer, she added, "Shuffling paper can get pretty boring. I like working with people a lot more."

They stopped behind Chick's truck, and Jud set down the cartons. His expression told her he knew there was more to the story. "You don't seem like the carny type."

Giving him what she knew was a nervous smile, she set her load on top of his. "Neither do you."

"Why don't we talk about it over that drink? I promise to bring you back early."

Before she could think of a neat way to turn him down, Chick appeared out of nowhere and stepped smoothly between them. One arm quickly circled her shoulders in a possessive gesture. "The lady isn't lacking for company, if you know what I mean. If she wants a drink, I'll do the buying."

Jud held up his hands and backed off. "I wasn't trying to poach on your territory."

Eden noted that Chick's grin didn't have its usual happy-go-lucky quality. His lips, stretched over his teeth, gave him an almost feral air.

"Good thinking, Nystrom. See you around sometime."

"I already got the message." An angry expression marring his smooth good looks, Jud met Eden's eyes. "Good night. I didn't mean to make trouble for you."

"Don't worry, you didn't."

She waited until the patch was out of sight, then wrested herself free of Chick's grasp and turned on him. "Was that rude behavior really necessary?"

"I was just making sure he didn't get it in his head that he could try anything with you."

"I am capable of handling some things on my own. Besides, Jud is a nice man. He's not oily like Sheets."

Shrugging, Chick pulled out his keys and unlocked the back of the truck. "If I hadn't gotten here in time to stake my claim, Jud would have tried to move in on you."

"Ugh. 'Claim.' You sound like some kind of prehistoric caveman! Trying to talk sense to you is useless."

Eden lifted the top carton and cash box, shoved them into the truck and climbed in, careful to keep her skirt from riding up. She was finally getting the hang of wearing the skimpy thing. She looked down at Chick, who was placing the other two cartons next to hers. He jumped up beside them.

"And speaking of arriving in time," she continued, "where *have* you been?"

"Around."

Eden moved her load to one of the shelves. "You've been 'around' all day, talking to the other jointees."

"Everyone is worried about the thefts," he said, stacking up the other two cartons. "I was seeing what was going on. I need to protect my own investment."

Something in his words didn't quite ring true—maybe his tone was a bit too nonchalant—but before Eden could figure out exactly why she wasn't buying his statement, Chick distracted her by stepping closer. Pinning her against the shelves with his body, he placed his hands on either side of her head.

"So, were you going to accept that offer for a drink?" he asked softly.

Chick was so close that Eden could feel his breath on her temple. "Not that it's any of your business, no." He had the knack of putting her off balance, making her uncomfortable, but she wasn't about to clue him in to the fact. He took advantage as it was. "You and I made other plans. Or have you forgotten?"

She didn't so much as flinch when he smoothed back her hair from her face and let his fingers run down the sides of her neck. His touch was provocative; her skin seemed to sizzle. Their gazes meshed for a moment, and when he leaned forward, Eden was sure that Chick meant to kiss her. The breath caught in her throat...but he was merely reaching past her to retrieve something from the shelf.

"I'm ready if you are," he said, drawing back.

"What's to get ready?" Eden was unable to keep from sounding prickly. Not that she really wanted to be kissed by Chick Lovett. She just couldn't help wondering what it might be like. "Until I meet Taffy, I don't even have a change of clothes. As a matter of fact," she said, looking down at the single skirt pocket that bulged with her wallet, "I don't even have enough room for a flashlight. You did remember to get them?"

"Right here." Chick showed her what was in his hand—two thin flashlights with focusing beams. "Sure you don't have somewhere you can tuck one of these away?" His eyes strayed to the top of her scoop-necked blouse.

She grabbed one and shouldered her way past him. "I'll find a place."

"You're sure you want to go through with this? We could be arrested if we're caught."

"Positive. If you don't have the nerve, you can back out now."

Chick's silence made Eden feel guilty. He'd agreed to the plan, knowing the risks, and he was exposing himself to danger in order to help her. She led the way out of the truck, jumped to the ground and waited while he locked up. She found that she could just slide the slender end of the flashlight into the pocket, next to her wallet.

"I'm sorry," she said as Chick finished. "Are you sure *you* want to go through with my plan? This isn't your battle."

"I made it mine, and I don't go back on my word. I just hope Maisie's clothes don't draw too much attention to us."

Eden looked down at the purple and yellow outfit. "Even if there's anyone around to notice, no one would blink an eye. That neighborhood has everything from yuppies to punkers to Clark Street hookers."

She thought he might make a smart remark, but he restrained himself. Verbally, at least. He slipped an arm around her waist and led her across the carnival grounds. By now she knew better than to fight him. As usual, he would have a good reason for getting close to her, even though the ride jocks seemed to have departed for that drink.

Chick picked up the conversation. "What if someone's on board?"

"We'll improvise. You seem to be good at that."

"Why, thanks, Toots. I'm flattered you noticed."

He slid his arm around her even more intimately. Eden was about to tell him off when she heard a familiar snicker. From the corner of her eye she spotted Sheets and Nickles in the shadow of a ticket booth. As previously instructed, she gave Chick one of those lovesick looks. He seemed first surprised, then delighted, and gave her ribs a squeeze. The back of her neck grew hot, and she couldn't wait to get to the street, where she could be free of him. He really was getting on her nerves.

Luckily, when they left the carnival grounds, an empty taxi was just pulling away from neighboring Lake Point Towers, the curved high-rise apartment building that dominated the Navy Pier area. Chick flagged down the vehicle. A five-minute ride later, they were on foot again at an intersection a block from Belmont Harbor. They proceeded through the moonlit night in silence, shoulders only inches apart.

"You've got a lot of guts doing this," he said suddenly.

She gave him a quick look. "Why? Because I'm a woman?"

"Because I don't think intrigue comes to you naturally."

"I'm certainly not trained for it. The only thing I seem to know how to do anymore is shuffle papers and prepare reports." She glanced around them to make sure no one would hear. They were alone. "Breaking into someone's yacht is the most creative and exciting thing I've done in years."

"What about your job with the Illinois Tourism Office?"

"The other assistant director gets to work with agencies that help promote the state more visibly. I would rather be working on ad campaigns and press releases like he is, than on neighborhood calendars of events or bed-and-breakfast lists."

"I'm surprised you work for the government at all. I would have guessed the private sector...an old family business, perhaps. I pegged you for a North Shore socialite. Or am I wrong?"

"Winnetka," she agreed stiffly, identifying the affluent suburb where she'd been raised. It nettled Eden that her background was still so obvious. "I think of myself as a Chicagoan, though. Some of us socialites have what it takes to make a decent life for ourselves, without depending on the family business or money."

"I wasn't criticizing. I know how difficult it is to remove yourself from family and all that it entails."

The obvious approval in Chick's voice mollified her. "Sounds like you've had experience."

"I ran away from home to join the Hurley-Gurley when I was seventeen," he said as they passed the harbormaster's office.

Eden was surprised by the statement and wanted to know more about Chick's past, but she was disappointed that she wouldn't have time now to hear more details. Still, she felt excited that she would finally be doing something to help herself out of an impossible situation.

"The harbormaster said the *Ambition* was docked at the north end of the basin with all the larger craft," she said in a low voice, looking in that direction. What she saw made her gasp. "Oh, no!" She hadn't been prepared for a security guard, yet there he was, making his rounds, sweeping a light across the decks of the nearby yachts.

"Don't panic." Chick's arm went around her shoulders so naturally that it felt as if it belonged there. "Pretend we're out for a romantic moonlight stroll."

He whispered the words into her hair, but the rumble of his voice didn't dissolve the lump of fear that was forming in her stomach. Eden tucked her head into his shoulder as the guard drew near. Her pulse picked up as the uniformed man looked their way, but he didn't say a word as their paths crossed. With relief, she sagged against Chick. He gave her shoulders a reassuring squeeze. They continued until she spotted the *Ambition*. A glance in the opposite direction assured her that the guard was out of sight, probably in the harbor office.

"How often do you think he makes his rounds?" she asked.

"I haven't the faintest idea."

He hopped on board the *Ambition* and offered her his hand. Eden allowed him to help her this time. The yacht bobbed on the water's surface with her weight, and she felt a little unsteady as her high heels hit the deck. She would be glad when she had access to footwear with more traction.

"Why don't you search the cabin?" she suggested. "I'll look around out here."

"Sure you don't want company?"

"I'll be fine, but thanks for the offer."

"Keep an eye out for that guard."

Eden fished out her flashlight as Chick tried the cabin door. Locked. But he found a nearby window that hadn't been secured. Sliding it open and reaching through the gap, he released the door. She concentrated on her own task, dropping to the deck to keep the powerful beam low, so as to minimize the possibility of their being spotted. All she found for her trouble was a crushed beer can that had gotten wedged behind the bench seat.

She stared at what had been a makeshift coffin and called up the nerve to check out its interior.

Her hand trembled as she lifted the padded seat. She couldn't stop the image from returning to her mind: Kim Quinlan's body tumbling, the seat top being replaced, a white arm sticking out at an unnatural angle. She closed her eyes for a second, then scanned the interior. It was empty. She felt a deep sense of disappointment.

But what had she expected to find? A purse...a shoe...a shred of cloth?

The beam revealed nothing; she focused it and double-checked every inch. About to give up, Eden decided she was still too far away to see anything. A closer inspection was in order, no matter how much the idea of exploring the storage area revolted her. Intending to run her hand along every inch of the inside, she leaned forward, then was startled by the sound of quick footsteps.

She whirled as Chick made a dive for her. The flashlight fell from her hand and blinked out. Before she could protest, he was lowering the bench seat and throwing her up against the stern of the boat in one smooth motion. His dark-clothed body immediately covered hers.

"Shh," he whispered into her ear.

But Eden didn't need the verbal warning. His actions spoke louder than words. Fright made her speechless. Chick had seen or heard something....

Her heart was pumping wildly, and she was having difficulty breathing. She didn't utter a sound, didn't move a muscle. His weight pressed her into the deck. After what seemed like a lifetime, she heard a double set of footsteps—and a moment later, the murmur of voices.

Chapter Five

"I could have sworn I saw a light coming from one of these yachts down here," a gravelly male voice stated.

The deck of the *Ambition* was illuminated for a few seconds, but the footsteps didn't falter. It was the harbor's security guard, not Barnes or one of his thugs. Eden would have breathed a sigh of relief—if she could have breathed at all. Chick was crushing the air from her, but she dared not try to convey that message to him.

"You're getting old, Toby, admit it," a second man said. "Your eyes are playing tricks on you. You probably just saw the reflection of headlights off Lake Shore Drive."

The footsteps continued on a few yards farther. Eden strained to hear every word.

"I thought maybe that couple I passed earlier was fooling around down here," the guard mumbled. His words made Eden's heart pound so hard that she thought he might hear it. "Maybe I was seeing things. I've been meaning to get to the eye doctor for a new pair of specs."

"C'mon. Let's go back and finish that hand of pinochle. There's no one out here."

"I guess you're right."

The two men moved past the *Ambition* once more. They exchanged sarcastic remarks about the effects of aging on various parts of the male body, including some Eden would rather not have heard about. Finally their voices faded and the night was silent, except for the occasional lapping of water against the dock. Chick waited several minutes longer before lifting his weight from her.

Eden gasped with the physical relief. "I feel as if my lungs are on the verge of collapse."

"I told you to keep an eye out for the guard."

All traces of Chick's laid-back carny attitude were gone. He sounded tough, almost menacing. Moonlight bathed his face with a silvery-blue glow that didn't manage to soften his expression. Eden bit back an irritable reply and told herself that he wasn't really angry with her. He'd gone through the same few minutes of tension-raising hell as she had, and had taken the same chance of being caught.

"I'm sorry. I'm new at this." To redirect his thoughts, Eden asked, "Did you find anything inside?" She could tell he was aware of her ploy. . . and that he was going to let the subject drop.

"Only the craft's registration," he said softly, his expression becoming neutral. "Rhonda Barnes owns the *Ambition*."

"Do you think that's important?"

He shrugged. "Doubtful. It probably means that our attorney general didn't want the yacht in his name because he might seem too affluent to his constituents. Some suspicious soul would think he was taking bribes to pay for the thing."

"I wouldn't doubt it. After what I saw, I wouldn't doubt anything where Stanton Barnes was concerned."

"We'd better get out of here while the going is good." Chick turned to the storage bench. "I'll get your flashlight."

Eden scrambled up next to him. "Not yet. I was looking for something."

"What?"

"I don't know. I was about to check out the interior of the bench more closely when you jumped me," she said, lifting the padded seat. "Looks like my flashlight is dead. Let me use yours."

Chick obliged, and flicking it on, Eden leaned in and ran her hand over the bottom of the box. She ignored the revulsion that knotted her stomach as she imagined a woman's body—still warm, though lifeless—encased in that darkness.

"Hurry it up, would you?"

The impatience in Chick's tone set her more on edge. The wood was damp and smooth under her hand... until she brushed by the corner. Something sharp and irregular scraped her fingertip. She leaned in farther and inspected the corner with the beam. A gold sparkle! She captured the tiny object.

"It's a clasp and a few links of chain from a necklace," she said, inspecting it under the beam. "This is very unusual—and it looks like real gold."

"How can you tell?"

In answer, Eden gave Chick a quelling glare. "Trust me. This is from a finely crafted necklace. And look," she said, her voice rising from its whisper. "A few strands of red hair are caught in it. The newspaper article said the Quinlan woman had a thin abrasion on her neck, but didn't suggest the cause."

"So?"

Eden could no longer contain her excitement. "Someone must have ripped a chain from her neck, but the clasp must have been caught in her hair. Don't you see? This is all we need to prove that Kim Quinlan was on this yacht!"

CHICK DIDN'T SEE how they were going to use the evidence Eden had so carefully collected. Even if the police matched the hairs to those on the dead woman's head, the authorities wouldn't necessarily believe they came from the *Ambition*. They had yet to prove a connection between the gubernatorial candidate and the model. He didn't voice his thoughts, however, because he didn't want to discourage Eden, just when she felt as if she had regained some control over her life.

While Eden found a small plastic bag in the yacht's galley, Chick kept an eye on the guardhouse. He was starting to get nervous as she emerged. The two men could return, and Eden and he might not be lucky enough to escape detection a second time.

"We'd better hurry, if you don't want your roommate to think you stood her up."

"I was just taking a last look around."

She snapped off the flashlight and began to stuff the plastic bag with the evidence inside her blouse. Chick's brows shot up. When she realized he was staring, Eden turned her back on him while she completed the procedure. Then she nodded toward land, and they made their way off the yacht as unobtrusively as they had boarded it.

"We'd better not go back the way we came," he whispered. "Instead of using the underpass, we'll have to take our chances crossing Lake Shore Drive."

"What are we waiting for?"

They ran up the grassy slope and made their way hand in hand across the highway, which had little traffic this late on Sunday night. Then they headed south, back toward Lincoln Park and their midnight rendezvous.

A quarter of an hour later, as they cut across the park's hilly lawn, Chick took his first easy breath since they'd left the taxi. If they'd been caught, they would have had a hell of a time explaining their way out of the situation. He'd had visions of them being booked at a local cop shop. He shook his head. The colorful carny language came back so easily, as if all those years since he'd last been part of the life hadn't happened. And in all those years something had been missing....

Eden tapped his shoulder and pointed. "I think I see Taffy and Hank. They're already waiting for us outside the gazebo."

He grabbed her before she could run to greet them. "Wait a minute." He pulled her into some nearby bushes and wrapped an arm around her waist. To anyone watching them, they might have been lovers.

Ignoring the image that that thought conjured up, Chick scanned the area as an extra precaution. He spotted a couple under a blanket near the lagoon. They were wrapped up in one another as well as the covering. A young woman was walking her black Great Dane. Mistress and canine passed the gazebo with barely a glance, the dog seeming more interested in the cars parked along the street. A nearby bench was occupied, but Chick didn't think the shabby-looking man stretched out there presented any danger. Everything seemed normal.

"You're sure you can trust this Taffy person, aren't you?" he asked.

"Of course I can," Eden whispered indignantly. "Taffy Darling and I have known each other practically all our lives and have been best friends since high school. She would never betray me, and before you make accusations about Hank, he's crazy about her. He would do anything she asked."

"I'm sure you're right."

"Being a carny must be real lonely, if you can't even be good enough friends with someone to have some trust."

"You learn to be cautious," he admitted.

"I'm not going to let your paranoia make me suspicious of someone I love." She wriggled out of his grasp and started down the hill. "I feel sorry for you," she called over her shoulder.

Sorry for him? That didn't sit well.

Putting aside his own reservations, Chick followed Eden and hoped she wasn't leading him into more trouble. He easily caught up with her, but didn't touch her this time. He'd been getting used to doing it. He liked the way she felt tucked into his side. They were three-quarters of the way to the couple by the gazebo when the woman spotted them. She waved excitedly, and Eden took off at a run.

Just the way she would run back to her own life and forget all about him, if she could, Chick thought. He refused to hurry after her, but watched the reunion as he closed the distance between them in leisurely fashion. The other woman's hair was pale in the moonlight. She was smaller than Eden and seemed to be full of untapped energy. The two women hugged, then stood still, directly outside the gazebo.

"What's this all about?" Taffy demanded in a light voice that made her sound incredibly young. "Why the secrecy? Why can't you come home?" Chick heard her say as he approached.

Before he could do anything about it, Eden was running off at the mouth. "A woman's body was found in the river yesterday morning. The night before, I saw that same woman being brought onto a boat. Stanton Barnes was there. I think he murdered her."

Chick caught up to Eden and slipped an arm around her waist. "The less your friend knows, the less she can tell."

"I'm not telling anyone anything." Taffy's dark eyes went from him to Eden. "Who is this guy?"

Her companion stepped to her side. "Want me to get rid of him?"

The guy didn't look as though he could get rid of a fly. He was clearly a lightweight, dressed in the latest fashion, his hair gelled and combed straight up.

"No, but thanks, Hank," Eden said quickly. "This is Chick Lovett. He's helping me."

"Helping you what?" Taffy demanded.

"Stay alive." Chick's statement earned him an elbow in the ribs and a glare from Eden. "I thought you wanted her to know the truth."

Taffy narrowed her eyes. "You sure you can trust him?"

"He asked the same about you," Eden replied.

Obviously insulted, the blonde pulled away from her boyfriend and moved in on Chick. She poked him in the chest. Hard. "I don't know who you are, mister, but I would never do anything to hurt Eden or to endanger her." She punctuated that with another jab.

"Neither would I," Chick said, and Taffy backed off.

"I told you so," Eden murmured.

"Now I want the whole story," Taffy insisted, "or so help me..."

Eden launched into a condensed version of the last forty-eight hours. When she got to the part about their search of the *Ambition*, and Taffy asked if they'd found anything, Chick's protective antennae rose once more.

Before Eden could mention the necklace clasp, he cut in smoothly. "We did learn that the yacht belongs to Rhonda Barnes rather than to Stanton himself."

"Rhonda Barnes." Taffy frowned. "Didn't she used to be Rhonda Lawrence...old-money Kenilworth family...mansion on Lake Michigan with a coach house big enough for a whole sorority?"

Chick said, "That's her."

"How would you know?" Eden asked, disbelief lacing her tone. "You don't exactly run in those kinds of circles."

Chick bit back his immediate irritation. He was beginning to think the woman was dense. Considering how much time they'd been spending together, one would think she could tell there was more to him than met the eye. But she'd merely accepted what he'd led her to believe, and was clearly too preoccupied with her own situation to investigate his more closely. He supposed he couldn't fault her for that.

"Even carnies read the newspapers," he finally told her, popping a toothpick between his lips for effect.

Hank spoke up. "You work at a carnival?" He made the place sound equivalent to a sewer.

Evidently sensitive about some things, Eden ran interference. "The Hurley-Gurley is part of Septemberfest down at Navy Pier. Several people there have been very nice to me, especially Chick. He's covering for me, pretending I'm his...uh...assistant, and he's letting me stay with him in the back of his truck on the carnival grounds."

"Back of his truck?" Taffy's eyes widened and she stared at her roommate. "I don't like the sound of this, Eden. Why don't you come home and we can figure out—"

"I can't go home, and neither can you. It isn't safe for either of us. That's why I made you promise to take such precautions when you left." She looked around, as if she suddenly realized Taffy and Hank might have been followed, anyway. "You did bring my clothes?"

"Of course. I left them right here in the gazebo."

Taffy led the way under the roofed pavilion, with Hank and a spooked-looking Eden directly behind. No doubt her imagination had been set off by the close call on the yacht, Chick thought, bringing up the rear. If anyone had followed her friends, he hadn't been able to spot the person.

Still, he thought, looking around intently, they couldn't be too careful....

LOU FARENTINO relaxed behind the steering wheel of his Oldsmobile as he listened in on the conversation the blond bimbo was having with the Payne woman.

"Here they are," she was saying. "There's a suit, a couple of blouses and two dresses in the garment bag, and your jeans, T-shirts, sweater and accessories in the case."

"Good grief, I only asked for a change of clothes, Taffy, not a whole wardrobe. Are you sure no one followed you here?"

"Positive. We took the stuff out to the loading dock. Hank left by the front door and pretended to go home. He drove around for a while, then picked me up around back. Those men that were staking out the place couldn't have been smart enough to figure that out."

Farentino laughed and addressed the receiver, as if he were talking to the blonde herself. "I was smart enough to break into your place and bug your telephone, sweetheart." Bugging the gazebo had been even easier than the apartment. "And I'm here, ain't I, listening to every word you say, just like I was right next to you."

He lifted the infrared binoculars and focused on Taffy Darling. If the Payne woman somehow gave them the slip, he knew he'd be able to find her again through the little blonde.

"You'd better stay with Hank for now," the Payne woman said, as if she could read his thoughts.

Farentino cursed. "Interfering broad." Now he'd have to follow them to find out where the pansy lived.

Taffy touched her friend's arm. "Come with us."

His quarry looked at the guy who was helping her. Chick Something-or-Other. The last name hadn't registered, but who would know that he'd heard it at all? Farentino thought. He would never tell.

"No," the Payne woman said. "I can't put you in that kind of danger. I'll call you soon."

"I don't like it, but I suppose I know where to find you."

"Don't try, Taffy, *please*. Promise me."

But the blonde wouldn't do any such thing. She folded her arms across her chest. Farentino snorted at her posture, even while he appreciated her guts. She sure was a feisty little thing.

Only half listening to the close of their conversation, he picked up the cellular telephone and dialed the number he'd memorized earlier. A last look through the binoculars assured him that the party in the gazebo was breaking up. The two women were hugging each other as if they might never see one another again. Odds were with that bet. He turned off the receiver as his call went through.

Two rings and the phone was lifted at the other end.

"Yes?" came the voice he'd expected to hear. "Did you find the Payne woman?"

"You got it," Farentino replied. "She's been hiding out at the carnival at Navy Pier. Want me to take care of the broad tonight, or what?"

Though he knew he would be well paid for it, Farentino was hoping he wouldn't be instructed to kill Eden Payne immediately. He took pride in his creativity.

"Don't do it yourself," came the surprising reply.

He wondered if he should take that as an insult to his professional prowess. "Who, then?"

"The Payne woman needs to be eliminated in a way that can't be traced back to us. Carnival people aren't the most upright of citizens, and they're always short on cash. Find someone who's desperate enough not to care how he or she earns a windfall."

That made sense. Mollified, he grunted, "You're the boss."

Farentino hung up, satisfied that he wouldn't have any difficulty following orders. When he'd been on the Payne woman's trail the other night, he'd chewed the fat with quite a few of the carnies. Instinct allowed him to recognize a kindred soul when he met one.

He knew exactly whom to contact.

TRYING TO ACT NORMALLY, feeling as if every eye would be directed at them, Eden led Chick into the State of Illinois Center just before noon on Monday. Of course, no one paid them any attention. Both were dressed for business and they blended into the crowd. Still, it didn't hurt to be cautious.

"This way," Eden said in a low voice, steering him in a semicircle to the left side of the atrium.

"Where are you taking me? The elevators are straight ahead."

"But the information booth on the other side is run by our office. Since I called in sick, I don't think I should let Marilee get a good look at me."

Eden took another look at Chick, still amazed by his transformation. She could thank Taffy for *her* clothes, but where had he gotten his? Not from the truck—she was sure of that. The only garments she'd seen in there had been his usual jeans and shirts. The suit he was now wearing looked like a silk blend, and his shoes had to be hand-stitched Italian leather. The distressed leather briefcase was a little unusual, something one might find at a Banana Republic store, but the tie was definitely Armani.

Chick had disappeared early that morning, then had shown up in his finery. She was hiding her hair under a brown curly wig that belonged to Maisie. When she'd questioned him about the source of his wardrobe, he hadn't answered, and had merely given her one of those impatient looks that always discouraged her from pursuing an issue.

They approached the banks of elevators. Chick pressed the Up button, while Eden continued to keep watch for anyone she knew. Luckily they were alone.

"I hope Barnes doesn't change his schedule and come back to the office while we're there," she said in a low voice.

"Our attorney general is undoubtedly too busy campaigning to see to his duties."

He'd made the statement with such authority—or maybe it was cynicism. Eden gave him a swift look of appraisal and couldn't help but admire the handsome profile that was accentuated by his neatly slicked-back hair. His hazel eyes met hers with an inquiring glimmer that made her drop her gaze.

The ding of a bell alerted her to an arriving elevator car. She moved closer to Chick and stared at his tie tack, which she would have sworn was studded with a perfect if modest diamond. "Amazing what they can do with zircons." Her senses clouded by the smell of his after-shave, Eden barely noted his frown. She was relieved when the doors opened and a dozen people exited, undoubtedly on their way to lunch.

Chick guided her into the empty elevator. "So far, so good," he said tightly.

Ignoring his tone, Eden breathed a sigh of relief. "Now if only the guard doesn't question my ID."

"Why would he?"

"The hair," she said, fingering the riot of curls as the doors closed. "It's not exactly me." But that had been the point of wearing the wig—as a minimal disguise, in case an acquaintance or coworker spotted her.

"Women are always changing their hairstyle. Besides, identification pictures don't usually do anyone justice."

"True." She dug into her purse and pulled the plastic-coated card from her wallet. Eden kept the conversation going to ease the tension that she felt building as she gazed out the glass wall at the open floors. "I took a closer look at that necklace clasp in daylight."

"And?"

"I think the piece it came from is old."

"You mean antique?"

"No. The design of the clasp was old-fashioned, but not that old. It reminded me of jewelry my mother used to wear."

"Kim Quinlan was a model. Maybe she bought secondhand jewelry and clothes to develop a particular style for herself."

Eden shook her head. "The dress she had on Friday wasn't secondhand. Maybe *someone* bought her unusual and expensive presents."

"Someone, huh? Don't you mean Stanton Barnes?"

The elevator slid to a stop. "If only we could get into her apartment, we might be able to verify that," Eden murmured as the doors opened with a whoosh. "But first we have to find out where she lived."

"In the meantime, where are you keeping the clue?" Chick asked, his expression devilish.

"On my person," she said, sweeping through the doors. "Where it'll be safe."

Eden ignored the low-voiced guffaw behind her and approached the guard station. This was one of the few floors in the State of Illinois Center that had built-in walls, doors that locked—and minimal security. All business, she produced her ID and lied about having an appointment with Barnes. The guard waved them on. If only the rest of their mission would go as smoothly, Eden thought. She'd called the attorney general's office first thing that morning and had tricked Barnes's administrative assistant into revealing she was taking an early lunch.

Hoping the woman hadn't changed her plans, Eden was disappointed to hear sounds coming from the area ahead. How were they going to explain their presence? she wondered, entering the outer office.

Behind the desk, a brunette hummed a rock tune as she worked on the computer. Forcing her lips into a smile that belied the shakiness of her stomach, Eden approached with Chick right behind her. "Excuse me."

The young woman looked up, and her eyes immediately slid to Chick. "Can I help you?"

"Are you Ms Kramer?" Eden asked.

"Nope. Ms Kramer is out to lunch." The brunette aimed a flirty pout in their general direction. "My computer is down, and I had to get this letter out today."

"We'll just wait, then," Chick told her, indicating the chairs a short distance from the desk.

"Sure. Make yourselves at home."

Their doing so seemed to slow down the secretary's progress. For every line or so she typed, the brunette sneaked a look in their direction while Eden stewed. She felt each minute that ticked by and wondered if Chick was as relaxed as he appeared. She couldn't tell. She didn't know for the life of her how they were going to get into that inner office before Ms Kramer returned, and sighed with relief when the young woman printed out her letter.

"Want some coffee?" the secretary asked Chick over the clacking noise.

"No, thanks. I wouldn't think of holding you up from lunch."

Eden gritted her teeth when he grinned; the brunette looked ready to melt. At this rate they would never get rid of the woman. She checked her watch. Unless Ms Kramer took more than the allotted lunch hour, Barnes's assistant would be back in ten minutes or so. Finally, with one last admiring glance at Chick, the secretary gathered her things and left for her own office.

"With our luck, she'll come back to see if she can swing lunch with you," Eden muttered as she jumped up from her seat.

"You sound jealous."

"Don't be ridiculous. I'm worried about getting caught."

"Then I'll stay out here and create a diversion if the young lady returns." When Eden gave him a startled look, he added, "It's a dirty job, but someone has to do it."

So searching the office was to be up to her. Well, it had been her idea. Clenching her jaw so that she wouldn't say something unflattering, Eden nodded and hurried inside. A rush of adrenaline lent sureness to her movements. Quickly she went through Barnes's files for anything personal. No luck there. She started on the desk and in the center drawer found a photo of his wife in evening wear, a mink draped over one shoulder.

Rhonda Barnes was still a very desirable woman, even though she was probably only a half-dozen years younger than Eden's own more mature-looking mother. The picture must have been taken some years ago, because Rhonda was no longer this slender. Eden had seen enough news photos and clips on television to know that. Thinking about the possibility that Barnes had been involved with the Quinlan woman, she wondered if he'd thought an extra twenty pounds sufficient justification for cheating on his wife.

Eden returned the photo to the drawer. About to give up, she decided to check his desk calendar. Two different hands had penciled in notes. As she turned the pages, an entry made the week before caught her eye—the initials K. Q., and a local phone number.

K. Q. Kim Quinlan.

Elated, looking for a piece of paper on which to copy the number, Eden panicked when the door opened. But it was only Chick slipping into the room.

"You'd better hurry."

"I'm trying." Frustrated when she couldn't find a blank sheet of paper, Eden ripped the page out of the calendar and flipped the pad to the correct date. She crossed to Chick. "What do you think of this?"

He had just taken the page from her when the door opened again. Eden found herself staring over his shoulder at a tall, middle-aged woman, who seemed shocked at their presence.

"What in the world are you two doing in here?" she demanded. "Explain yourselves immediately, before I call security!"

Chapter Six

Aghast, Eden stared at the formidable Ms Kramer and tried to make her mind—and mouth—function. Chick gave her a warning look. He hid the phone number in an inside breast pocket and turned to face the woman.

"You must be the attorney general's assistant—"

"I know who I am."

"But you don't know me." With a practiced smile, Chick held out his hand. "I'm Charles Lovett of Lovett Promotions. I'm sure you've heard of us."

Eden contained the gasp that threatened to loose itself from her lips, while Barnes's assistant looked doubtful and ignored Chick's hand. He finally placed it in a trouser pocket without looking in the least awkward.

"I don't know...well, maybe I have heard of Lovett Promotions," the woman said stiffly. "That doesn't explain what you're doing in Mr. Barnes's office."

Eden figured Ms Kramer was trying to cover, in case she ought to have heard of the supposed agency.

"I was looking forward to meeting your employer," Chick explained. "I've worked on other political campaigns in the past several years and was hoping I could interest him in hiring our firm. I have no doubts I can promote him right into the governor's seat."

IT'S A HARLEQUIN HONEYMOON—A SWEETHEART OF A FREE OFFER!

HERE'S WHAT YOU GET:

1. **Four New Harlequin Intrigue® Novels—FREE!**
   Take a Harlequin Honeymoon with your four exciting romances—yours FREE from Harlequin Reader Service®. Each of these hot-off-the-press novels brings you the passion and tenderness of today's greatest love stories . . . your free passports to bright new worlds of love and foreign adventure.
2. **A Lovely Bracelet Watch—FREE!**
   You'll love your elegant bracelet watch—this classic LCD quartz watch is a perfect expression of your style and good taste—and it is yours FREE as an added thanks for giving our Reader Service a try.
3. **An Exciting Mystery Bonus—FREE!**
   You'll be thrilled with this surprise gift. It is elegant as well as practical.
4. **Money-Saving Home Delivery!**
   Join Harlequin Reader Service® and enjoy the convenience of previewing four new books every other month delivered right to your home. Each book is yours for only $2.24*—26¢ less per book than the cover price. And there is *no* extra charge for postage and handling. Great savings plus total convenience add up to a sweetheart of a deal for you! If you're not completely satisfied, you may cancel at any time, for any reason, simply by sending us a note or shipping statement marked "cancel" or by returning any shipment to us at our cost.
5. **Free Insiders' Newsletter**
   It's *heart to heart®*, the indispensible insiders' look at our most popular writers, upcoming books, even comments from readers and much more.
6. **More Surprise Gifts**
   Because our home subscribers are our most valued readers, when you join the Harlequin Reader Service®, we'll be sending you additional free gifts from time to time—as a token of our appreciation.

START YOUR HARLEQUIN HONEYMOON TODAY—JUST COMPLETE, DETACH AND MAIL YOUR FREE-OFFER CARD

*Terms and prices subject to change without notice. Sales taxes applicable in N.Y. and Iowa.

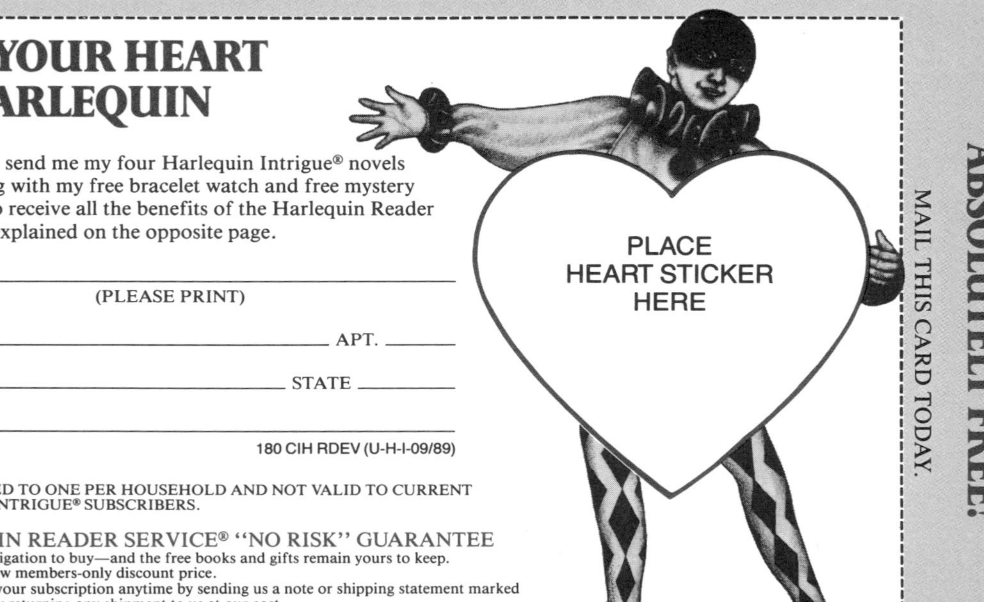

PLACE
HEART STICKER
HERE

"Such confidence... So you just came in here and made yourself at home?"

"Actually, Edie and I were waiting outside, while a very nice young woman finished printing out a letter." Chick switched gears faster than greased lightning. "Pardon me. I haven't introduced you." He wrapped a hand around Eden's upper arm and urged her forward. "Edie is my assistant."

Edie? His assistant?

Eden smiled and nodded and kept her mouth shut. The veteran carny was working his play, and she wasn't about to interrupt his rhythm. All she wanted to do was get out of the building without a uniformed escort.

"Mr. Lovett, you still haven't explained what you're doing in this office."

"Getting the lay of the land, Ms Kramer. It helps to know a potential client from the inside out, and since I've never had the pleasure of meeting Stanton Barnes, I took the liberty of looking around. Every detail of a candidate's life is on display, you know. He could use some help, starting right here in this office."

Eden could tell Chick's story was working. Before he could overplay his hand, she addressed the woman herself. "Mr. Lovett can be a bit peremptory at times. Consider it a fault or a blessing, but know that's why he's so successful. I'm sure Mr. Barnes appreciates a man of action. If you could just make an appointment for us to see him, we'll leave without further ado."

"An appointment." Ms. Kramer sighed, and Eden knew they had her. "All right. Let's see what time he has available next week."

"This week," Chick insisted. "The sooner I'm working on his campaign, the happier your employer will be."

Afraid that he was pushing too hard, Eden felt her heart skip a beat before the woman nodded and turned to the door. Chick winked at her. Not about to issue congratulations until they were safely out of danger, she gave him a stiff smile and followed Ms Kramer, who scheduled an appointment for Wednesday.

A few minutes later they were walking east on Randolph, and Eden let herself sag with relief. "Thank goodness we're out of there. Pretending you had your own PR firm was fast thinking." Chick grinned until she added, "I never would have believed you could have pulled something like that off."

"Right," he said, stopping despite the heavy pedestrian traffic. "Who would have thought someone like me could impress a woman of Ms Kramer's background and intellect?"

Realizing she'd somehow insulted him, Eden tried to smooth things over. "Listen, I didn't mean—"

"I know exactly what you meant." His tone cool, his mouth pulled in a straight line, Chick stared at her. "I've got a few things to take care of. I'll meet you back at the Hurley-Gurley later."

Eden put a staying hand on his arm. "When?"

He shrugged off her touch. "When I get there."

He stalked off without another word and left Eden staring as he disappeared into the crowd. Now what had gotten into him? He'd been having a hell of a good time playing the big shot promotions man and now he was sullen. Go figure! Telling herself she couldn't worry about some ego difficulty that she didn't comprehend—she had more serious problems to resolve—Eden walked on. Where to next?

The answer came to her immediately. It had actually already occurred to her, before Chick volunteered his assistance. She wasn't sure what Dennis Cameron could or would be willing to do for her, but she was going to pay a visit to her former fiancé.

Eden turned and backtracked toward LaSalle Street, thinking how she hated to do this—to give in and ask for support from someone she had rejected along with all that he had to offer. Dennis was a good man, the *right* man for her, if she were to believe her family, friends and Dennis himself. She'd gone along with the program for a while, had tried to believe that everyone else was correct.

But eventually she'd faced the truth.

Eden wanted more from life than what her mother and many of her own contemporaries had settled for, more than a successful husband and family, social position and money. She demanded more of—and for—herself. Self-reliance, pride in her own achievements, a sense of being really alive, and someday the love of a man who thought of her as an equal partner rather than an accessory—those were her heartfelt desires.

Dennis had seemed to understand her needs and had remained her friend, even after she'd broken off their engagement.

And Dennis would understand what she needed now, two years later.

Or so Eden told herself as she approached the high-rise building that housed the law firm of Fairmont, Zide and Cameron. A quarter of an hour later she found herself in her ex-fiancé's posh office, saying that she was in serious trouble, but not giving him the details. She was asking Dennis for his help. And his silence.

"I'll do whatever I can. You know that," he said.

Eden nodded. "I wouldn't be here otherwise." She hesitated only a second before making her plea. "Tell me what you know about Stanton Barnes."

A frown crossed Dennis's perfect tanned features. He worked for the Democratic committee and was already enmeshed in the party's political machinery. With his golden good looks, faultless style and political savvy, her ex-fiancé would soon have a second office . . . in Washington.

"You really are in trouble," he said at last. "What do you want to know?"

"The kinds of things that I can't read about. The kind of man Barnes is. His habits."

"Personal things?"

"If you think that will help."

"I could help more if I knew what was going on."

"But I can't tell you more. I'm sorry."

"One of your favorite phrases."

An awkward silence stretched between them. Eden hadn't thought that coming to him would be a mistake, but people changed. She started to rise.

"Don't go," Dennis said hurriedly. "That wasn't fair of me. You did what was best for us both."

"You're sure?"

He nodded, and she sank back into her chair. Falling silent again, Dennis stared at her as if he couldn't get his fill. An old guilt whispered through her, but Eden pushed the uncomfortable feeling aside. As he had admitted, she had done what was best for them both.

"Stanton Barnes is a very ambitious man, but I'm sure you know that," Dennis began. "What you may not know is that his wife Rhonda is even more power hungry. She's the driving force behind Barnes. She'll push her husband right into the White House if she can."

A murderer for president, Eden thought with a shudder.

"So they're happily married for the public and press. What about behind closed doors?"

"I don't know anything for a fact, but rumor has it that neither is happy with their union, and that both may have had discreet affairs."

Hauling a dead woman's body around wasn't exactly discreet, but Eden couldn't express that opinion to Dennis without further explanation. "You couldn't attach names to those rumors, could you?" she asked, though to her mind he'd confirmed what she'd already assumed was going on between Barnes and the Quinlan woman.

"I'm afraid not. Wylie Decker is an expert at handling unpleasant tasks, including keeping nasty rumors to a minimum."

Dennis wedged a hip on the corner of his desk, and his leg brushed against her knee. Not knowing if he'd done so on purpose, Eden shifted discreetly in her seat. The motion didn't go unnoticed. She could have sworn that disappointment shadowed Dennis's brown eyes.

Eden was fond of the man and hated to feel as if she were using him. Still, she pressed on. "Who's Wylie Decker?" she asked.

"Barnes's campaign manager. He's good at what he does, but I would never consider having the man on staff myself. His tactics can be questionable."

Knowing the campaign manager had been the man she'd first seen along the river—he'd been on the front page of the newspaper with Barnes and the others—Eden inquired, "What kind of questionable tactics?"

Dennis gave her an odd look. "What are you doing here in my office, when you should be at work, anyway? You haven't quit your job and gone undercover, have you? I never thought you would work for a rag."

Eden laughed nervously. "No, Dennis, I'm not a reporter, so relax."

They talked for a while longer, but Dennis didn't know Barnes or his staff well enough to give her any other information of value. When she was satisfied that she'd heard all he had to tell, Eden worked the conversation around to a few pleasantries before excusing herself. Dennis insisted on walking her to the elevator.

"If I think of anything else, I'll give you a call."

About to say that was impossible, Eden changed her mind. "Sure. I would appreciate that." Her answering machine would take the messages, and she could pick them up from a Touch-Tone telephone. A sharp ding announced the elevator's arrival. "Take care of yourself."

Before Eden could step inside, Dennis managed to plant a kiss on her cheek. She smiled and pulled away. She had the feeling that Dennis would take her back if she said the word... but she was already thinking about another man.

What was Chickie-Loves-It up to now?

CHICK THREW HIMSELF into the leather chair that faced Lake Michigan and raised his stockinged feet to the windowsill. He'd never thought of thirty-six as being old, but the comfort factor of the chair compared to that of the truck's floor was almost as seductive as Eden Payne. Or as seductive as she could be when she wasn't irritating him. He was still ticked at the surprise he'd heard in her voice while she was congratulating him. She'd inadvertently insulted him by not recognizing what was right in front of her patrician nose.

If there weren't so much to do, he would be tempted to relax and stay put for a while. Let Eden stew and wonder where he might be. Instead he picked up the telephone, and while watching a young man run his dog along the lake's edge, placed his call.

"Wabash Directory," came the impersonal reply.

Chick read the telephone number off the paper he still had in his possession. In return, the operator gave him a name—Kim Quinlan—and an address.

"Bingo."

Hanging up the receiver, he savored the luxury of the chair for a moment longer. Then he slid into his shoes and mobilized himself, not stopping until he reached the master bedroom closet, where he selected a change of clothing that he would take with him. He was packed and in the hallway within minutes. Leaving the third floor of the graystone mansion that at one time had been home to a single family, he hit the sidewalk as an empty taxi came cruising by. He waved it over and hopped in.

The chunky Pakistani behind the wheel asked, "Where to, bud?"

Peering out the taxi's windshield, Chick could see the oddly shaped building that loomed over the carnival grounds. "Lake Point Towers," was his reply.

EDEN RETURNED to the carnival grounds by way of the back lot. She wanted to avoid being seen, if possible. She doubted that too many women associated with a carnival owned a professional-looking suit, and she didn't want the others to be suspicious of her. Glancing around to see if anyone had noticed her, she almost missed the furtive sound that came from the back of Chick's truck. Was that the sound of a lock being tampered with? She stopped and listened.

Someone was definitely sneaking around, but why?

Suit or no suit, she decided to find out. But as she rounded the cab, the person moved on and slid between two other vehicles. She caught a flash of a man's bare forearm . . . and the dark green tail of a familiar tattoo.

Gator Yost.

She tried to catch up with him, but to no avail. He disappeared as if into thin air, but coming from the area of the rides was Sheets Iaconi, his dark eyes glued to her. For once his unpleasant companion was nowhere in sight.

"Hey, sweetheart, what's the hurry?" Sheets called out. "And where'd you get the fancy duds?" He was looking her over as if she were a foreign but appetizing dessert.

Thinking quickly, Eden said, "I was looking for a job, if that's all right with you."

"Oh, yeah? Your old man know about this?"

"Maybe."

"I didn't think so." Now at close range, the ride jock looked her over more carefully. "A sucker job, huh?" he said, not bothering to hide his contempt.

"It's almost the end of the season. A sucker job pays good money. What do *you* do to get through the winter?"

Sheets grinned and moved in on her. "Keep some babe with money happy."

Though the man made her uncomfortable, Eden held her ground and took the offensive. "Oh, yeah? Who?"

"I haven't picked this year's lucky lady yet." He backed her up against the truck and played with the ruffle on her blouse. "But if you're going to be making all that money, I might pick you. Believe me, sweetheart, I know exactly how to keep you happy. Sheets Iaconi has never had a dissatisfied lady yet."

"I guess I'll never know, because I'm not interested." Intending to unlock the back of the truck and take refuge inside, Eden turned her back on him and his blatant come-on.

"Hey, wait a minute," Sheets growled, grabbing her by the arm and whipping her around.

Eden was so surprised that she stumbled and crashed into the man's chest. His hungry expression made a spurt of fear well in her throat.

"Let me go!" she croaked.

"Or what?"

Suddenly he looked dangerous, and Eden chastised herself for not handling the ride jock differently. But she couldn't back down now.

"Just let go and I'll forget this ever happened."

"Maybe I don't want to, and I know your old man's not around to make me. So what are you going to do about it?"

Eden's heart began thudding in her chest, and she could feel her pulse surge with her anger. She was preparing herself to bring her high heel down on the ride jock's instep, when a male voice stopped her.

"The lady asked you to let her go."

Thank goodness. They weren't alone, after all, Eden thought.

"I'M HERE to see Alex Ryan." Chick gave his acquaintance's name to the security guard in the lobby of Lake Point Towers.

"One moment. I'll check to see if Mr. Ryan is in."

As the guard checked the directory column, Chick set down his suit bag on the counter and surreptitiously leaned forward to scan the list printed on a large plastic inset that was part of the console. Though reading upside down was a bit awkward, he found what he was looking for. Kim Quinlan was the only *Q* in the directory. He memorized the apartment number even as the other man placed the call to Alex Ryan.

Knowing the guard was wasting his time, because Ryan wouldn't be home in the middle of the day, Chick took the opportunity to absorb the details of the security station. A bank of monitors switched from camera to camera, giving the viewer fleeting images of hallways, garage and loading dock areas. He'd always liked challenges, but this situation looked pretty impossible without involving Ryan.

Besides, if he introduced Eden to Ryan on some pretext to get them into the building, she would know the truth about himself, something he wanted her to figure out on her own. They would have to find another way in.

"Nope." The guard set down the receiver and shook his grizzled head. "Mr. Ryan's not in yet."

"Okay, thanks. Sorry to have bothered you."

Sliding his suit bag over his shoulder, Chick quickly left the building, bought the daily newspaper from the box at the bus stop and crossed the street to the carnival grounds. He hopped the wood and wire snow fence that had been set around the vehicles and trailers and approached his truck. The scene that was being played there stopped him cold.

Sheets Iaconi was skulking off, his expression resentful as he looked back at the couple standing by the truck. Then Eden placed a hand on Jud Nystrom's shoulder, and spoke to the patch, her face wreathed in smiles. Too far away to hear what they were saying, Chick felt a surge of an emotion that he could only identify as jealousy.

His teeth clenched, and his free hand curled into a fist that itched to come into contact with Nystrom's perfect jawline. He had to force himself to relax. What was wrong with him, anyway? He couldn't possibly be jealous. He was attracted to Eden, but he certainly didn't have any claim on the woman.

But Jud *thought* he did, Chuck reminded himself with a testy little smile.

"Nystrom!" he shouted as he strode toward the couple. To his satisfaction, Eden's hand dropped to her side, and both seemed startled to see him. "You don't have a long memory, do you?"

"Listen, Chick—"

"No, *you* listen." Chick moved in aggressively on the other man. "Eden is not available to the highest bidder. She's mine, and she's going to stay that way. Got it?"

"Chick!" Eden protested. "Jud was only trying to—"

"I don't care what he was only trying to do. Get your fanny in the truck. We'll discuss this, after I get rid of him."

With fury written all over her face and rigid body, Eden visibly wavered before making up her mind. Finally she stormed past him and fumbled with the lock.

Chick turned back to Nystrom, whose expression was closed. "That was your invitation to get lost, in case you didn't recognize it."

The patch ignored him. "Eden, you don't have to follow his every order, you know."

It must have galled her to do so, yet Chick heard her say, "Yes, I do, but thanks for being there, Jud." And then she disappeared inside the truck.

Now that his aggravation had abated, Chick had a moment's unease. Nystrom gave him one last look and turned to go.

"Don't try to interfere between me and Eden again," Chick said softly.

Nystrom glanced over his shoulder but said nothing. Chick waited until he was out of sight, then climbed into the back of the truck. Something large and soft hit him square in the face—one of the stuffed polar bears.

"Was that really necessary?" he asked, picking up the prize with his free hand.

Eden crossed her arms and glared at him. "Was your behavior really necessary? Jud was not coming on to me. He just saved me from an uncomfortable situation with Sheets.

But you couldn't wait for an explanation. You had to jump in, all macho male. Such ridiculous behavior doesn't become you."

Amused, Chick hung up his suit bag and got rid of the newspaper and bear. Before Eden could figure out what he was up to, he'd pressed her back against the steel shelving and trapped her there. "So you don't think macho fits my personality?"

She refused to answer, but Chick could see her jaw clench. Her lips tightened in a straight line, making him imagine them softening under his own.

"It's the suit," he went on in a low, purposely seductive voice. He pressed closer, so that all each could see was each other's face. "Kind of distorts my real image. Maybe I should take it off and let you see the real man."

"Where did you get the suit?" she asked with a frown.

"Changing the subject, because you're afraid you might enjoy yourself?"

"Don't be ridiculous."

"What's the matter, Toots? You don't enjoy men's bodies?"

"I didn't say that, and you know it."

"Then you *do* enjoy men's bodies?"

Eden refused to rise to his bait, but her body answered for her. He could feel her blood racing where her breasts touched his chest, and she wasn't breathing normally. Unless he was crazy, she wanted him to kiss her. It took every ounce of willpower he possessed to move away.

"Maybe I was only playing my part with Nystrom," Chick said, his even tone belying the physical quickening he couldn't easily censor. "As were you."

"I wonder."

"About what?"

"About your mental stability—why you left me alone on the street earlier, for instance."

Chick tried not to let the reminder bother him. He turned on a battery-operated light, picked up the newspaper and forced himself to focus on the front page instead of on her.

"Well, well, well. The leading lady in our drama made the news again."

"Let me see." She pressed close to him, as if her anger were suddenly forgotten.

Chick tapped the second paragraph of the article. "The coroner says she died of a broken neck. Hmm. Her arm was broken in three places as well."

Eden made a choking noise, and her face suddenly looked pale, even in the subdued light. "What about the necklace?"

He glanced back at the article. "'Quinlan's throat was marked by twin abrasions, possibly caused by a necklace—'"

"I knew it!" she interjected.

"'—that had been pulled violently from her neck prior to her death,'" Chick continued. "'Shattered fragments of bone indicate Quinlan received a powerful blow, instrument undetermined. The police say they have no suspects at this time.'"

"Maybe Barnes struggled with her to get the necklace back, because it could identify him somehow."

"And then broke her neck with his bare hands?"

"I don't know. It doesn't sound logical, does it? He could have delivered the blow, then taken the necklace before she actually died. Maybe they had an argument, and he just lost control."

"Could be. I can't imagine he wanted his mistress attending an important fund-raiser for his campaign."

"Do you think she just showed up? That she was trying to make trouble for him there with all those witnesses?" Eden asked. "Not to mention the presence of his wife."

Noting that Kim Quinlan had worked as a model through the Yorke Agency, Chick folded the paper and set it on the shelf. "Your guess is as good as mine."

"Our guesses might be better if we could search her home."

"We can."

"You got the address, using the phone number?"

"You can be quite insightful when you want to be."

A puzzled expression crossed her features, but Eden didn't ask him to explain. "So where did she live?"

"In a condominium across the street."

"Across...you mean Lake Point Towers?" When he nodded, her eyes widened. "But we'll never get past the security guard."

"We're not going to walk in the front door."

"I assume you don't mean to climb the thing."

"I was thinking more in terms of getting in the back way, through the garage."

"And how are we supposed to get into the apartment itself?"

"By picking the lock, of course."

"I should have figured. Tell me, just when did you learn this skill?"

"When I first joined the carnival. The Hurley-Gurley wasn't a forty-miler then. We were on the road, going through small towns that had motels with vacant rooms going to waste." He realized she didn't get it, so he explained further. "Carnies sometimes use motel rooms they can't exactly pay for. Assuming we can get into the building, I'll give odds on being able to do the lock. People in buildings with security guards don't necessarily make their apartments into fortresses."

Eden was looking at him as if he had two heads.

"What now?" Chick asked, irritated anew.

"I was just wondering what I've gotten myself into. Stacking joint odds in favor of the house is one thing. But breaking and entering?"

"Getting into Kim Quinlan's apartment was *your* idea," he reminded her.

Eden didn't have an answer for that, but even so, he could sense her disappointment. It was as if his knowing how to pick a lock brought him down a notch in her estimation. Hell, he couldn't win, couldn't stack the odds in his own favor, no matter what he did, so why didn't he stop trying?

One look at the desirable if disapproving woman opposite answered that question. As for telling Eden the whole truth about himself...

Chick knew she was attracted to him, and he was certain she hated the fact. That she continued to judge him by appearances and didn't search for the real man beneath the carny act not only hurt his feelings, but got his back up, as well.

"Look, Eden, it's up to you. Say the word, and we forget about Kim Quinlan's apartment."

Though she looked as if she wanted to do just that, Eden didn't speak.

"HOW LONG are we going to have to wait out here like this?" Eden whispered as they hid behind Lake Point Towers.

She was worried that someone would spot them, since it wasn't yet completely dark. She'd wanted to wait, but Chick had thought they'd have a better chance of getting inside right after rush hour rather than late at night.

"Patience, Toots. We've only been out here a few minutes."

His sharp tone cut Eden to the quick. Didn't he realize how nervous she was? She hated hiding behind a clump of bushes like some common thief. If she dared tell him that, though, he would undoubtedly find reason to take offense again.

Adding to the strung-out state of her nerves was the physical discomfort that her clothes were causing. Chick had insisted that in this particular apartment building they would blend into the scenery better in suits than in more comfortable jeans and T-shirts, especially if the guard caught a glimpse of them on one of his monitors. She knew Chick was correct, but she had to wonder where a carny had gotten that kind of savvy.

"I think something's coming now," he whispered.

Listening intently, Eden heard the muffled sound of a car engine. "I do, too." As the sound drew nearer on the other side of the garage door, a mixture of excitement and fear washed through her and made her nerve endings tingle.

"Wait until the car has passed us," he told her. "Then we'll get in before the garage door can close again."

And hope and pray no one was getting into a car inside the garage to see their furtive entrance, she thought. They would already be taking their chances with the security cameras. The power-operated door rattled, and Chick took her hand, squeezing it reassuringly. It was the first comforting gesture he'd made since their argument in the truck. She didn't have any more time to think about his disposition, however, for a Porsche sped out of the building faster than she'd anticipated.

Then Chick was moving, taking her with him. The garage door was already lowering. He sped up and hunched over. She was forced to do likewise. Her feet moved as fast as they had when she'd outrun Barnes's thugs on Friday night. Peculiar how fear heightened one's abilities. They flew under the closing metal door almost in a crouch.

"Made it!" she gasped in sync with the sound of metal meeting concrete.

Chick jerked her to her feet and pulled her into a dark corner; there he wrapped his arms tightly around her back so that she couldn't move.

"The camera," he whispered into her hair. "Above us to your right."

Still pressed against him, trying to ignore the physical attraction he'd stirred up in the truck, and which was now multiplying by leaps and bounds, she peered over her shoulder. The camera seemed to point directly at them before finishing its sweep of the area.

"Think it picked us up?" she asked softly.

"Let's hope not. Come on."

He drew her from their momentary resting place as the camera started its reverse sweep. They were barely able to beat it to the door that let them out of the garage area. The hallway led them to the elevators. Eden's heart began to pound in earnest when she realized they had to cross behind the security guard with only the glass doors between them as cover. Chick didn't give her time to think about what might happen, but slid an arm around her waist and kept her moving.

Telling herself that the uniformed guard could hardly know each of the several hundred occupants of the building was of little comfort. Nor did seeing the person who was keeping the man's attention off the monitors.

Zelda Hurley.

What in the world was the fortune-teller doing there, and in her gaudy costume, at that? What if she saw them?

They were in the elevator and Chick was punching a floor button, before she realized that Zelda knew. Her odd gray eyes met Eden's directly for a second—as if in complicity—and then went back to the guard. As soon as the doors closed, Eden turned on Chick.

"What's Madam Zelda doing here?"

"Playing decoy for us."

"I don't understand.... You *told* her we were breaking into the building?"

"How else was I supposed to get her cooperation?"

Sudden anger made her voice shrill. "What else did you tell her? All about me?"

"Only that you're in trouble, and I'm trying to help you."

"I don't believe this!" Anger burned away the fear that had had her in its grip only moments ago. "I trusted you."

"You can trust Zelda, as well," Chick said grimly.

How dare he come on like the injured party? Eden thought. "Is that why you didn't tell me what you were planning?"

"I figured you would make a fuss." He ground out the words. "I was right."

Eden couldn't think of a rejoinder fast enough. The elevator stopped and the doors opened. Without thinking, she rushed ahead of Chick and was halfway down the hall before she realized she didn't know where she was going. He hadn't told her the apartment number. She turned back to see him standing right behind her at the last doorway. He slipped a small leather case out of his breast pocket. From it he took two tools, one with an L-shaped piece of metal wire, the other with a curved head. Good Lord, the tools looked professional!

She was about to demand an explanation, when another door opened a short way down the hall. Chick palmed the tools and pulled her into his arms.

"See you tomorrow, Bev," a young female said, as Chick shoved Eden against the door and concealed her with his own body. Then the voice lowered to a whisper. "There's a couple of strangers down the hall."

"Where?" came another voice, equally young. "Let me see."

Eden felt a moment's panic. What if the other girl decided to call her parents to the door? Or what if she alerted security? Before she could lose her cool, Chick's mouth brushed her cheek and settled at her ear.

"Pretend I'm your lover," he whispered. "And make it look believable."

Chapter Seven

Eden was so rattled that she didn't react at first. She'd wondered what getting closer to Chick might be like, but had certainly not imagined a situation like this.

"Don't worry, Joyce, they're just a couple of love-birds." The statement was punctuated by a giggle. "You'll be safe walking to the elevator."

"And entertained."

Chick trailed his lips along Eden's jawbone. His warm breath made her shiver.

"You heard her," he murmured. "She wants to be entertained. Loosen up."

Eden hadn't realized how stiffly she was holding herself against him until light footsteps approached. She forced herself to relax and slipped her arms around his neck. She kissed Chick chastely, but he nudged her lips open. A thrilling warmth flowed through her, and her nerve endings vibrated with pleasure. She swayed into Chick with a moan.

What sounded like a smothered giggle prompted her to fight losing her head. Eden told herself this was only an act, but even though she vaguely heard the elevator arrive and the doors open and close, she had no thought of ending the embrace.

It was Chick who set her aside.

Feeling oddly bereft, her knees seeming incapable of holding her up, she stood in silence. Chick used the burglar tools on the lock without so much as a hand tremor, while her insides continued to quiver. He caught her staring, and his knowing grin was enough to prick her indignation; heat rose up her neck. She bit her tongue, so that she wouldn't say something foolish. But she knew that one wrong word from him would set off her temper again.

As the tumblers clicked, however, she got her emotions under control. She was in enough of a predicament already, and wasn't about to make things worse by falling for a fast-talking, nimble-fingered con man, no matter how tempting the opportunity.

Chick allowed her to precede him into the apartment. He followed, closed the door and found the light switch. The table and floor lamps added to the final glow of daylight that was coming through the curved floor-to-ceiling windows.

"We did it," Chick said.

"*You* did it."

Her nose slightly out of joint at his blasé attitude toward the embrace, Eden walked away from him and through the long space that was both living and dining room. She looked around curiously. The odd furnishings gave her a feeling as unsettling as the kiss had been. Eurostyle was freely mixed with lacquer veneer, Scandinavian teak and other pieces that were probably meant to be art, rather than practical furniture. The room reeked of money and newness, yet the individual furnishings didn't blend. The only statement the place made was one of poor taste.

"Something wrong?"

"I don't know. It's just the way this room is decorated, as if several people had just moved in and couldn't agree on anything. It's kind of bizarre."

"I see what you mean," Chick said as he looked around. "Kim Quinlan might have been a beautiful woman, but she didn't have the style to go with her looks."

"Odd, considering her career as a model."

"She didn't design garments, she merely wore them. This isn't going to help us prove anything, so we'd better start searching."

Both knew they might be on a fool's errand. Undoubtedly the place had already been gone over with a fine-tooth comb both by Barnes and his minions, as well as by the police. Nonetheless, who knew what another search might reveal to a fresh eye? Chick worked on the larger area, while Eden went through the more personal rooms.

She began with the bath, then moved to the bedroom, made quick work of the drawers and progressed to the closets. The same lack of harmony that characterized the furnishings was reflected in the dead woman's clothing. Geoffrey Beene, Norma Kamali, Christian Lacroix, Claude Montana—most of the top designers were represented, yet again without apparent rhyme or reason in the way of creating a personal statement. Eden was checking tags on several of the garments when Chick entered the bedroom.

"Find anything?" he asked.

"A lot... but not anything concrete. Even if Kim Quinlan was lacking in personal style, she liked to spend money. There are things in this closet that have never been worn. The price tags are still attached."

"She probably did exceedingly well as a model."

"Maybe," Eden agreed. "But if Kim Quinlan had hit the big time, I'm certain I would have recognized her from *Vogue* or *Elle* or even *Cosmopolitan*. I just have the feeling she's received a lot of expensive presents. Stanton Barnes is rich enough to afford all this—"

"I hear a 'but' in there somewhere," Chick interjected.

"This is probably silly."

"Try me."

"All right." This wasn't a subject she would have chosen to discuss with the man, but Eden had to take a deep breath and just say it. "We've assumed Kim Quinlan was Stanton Barnes's mistress, right? Well, I've looked through her closets, her medicine cabinets and all her drawers. I didn't see anything that made me think a man has been around. No robe, no after-shave..." She hesitated a second, then added, "No birth control."

Chick's startled expression made her redden.

"I told you it was silly," she rushed on. "Forget it." Eden was afraid he would pursue the subject, anyway, but for once Chick decided to spare her.

"Anything else?" he asked.

"Only that every piece of jewelry in her collection is modern. Nothing with a clasp like the one I found. What about you? Any luck?"

"There were a couple of things I looked for, as well," Chick told her, conducting his own quick search of the room. "A photographic portfolio is a pretty large item, difficult to hide. A model usually can't do business without one, but Kim Quinlan seems to have been the exception," he said, checking the closet. "Not in here, either. Either she's an exception," he repeated, "or someone removed it."

"How strange. Maybe she left it at her agency."

"That wouldn't make sense. She'd need it if she were sent out on a possible assignment."

"Are you sure you looked everywhere she might have kept it?"

"Positive. I couldn't even find professional photographs of the woman, as if someone were afraid of the wrong person seeing them." Now he was making a cursory inspection of Kim's drawers. "As a matter of fact, I didn't see pictures of any kind. No scrap albums, no personal telephone directory, no references to friends or family...." He paused to face Eden. "It's as if our victim had suddenly dropped into existence out of nowhere."

"You're right," Eden said thoughtfully. "I didn't come across anything really personal, either."

"But I did find this." Chick reached into his inside breast pocket and, with a flourish, presented her with a piece of legal-size paper.

Eden took the document from him. "A lease on this condominium, dated May 1."

"Look at the name of the lessee."

Her eyes widened as she read, "W. Decker. Barnes's campaign manager. This is it—the link we need!"

"Not a direct one, but we're getting closer."

For the first time in days, Eden felt as if she could see the light at the end of a long, dark tunnel. "We're going to find everything we need to nail Barnes. I just know it. How could the police have missed this?"

"They didn't take a good enough look at the pile of fashion magazines on the coffee table." Chick took the document from her and returned it to his pocket. "I found the lease stuffed in a copy of *Vogue*."

"What in the world made you look in a magazine?"

"Sheer ignorance of correct procedure, mixed with frustration at coming up empty-handed."

With a tired sigh, Eden shut the closet doors. "All of a sudden I feel as if my adrenaline has crashed."

Chick placed an arm around her shoulders and steered her out of the bedroom and into the living room. "What you need is a drink. The portable bar over by the windows has every kind of wine and liquor imaginable."

"Do you think sticking around is a good idea?"

"No worse than breaking in here in the first place. I don't think the police are going to come back tonight, and Barnes isn't going to be taking any chances. Besides, he probably ordered this place stripped of anything incriminating. We're just lucky the Quinlan woman had a unique filing system. I don't know about you, but I sure could appreciate getting comfortable on one of these plush sofas for a while."

Eden suddenly felt too exhausted to argue. Sitting down, she watched him open a bottle of cognac. Her brain was only half functioning, yet it refused to shut down the way her body had. The furniture and clothing weren't the only things around that presented her with contradictions.

Chick was every bit as confusing.

He wasn't the typical carny. Well-spoken, he handled himself as if he was used to dealing with more than the public that strolled across the carnival grounds night after night. He seemed as comfortable in a suit as he did in jeans. Maybe he had a sucker job in the off-season. Or maybe he just came from a better environment than most of his co-workers.

It was natural for Eden to wonder about Chick's background. She couldn't help but feel that he had options other than running a One-Ball joint. She had a thing about people living up to their potential—perhaps because no one had ever expected it of her.

But Eden had expected the best from herself and could ask no less of a man she cared about. Perhaps that was why she'd considered marrying Dennis—a man with high objectives for himself—despite the parts of the relationship that hadn't worked. Chick, on the other hand, seemed content to take life as it came. She couldn't see herself seriously involved with a man who didn't have goals.

Startling her from her thoughts, Chick handed Eden a bowl-shaped glass with a splash of amber liquid in it, and made himself comfortable on the couch opposite her. She assessed him surreptitiously. Any woman would find the man attractive as he was, but she had to admit that he looked even sexier in his carny guise. She sipped her drink, and the fiery liquid trickled down her throat. Its effect on her system was almost instantaneous. The inner warmth relaxed her...and made her brave one of the questions that had been flowing through her head since he'd first made that personal confession.

"Why did you run away from home to work for a carnival?"

"I was a rebellious teenager." Chick looked surprised at her question. "My father always expected so much of me. I had to get the highest grades, be the top athlete, win the popularity contest."

Eden didn't think that sounded so bad. "At least he's a parent who wanted the best for his son."

"It was more than that. Sometimes my old man acted as if he were living his life through mine. I always came through for him, until he tried to lead my life in earnest. During my last semester of high school, Father mapped out my future...only he forgot to consult me. I was going into the family business, and that was that. He turned a deaf ear to my objections."

"What kind of business?"

"The kind didn't matter. My father's attitude did."

Eden could tell that Chick wanted to drop the subject, but she felt this was her first glimpse of the real man underneath the happy-go-lucky facade. Since she wanted to get a handle on him, she persisted. "I guess a carnival would seem exciting to a teenager. Weren't you afraid to leave everyone and everything you knew behind?"

"Fear is a healthy emotion," he answered in an aggravatingly roundabout way.

"Weren't you lonely?"

"I made friends. Abe and Zelda unofficially adopted me."

"What about your real parents?"

"I wrote to my mother a few times, to tell her I was safe."

"You mean you've never seen your mother or father since?" Eden asked.

She couldn't help but sound shocked. She might have taken a different route than the one her parents would have chosen for her, but she would never think of writing them off.

"Of course I've seen them. And before you go on worrying about it, my father and I have mended our fences." Looking down into the glass he'd set in motion so that the liquid swirled against the rounded sides, he deftly turned the focus of the conversation back to her. "What about you? What are you running away from—other than a murderer?"

Add "perceptive" to the list of qualities that made Chick so intriguing. "Not from, *to*," Eden corrected him. "There was no way I could have lived with myself, had I chosen to follow my mother's profession. Though it was a very honorable one," she added quickly.

"Which was?"

"Wife and staunch supporter of my father. I would have been pleased had he allowed me to work in the family business. Until he retired recently, Dad owned and managed a printing plant that did work for some of the major agencies and magazines. He didn't approve of women being too ambitious. He thought hard work at something other than charitable causes might chase off future husband material," she said lightly, though she hadn't forgotten the difficulty of breaking free of the mold.

When she'd announced she'd been hired for her first job, her father had cut off her more than generous stipend. He didn't understand that she hadn't considered it a punishment. And when he'd come around, he'd been shocked to learn that she hadn't wanted it reinstated. Then he'd set up a trust fund for her, one that she still refused to touch.

"So you have something against marriage," Chick said.

"I have something against marrying for the wrong reasons."

"What would be the right reason?"

Eden didn't even have to think about the answer, but discussing the subject with Chick made her uneasy. She rose and walked to the glass wall. Her back to him, she said, "Being in love with a person who respects and supports you, no matter what you want to do with your life, even if that doesn't agree with his carefully laid-out plans."

"Sounds like experience speaking."

"I was engaged for more than two years. My friends approved, my family was ecstatic, I wasn't sure. I postponed the wedding three times."

Eden took another sip of cognac and stared out at the lake and the city. Dusk had fallen, and building lights outlined the cityscape. The view would have been romantic, if she could have forgotten that it had belonged to a woman who had been murdered. The thought gripped her, reminding her of why she was there. Chick's voice directly behind her was startling.

"So what happened?" he asked.

"It didn't work out." He was standing too close—she could see his reflection in the glass. If only he would move a foot or two away, then her insides would settle down again. "Dennis wanted me to center myself around his career rather than the two of us building a life together. I wanted a husband, not a new employer. Working in the state tourism office might not be the most exciting job in the world, but it's mine." She hesitated only a second before adding, "I saw him today."

"You ran into your ex-fiancé?"

"I went to his office." Eden turned to Chick. "Dennis Cameron is a lawyer with connections in the Democratic Party. It's ironic that I left him, because I didn't want to be a camp follower, and now I've asked for his help because of his involvement with politics."

Chick frowned at her. "How much did you tell him?"

"Only that I was in trouble, that I needed information on Stanton Barnes. He couldn't help, except to confirm what we'd already guessed. Stanton and Rhonda are unhappily married. Both have had affairs—Dennis had heard of no names, of course."

"You didn't tell this Cameron character where to find you?"

"No." Eden realized that Chick had tensed, undoubtedly because of the danger Dennis's involvement might bring to them. "Don't worry. If he learns anything new, he'll leave a message on my answering machine."

"You're sure you can trust him?"

"Are we going back to that again?" Eden moved away from Chick and set down her glass on the bar, aware that he followed. "I must be a pretty good judge of character. I trusted you, didn't I?"

Chick didn't answer, merely downed the remainder of his cognac and poured himself a refill, as if he were considering her statement. Eden still didn't know why he was helping her. She'd like to think he had a better reason than feeling sorry for some poor, helpless woman. They had something in common—or had in their youth. Both had been defiant of authority and had refused to conform to their parents' idea of what they should do with their lives. Maybe Chick had recognized a kindred spirit in her.

"So what do you think we should do next?" she asked, when she realized he was staring at her, his drink forgotten.

"I can check with the Yorke Agency tomorrow morning, before the carnival opens. The newspaper said Kim Quinlan worked through Yorke."

"I'll go with you."

"No," he said quickly. "It would be a waste of time for both of us to go. You can open up the booth."

"Why don't I go and you open the booth?" Eden asked.

"Because it was my idea."

"It's *my* problem."

"Are you saying you don't want my help?" Chick inquired. "If you'd rather go this alone, speak up now. Otherwise, just relax and let me handle this one. I might be able to get more out of Rebecca Yorke than you would." He raised both eyebrows. "Some women find me charming."

There was no denying his charm, Eden thought. But she wasn't about to give him the satisfaction of agreeing. As for going it alone...she certainly wouldn't look forward to that. She hadn't realized how quickly she'd learned to depend on Chick's support.

"What?" he asked, a grin tugging at his mouth. "You're not going to set me down with some clever retort?"

She couldn't keep herself from grinning right back at him. "I'm thinking."

"Let me help."

Instinct told her exactly how he intended to do that, and curiosity kept her from moving away. Surely he couldn't affect her so completely, twice in a row.

Chick didn't have to prompt her to make the kiss look real. Eden couldn't stop her arms from wrapping themselves around his neck. And her lips parted of their own volition. The eroticism of his mouth brushing across hers, lightly at first, then with more hunger, fueled her senses. His muscular body pushing her back against the bar made her all soft and pliant inside. His hand found her breast and feathered her nipple. It took her breath away.

He was far more intoxicating than the cognac.

Cognac. She could smell the expensive French brandy on his breath, taste it on his tongue. They'd shared a dead woman's liquor. Now they were becoming intimate in a dead woman's apartment. The thought made her stiffen, made her pull away from Chick so sharply that the force of her weight jerked the portable bar out of position.

"We can't do this here!" she gasped over the noise of clinking bottles.

"Then let's get out of here," Chick whispered.

His voice was low and dripping with such sensuality that her body was forced to respond. He backed her into the bar again and pinned her there, not with his arms, but by the sheer force of his will. His fingers found the hair grazing her temple and brushed it from her forehead.

"We can find another place that's more romantic."

Like the night skies, his hazel eyes had darkened. Eden grew more and more uncomfortable under their penetrating stare. She lowered her gaze and focused on the small scar on his chin, wondering how he'd gotten it. In a desperate attempt to break the invisible bond between them, she pushed again at the portable bar. Even his reflection in the glass momentarily mesmerized her.

Still, she forced herself to be practical. "Let's just clean up these glasses and go."

She knew exactly when his expression closed; her chest heaved in a sigh of relief.

"So that's the way it is," he murmured.

She wasn't rejecting him. Not exactly. She was merely uncomfortable. The place wasn't right. The timing wasn't right. Nothing was right. She'd been an unwilling witness to a murder cover-up. She couldn't get romantically involved with anyone. Not now, not under these circumstances. He could accept it or not, but that was the truth.

Or so Eden tried to convince herself.

SURROUNDED BY DARKNESS, silence thick between them, they left the building through the garage and headed for the truck. How could Chick help but be teed off? While he turned on the class act, Eden wouldn't give in to what she was feeling, because she thought he wasn't good enough for her.

Would he really have to give her his personal bio and résumé to impress her? Chick wondered as they entered the back lot. Would he have to show her his diplomas?

As they approached the truck, he stopped and held out his arm in front of Eden.

"What?" she whispered.

"The truck door's not completely closed."

"Impossible. I watched you lock it."

Chick gestured to Eden to stay put, but as he advanced on the vehicle and a conceivable intruder, he sensed she was right on his tail. Damn the woman! He didn't need to be distracted. She didn't need to get herself hurt. He glanced over his shoulder, but if Eden noted the impatient look he gave her, she ignored it.

He focused on the door and found the flashlight he'd stuck into a suit pocket, in case the electricity in the Quinlan woman's apartment was out. His ears were attuned to the night, but the only sounds he heard were those of distant traffic, faint strains of laughter and the muted sound of the lake lapping at the nearby shore.

Before clicking on the flashlight, he buried the lens face in his jacket, so as to give no warning. He reached for the bottom of the door... then threw it open, as he thrust the light into the cavernous interior.

Empty.

"Damn!"

Chick swore out loud this time, and made the opening in a single leap. He rushed to the shelving, knowing what he would find even before he got there.

"What's going on?" Eden demanded, scrambling into the truck behind him.

"Someone was busy while we were gone." He flashed the light toward the shelving and focused on the empty cash box. "We've been robbed."

LOU FARENTINO parked the car within sight of the building at Sheridan and Diversey. He had a free evening ahead of him as soon as he placed the call. He picked up the telephone and dialed, content that he could sit and watch for the blond bimbo all night if necessary. He wasn't in any hurry. Foreplay with an unwary victim was the best part.

"Yes?" came the voice at the other end of the line.

"It's done. You can relax about the Payne woman."

"Everything is arranged, then. You're sure there won't be any last-minute hitches?"

"Money talks," Farentino said, adjusting his seat to a more comfortable position. "And kills. The Payne woman doesn't know it yet, but she's bought herself a ticket to nowhere."

Chapter Eight

"Charles, how nice to see you again," Rebecca Yorke said, her attractive face lighting with pleasure. Her hand lingered in his a few seconds longer than necessary. "And you've come to see me in person. I'm so flattered. You must have a very important assignment that you want to discuss. Sit." She indicated a chair on the other side of her desk. "Can I have Alycia get you a cappuccino?"

"No, thanks." Chick made himself as comfortable as he could in the ultrafeminine surroundings. Rebecca gravitated toward delicate furniture, pastel colors and lots of frills. Expensive ones. "Actually, I'm not here on business, but to ask you a personal favor."

"Hmm." She raised her brows. "That sounds promising."

Rebecca was a professional flirt as well as a sharp businesswoman. She had honed both skills during her own modeling days, when Chick had first met her. Though she was several years older than he, time had been generous to the silver-blond beauty, and she had used both her experience and her looks to help make the Yorke Agency a success. Chick had worked with Rebecca's models many times in the past several years. That was why he'd avoided bringing Eden with him. She would have immediately known the truth.

"I need information on Kim Quinlan."

"Well, well." Rebecca sat back and scrutinized him. "You and the police. You wouldn't want to tell me what your interest is, would you?"

"I would... but I can't just yet. I'm dealing with a very delicate situation."

A speculative gleam shone from her large gray eyes. "I suppose so... considering the woman was murdered."

"Don't let your imagination run wild. I didn't even know Kim Quinlan, or I wouldn't need your help," he assured her.

"I've always thought you an intriguing man, Charles, and now you've confirmed my opinion." She tapped her desk top with long, pale pink nails. "I don't normally give out personal information about my girls, but since Kim met such an untimely demise... I guess it wouldn't hurt. What do you want to know?"

"Everything you do. Start from the beginning. How long did she work for you?"

"Only since last March."

And the lease had been dated May 1. Chick wondered if that meant anything. "Did someone refer her?"

"A photographer. He's new, but you may have heard of him. Paco Jones."

"I recognize the name. Kim Quinlan did some work for him?"

"As far as I know, she never even thought of modeling until she met Paco at a social gathering," Rebecca explained. "He was so impressed by her scintillating look that he called me personally and arranged a time for us to meet. I was quite grateful to him. Kim Quinlan's combination of innocence and sexuality was salable."

"So she was successful."

"Modestly so. She wasn't as young as most of the girls starting in the business. Kim insisted she was only twenty-one, which would still be seasoned, but I never believed her. Add at least two or three years," Rebecca said with certainty. "She did well despite her age, but as you know, building a reputation takes time, something she ran out of."

"Considering she was living at Lake Point Towers, she must have had some money of her own."

"Hardly." Rebecca laughed. "The first time we met, she was wearing an outfit that couldn't have cost her fifty dollars. That changed quickly enough. Within a couple of months, she began showing off designer garments and kept talking about her ship coming in soon—and that if she wasn't famous by then, she would get out of the business. Patience was not one of her better qualities. Anyway, I assumed a man was involved."

"But you don't know for sure."

"Kim was very secretive."

Having an affair with a married gubernatorial candidate wasn't something either would want to broadcast, Chick thought. Was it possible that Kim had hoped Barnes would dump his wife for her, after he won the election?

"You're sure she couldn't have been getting money by some other means? Something...not exactly legal?"

"Like drugs?" Rebecca pulled a face. "If so, Kim wasn't using what she was selling. You know how common that is in this business. Believe me, I recognize the signs when I see them. Besides, that kind of thing gets around. No, I think my instincts about a man were correct."

"What about friends or family? Did she ever mention them?"

Rebecca thought about it for a moment. "Like I said, she was secretive. She didn't volunteer anything about her background and she seemed to be a loner. I once jokingly told her I thought she'd been dropped out of the heavens fully grown. Kim laughed and said that in a way I was right."

An odd comment, Chick thought. He didn't think Rebecca could shed any more light on the woman. Kim Quinlan was turning out to be something of a mystery. Maybe Paco Jones could tell him more. He'd never met the photographer, but that wouldn't stop him. His reputation opened all kinds of doors in the city.

"Rebecca, you wouldn't have a couple of spare photographs of Kim Quinlan, would you?"

"I have a few. What do I get in trade?"

"First consideration the next time I need to use models for a promotion."

"Done."

Rebecca not only found him the photographs, but set Chick up with Paco Jones as well. An envelope of eight-by-ten glossies under his arm, Chick left the office, hailed a taxi and headed for the photographic studio, located in an area west of the Loop that had not yet been yuppyized.

On the outside, the graystone two-flat looked as worn as its neighbors, but the inside had been gutted and transformed. Paco had set up the entire first floor as a combination office and studio, with a darkroom in back. While he offered Chick a director's chair, the photographer sat on a pile of cushions that lay heaped on one of his sets.

"There's not much I can tell you about Kim," Paco stated. His dark eyes narrowed as he studied Chick. "But I would like to see the bastard who killed her hang." He paused, as if expecting a reaction. When he got none, he said, "So you're not talking. Rebecca warned me."

"I have my reasons."

Paco nodded. "Okay, shoot. Questions, that is. I'm the photographer here." He laughed at his own joke.

"Rebecca said you met Kim at a social event."

"A fund-raiser."

Chick knew the answer before he asked his next question. "For whom?"

"Stanton Barnes."

"Did someone bring her?"

"Nah. Kim told me she crashed the party. Wanted to see how the other half lived. She was impressed."

"So you introduced her to Rebecca, and she started living like the other half herself. Do you have any idea where she got the money?"

"I only photographed her a few times. I didn't know her that well personally. No one did. Poor kid." Paco shook his head. "Leaves the nice, quiet country life to find her 'true place' in the big city, and what she finds instead is trouble... the permanent kind."

"So she wasn't from Chicago. Where then?"

Paco's brow furrowed and he shook his head. "All I remember is something about her being raised on a dairy farm. Probably why she had such a perfect complexion. Photographers dream of finding models with skin like that."

Though Chick spent another quarter of an hour talking to the man, he didn't learn anything more of value, so he headed back to the carnival.

At least he'd discovered that the Quinlan woman had met not only Paco Jones but Barnes as well at the fund-raiser. That fact added to the lease and the necklace clasp would help to corroborate Eden's story. If only he could convince her that it was enough to make a case, so that she would step forward. A murderer with high visibility wouldn't be sitting on his behind, twiddling his thumbs, when a witness to his crime was on the loose.

Chick had a gut feeling that Eden's time was running out.

BORROWED WIG in hand, Eden knocked on the Washingtons' trailer door about an hour before the carnival was scheduled to open for the afternoon. "Maisie, it's me."

"Let yourself in," came the cheerful reply.

Eden did so, and found the other woman bent over the stove, taking something out of the oven.

"Mmm, smells wonderful."

"Cranberry orange muffins. I got coffee to go with 'em. Wanna be bad?" Maisie asked.

"My mouth's already watering, and I just realized I forgot to eat lunch. I would love to be bad," Eden admitted. "Oh, I brought your wig back. Where do you want me to put it?"

"Bed's good enough, baby."

After depositing the wig in the tiny back room, Eden helped get things ready. She placed the coffeepot, mugs, milk and sugar on the table, while Maisie loosened several muffins from the tin.

"You never did say why you needed to borrow that thing, anyway."

Eden had hoped she wouldn't have to explain. "I went looking for an off-season job." She found it difficult to lie to the woman who had been so kind to her, but didn't want to involve Maisie in her troubles any more than she had to. "My hair was just such a mess, you know?"

"Mmm-hmm."

Rolling her dark eyes, Maisie slid onto the bench behind the table. Obviously she didn't believe the story. Eden sat down opposite her and changed the subject.

"I assume you heard about the robbery last night."

"Sure enough." Maisie filled the two mugs of coffee, then added milk and three teaspoons of sugar to her own. "Chick stopped by early this morning and told Felix and me all about it. I can't believe the thief got him, too. That makes three robberies in one week. No one's safe these days. If only we could catch the fool, I'd whomp his butt good."

Too worried to find the statement humorous, Eden bit into her muffin and sipped her coffee. Why did something like this have to happen now? She didn't need another kink in her overly complicated life. She'd told Chick about seeing Gator around the truck the day before, and he'd already passed on the word to Abe and Zelda. They'd all agreed that Gator needed watching, especially since Felix had been robbed while he'd been playing gentleman by helping out Ginger. That was one reason Eden didn't say anything about Gator to Maisie. The other was that she hated repeating gossip.

"I just hope the thief doesn't succeed in driving the Hurleys out of business," she said, nibbling on the muffin. "By the way, this is delicious."

"Thanks, baby." Maisie had already finished her first muffin and was reaching for a second. "These crimes have been hard on that poor old couple," she said. "They've lost three jointees this season because of the robberies. Good thing Chick was available to take over the One-Ball booth when the last one left."

Eden stopped chewing and swallowed the mouthful before speaking. "He took it over? You mean he hasn't been with the carnival the entire season?"

The other woman gave her a strange look. "He only started last week, a few days before you showed up. Must have come from one of the other forty-milers working this area. Chick didn't tell you?"

"No."

Eden wondered why. Chick had given her the impression he'd been with the Hurley-Gurley since he ran away from home as a teenager. That he'd omitted some very important information made her uneasy. One more piece to complicate the Chickie-Loves-It puzzle.

Distracted by the thought, she checked her watch. "Goodness, it's later than I realized. If Chick isn't back yet, I should start setting up the booth without him."

"I'll give you a hand."

"Maisie, you're always feeding or helping me. How will I ever repay you?"

"Makes no nevermind. Things'll even out. The good Lord sees to that."

Hoping she was correct, Eden didn't argue. The other woman's generosity was boundless. She had to accept that and hope things would indeed even out in the end. No—she would make sure they did.

After washing the cups and cleaning the table, they retrieved the boxes filled with stuffed animals and headed for the One-Ball booth. Eden intended to come back for the last box filled with milk bottles and balls after setting up the prizes. Down the midway, several ride jocks and jointees stood in a cluster, their heads together as if in conspiracy. Laughter spilled from the small knot of people.

"Something must be going on," Eden commented.

"Up to no good, if you ask me."

Curiosity prompted Eden to keep her eyes on the group as she set down her box in front of Chick's joint. A few of the carnies glanced her way. More laughter. She began to get uneasy as she unlocked the gate that would let them inside the booth, then realized that Nickles Vogel had separated from the pack and was trotting toward them.

"Uh-oh, trouble," she muttered to herself.

"Nothing you can't handle."

They'd just set the boxes on a counter inside when Nickles caught up to them. He was unkempt as usual; his beady eyes barely grazed Maisie, then settled on Eden.

"Got an invitation for you."

"Really?" she asked, stepping out of the booth. "What kind of invitation?"

"You ain't had time to try out no rides yet. Sheets wants to make up for gettin' you riled. He figures his Astro-Rocket's the ticket."

Knowing they were up to something, Eden shook her head. "That's all right. Tell him I accept his apology."

"But he wants you to have a free ride," Nickles insisted, his shifty eyes narrowing.

Now Eden knew the other carnies had something unpleasant planned for her. "I'm not in the mood."

"Why not? Think you're better'n us?"

"I didn't say that."

"Then why're you draggin' your feet?"

Behind her, Maisie tugged at the sleeve of her T-shirt and whispered, "Go on. Get it over with, baby. They won't leave you alone till you do."

Realizing this was to be an initiation of some sort, and sensing that Maisie didn't seem worried, Eden figured the ride thing was a ritual for newcomers. No doubt Sheets figured he could scare her and entertain his buddies at the same time. Little did they know she loved carnival and amusement park rides—the wilder, the better.

"All right," she finally told the sullen man. "I'd enjoy a ride."

Nickles smiled, showing green- and brown-stained teeth. To her disgust, he wiped his nose on his sleeve, trying to muffle his snicker as he turned to go. Maisie patted her shoulder comfortingly.

Eden secured the booth, and they set off down the midway after him.

Several hundred feet down the line loomed the Astro-Rocket—a long, girderlike structure with two passenger capsules at each end. She'd seen the thing at work. The main structure turned on its axis, while the capsules both circled each other and individually whirled in tight circles. That meant she'd be turning in three directions at once.

Eden was thankful she'd only had one of Maisie's muffins.

Every person she'd met at the carnival and some she hadn't were gathered at the ride's base waiting for her. Sheets was on the platform at the head of the crowd. Only Abe and Zelda stood away from the others, as if they didn't quite approve of their employees' antics. Some of the carnies were watching her approach expectantly, while others were trying to appear casual... as if she wasn't supposed to suspect what they were up to.

Fat chance!

Drawing closer, Eden felt her stomach do a queer little dance, despite her love of anything that turned, dipped or whirled. Intuition told her that this was going to be the roughest ride of her life. Nevertheless, she was determined to be a good sport and not spoil their fun.

Maisie left her side to join Felix. "Godspeed."

"Thanks," Eden said, knowing that "speed" was the operative word.

She marched up to the platform where Sheets waited for her, then challenged her audience. "Anyone brave enough to join me in this death trap?"

"The babe's afraid," Gator said. He pushed his stringy hair away from his face and straightened his thin shoulders. "I'll be happy to hold your hand."

"You do, and I'll break it!" Ginger promised.

He stepped forward, anyway, and the orange-haired woman grabbed him by his suspenders.

"Shrew! Get your hands off me!"

"I'll volunteer!" yelled a short, rotund man Eden didn't know.

Jud stepped in front of the squat stranger. "How about me? I've always liked fast women and fast rides."

"Jud, hush!" a middle-aged woman cried. "You know she's got to do it alone."

When it seemed as if he would ignore the woman, several people at once began giving him a hard time.

The patch laughed and held out his hands. "Sorry, Eden, I guess I'm outvoted. This ride's for you."

Eden made a clucking sound like a chicken that earned her a few laughs.

Stepping past her, Sheets opened the capsule's door. "Your chariot awaits, sweetheart."

Eden climbed inside and sat in the center of the padded bench. A cigarette hanging from the corner of his mouth, Sheets secured the seat belt—a combination of metal bar and webbing—that would hold her securely in place.

His eyes held a wicked glint as they met hers. "You have a good one, now, hear?"

"I'm sure you'll do your best to make it as good as possible."

"Got that straight."

He slammed the door and disappeared from view. A moment later, the ride was set in motion.

Eden let her head relax against the cushioned backrest, took a deep breath and held onto the metal bar as she was lifted skyward. The girder turned, and the two capsules rotated around each other. Next, her capsule started spinning, slowly at first, then so fast that her head started spinning too. She screamed and heard a roar of approval from below... whichever direction that was.

As the AstroRocket was jacked up to full throttle, Eden's glimpses of the carnies waving and yelling at her grew shorter and shorter. Just when she thought the ride couldn't get rougher, it stalled for a few seconds, then started up again, making her stomach lurch and her head and right shoulder whack against the capsule's side. She let out another scream, this one louder than the first.

That was, apparently, exactly what the audience was waiting for. They whistled and clapped and shouted. The ride stalled again, this time leaving her hanging upside down, until she thought she couldn't bear it. If she started yelling at Sheets to let her down, he would torture her even longer. Stoically she kept her mouth shut.

The ride jerked to a start and Eden felt something give. The webbing against her waist eased, and the metal bar moved in her hands. The hinge must somehow have worked loose.

"Wait a minute!" she cried, her heart pounding. "Stop! Something's wrong with the safety belt!"

But either no one understood her...or no one believed there was a problem.

Trying not to panic, Eden braced herself as best she could, but the next stop and start did more damage to the hinge. The webbing gaped, and she began sliding around in the seat. Her gorge rose, and she tasted the bile of fear until she could barely think straight.

Bombing downward...I'll pass the ride jock...have to get his attention.

"Sheets, help!" she shouted. He had to listen, to believe her. "Sheets, something's wrong!"

He waved as she went careening by.

When the capsule was as high as it could go and upside down, the ride once more came to a dead stop. Eden wedged her feet against the opposite side of the chamber and tried to keep her weight from pressing on the damaged safety belt and bar, but the webbing gave, and the metal ripped free.

The AstroRocket started again, and centrifugal force sent her bouncing from one metal wall to the other.

Screaming in terror, she clawed at the seat and tried to control her body, which was being thrown around like a rag doll. The next whirl of the capsule sent her flying at the cage door. Instinct made her wind her fingers through the heavy metal mesh and hold on for dear life.

Another sharp jerk—and the door's latch gave with her weight.

"He-l-l-lp!" she screamed as the door swung open. With a rip of material, her lower body shot into space.

"Look!" someone yelled as her legs dangled and twisted in the air.

"Sheets, get her down!"

Eden's fingers were screaming with the agony of holding on. The ground was coming toward her at a dizzying speed. The ride was slowing, her head spinning. Then the thing she feared most happened.

Her fingers began to slip....

Chapter Nine

Wylie Decker passed a worried-looking Stanton Barnes and slid into his favorite wing chair in the Gold Coast town house. Sitting there had become second nature, so that he sometimes forgot it didn't belong to him and never would. His excursions into fantasy didn't last long, however. He was honest with himself, if with no one else.

He might not have what it took to be a Governor Stanton Barnes—breeding, old money, social position—but he had what it took to make one.

He was an old-style promoter without scruples; he was proud of the fact.

Before he could get down to business, Rhonda swept into the room and addressed him without preamble. "Are you positive the Payne woman can be bribed to keep her mouth shut?" She gave him a tight little smile. "Assuming you ever find her."

Decker clenched his jaw so he wouldn't say something to make her turn on him, but he was getting weary of Rhonda questioning his abilities to get a job done. "Everyone has his . . . or her price."

"Sometimes the price is too high," Barnes interrupted. As was common lately, he was pacing the room to work off nervous energy. "We already know that firsthand."

"Kim had proof that could hurt the campaign," Decker said calmly. "Eden Payne doesn't. No one can make the connection. The apartment's clean, and the owner of that unit will be in Japan for another year or so."

"So when we find Eden Payne, we'll tell her Kim's death was a mistake—an accident—play on her sympathies, make her see she can't prove a thing." With each word, Barnes's tone gained assurance. "She'll be happy to come out of hiding. Maybe she'll even choose to leave town."

Decker wondered if Barnes was serious, or purposely playing dumb.

"You're dreaming, my pet," Rhonda told her husband with a contemptuous laugh. "This whole thing is a nightmare that just keeps getting worse. If we're not careful, it'll explode in our faces."

Though she had other flaws, Decker thought, at least she wasn't naive. "You have a point, Rhonda," he said. "But even nightmares end sometime."

CHICK ARRIVED at the carnival grounds, changed into jeans and a shirt and headed down the midway, just in time to hear shrill cries coming from the knot of carnies who were looking up at the AstroRocket. Something was very wrong. He began to jog, and when he saw the jeans- and T-shirt-clad figure suspended in midair, he ran.

"Eden!" he cried softly, not wanting to distract her from holding on.

Something lodged in his throat and squeezed his chest tight. If anything happened to her... No, he wouldn't think about the possibility.

As he got to the fenced side of the platform, the ride was stopping and bringing her closer to safety. He thanked God, but suddenly she lost her grip and fell the final ten feet to the ground with a heartrending scream. Voices rose as everyone pressed in on her. At the back of the small crowd, Chick was unable to see anything. Was she all right? Even conscious? He shoved his way through the cluster of bodies surrounding her prone form.

"Eden, say something!" he urged.

Her eyes were open and she was trying to sit up. Jud was helping her on one side, Maisie on the other. Chick knelt next to the patch. Neither said a word as Chick took over and gathered Eden into his arms.

"I'm . . . all right," she said with a groan.

"Don't try to talk."

"You just told me to say something." She tried to pull away from him.

"Stay put!" Amazingly, she stopped struggling and lay docilely in his arms. He looked around at a dozen guilty faces and stopped when he saw Sheets. "Well, what the hell happened?"

"I don't know," the ride jock insisted. "We were trying to give her a hard time, not to kill her."

"It was just an initiation," Ginger stated. "We've all gone through them."

Gator put his arm around his old lady. "The babe wasn't even afraid until something went wrong."

"The safety bar and belt came loose," Eden said, and Sheets whirled, heading for the ride.

She touched her temple and winced. Chick noticed that the area was already starting to discolor.

"Do you hurt bad?" he asked, wishing he could take the pain away.

"Only all over." She gave him a disgusted look that he found encouragingly normal.

"I meant, do you think anything is broken?"

Eden began moving her body, all the way down to her Reebok-covered feet. "Nope. I'm just one big sprain." She tried to free herself again, and when he held her fast, she said, "I don't have enough energy left to fight you today, so give me a hand, would you?"

He and Maisie helped her to her feet as Sheets returned, safety bar in hand.

"I don't understand," the ride jock muttered, holding out the thick length of metal piping, which seemed to be in perfect condition. "Nothing is broken. Somehow the bolts securing this side to the hinge worked free."

"When was the last time you checked your equipment?" Chick asked.

Sheets hefted the metal squarely in his hand and gripped the bar so hard that his knuckles whitened. "You trying to accuse me of negligence?"

"If the damn thing could come apart so easily—"

"Hold on here." Jud stepped between the two men and took the potential weapon from the ride jock. "Fighting isn't going to solve anything. Accidents happen."

Chick had seen a few accidents in the years he'd worked as a carny, but he'd never been personally involved. He turned his full attention back to Eden. She looked shaken, but determined to hide from him what she probably saw as a weakness. How easily he read her.

And how thoroughly he was involved with her—more than he'd ever meant to be.

"Can you walk, baby?" Maisie asked sympathetically.

"I think so."

Holding onto the two of them, Eden took a few experimental steps. She was limping, and almost tripped on the denim material that was now trailing on the ground in front of her. They stopped near Abe and Zelda, who were huddled together, looking horrified.

Abe patted Eden's arm with a shaky hand. "I'm so sorry. I wouldn't have let them do this to you if I'd thought—"

"I know you wouldn't," Eden interrupted. "I don't blame you. I know everyone only meant to have some fun." She turned toward the others. "Aah." Wincing, she shifted her weight off her right foot. "I'll be okay. You don't have to stick around. The carnival is scheduled to open in a few minutes, so you'd all better get to work."

The crowd broke up, leaving behind only the Hurleys and Washingtons.

"Chick." Zelda's voice quivered on his name. "I think you should take her to an emergency room."

"No!" Eden looked from the elderly fortune-teller to him. "I don't need a hospital."

Chick frowned. "Maybe Zelda's right. You could have internal injuries or a concussion."

"My insides will be fine, once they have a chance to settle down," Eden insisted, "and if my head hurts, it'll be your fault for aggravating me. I just want to get cleaned up and maybe lie down for awhile. Okay?"

"A hot shower will do her good," Maisie stated.

And Felix added, "She can come to our place and stay there as long as she wants."

Chick knew when he was outnumbered. And he figured Eden wouldn't set foot in a hospital, unless he dragged her there kicking and screaming. Undoubtedly, she was afraid they'd have to answer too many questions and was paranoid about Barnes being able to find her. He guessed he couldn't blame her, no matter how impossible that sounded.

"All right," he said finally. "I'll make a deal. I'll drop the hospital idea for now, and you promise to let me know if you start feeling worse. If you do, you'll see a doctor without any more arguments."

"I promise."

Chick was about to help her to the Washingtons' trailer, when he felt a restraining hand on his arm. Zelda.

"I must speak to you," she said, her tone urgent.

"Let me take care of Eden. Then I'll come find you."

"This is important," Zelda whispered; her tone made Chick uneasy.

"Listen, you and Madam Zelda have that chat, while Maisie and me bring Eden to our place," Felix suggested.

"Enough already!" Eden mutinously shrugged away from them all. "Stop acting as if I'm unconscious or something. I don't have a concussion. Nothing's broken. Okay?"

With that, she turned from them and limped off.

Maisie rolled her eyes and signaled to Chick to remain where he was. She and Felix hurried to catch up to Eden, one on either side, but neither offered to help her. Worried as he was, Chick figured that it would be adding fuel to the fire if he went after her himself.

Zelda stroked his arm in a soothing gesture. "She'll be fine, Chick. *This time.*"

Furrowing his brow, he looked down at the small woman. "I don't like the way that sounds." Her words worried him, especially since he hadn't told her the kind of ordeal Eden had been going through. He had the distinct feeling that he was dealing with something intangible—Zelda's intuition—when he asked, "Do you know something you're not telling me?"

"I sensed your Eden was troubled, even before you asked for my help yesterday. Her aura was cloudy, the particles in the surrounding atmosphere disturbed. I had no idea the source of disturbance was here, among us, until a short while ago."

"What do you mean?" Chick asked.

"Zelda tried to get me to stop Eden's initiation," Abe told him. "She knew."

"Knew what? Zelda, do you think someone tried to harm Eden on purpose?"

"I felt disturbing vibrations all morning." Her odd gray eyes had a faraway look, as if they had turned inward. "And now I sense danger beyond a carnival prank...."

"Wait a minute," Chick protested. "Eden's problems have nothing to do with anyone here."

"I am only interpreting the atmospheric vibrations," Zelda insisted. "And the tarot cards. Eden is in great danger. A malevolent force was at work here today."

"Who?" Chick asked.

"That I don't know. There were too many psyches to distinguish."

Abe circled his wife's waist. "But Zelda's still onto something."

"Maybe."

Chick might have been convinced, had the elderly woman been more straightforward about her intuition. But tarot cards? Malevolent forces? He couldn't help but wonder if she wasn't getting carried away, mixing up reality with the part she played as Madam Zelda, Fortune-Teller.

"I'll watch out for Eden more carefully from now on," he promised. That was the truth.

Zelda closed her eyes and sighed.

"Good," Abe said. "We'll both sleep better tonight, knowing that. I'm beginning to wonder if it isn't time for us to retire. First the robberies, now this. When are the problems going to end?"

When he came through for them, Chick thought. And when he fulfilled his promise to nail Barnes. If anything happened to Eden...

"Go to your Eden," Zelda said, as if she knew what he was thinking.

Chick kissed her on the cheek and clapped Abe comfortingly on the shoulder before he took off for the back lot. He stopped by the truck just long enough to grab the envelope of photos Rebecca had given him, then made for the Washingtons' trailer. Felix was just leaving. Seeing Chick, he called to Maisie, who came outside immediately.

"Mmm-hmm. That woman can go through clothes like nobody's business," she said. "I left her one of my old dresses to change into on the bed."

"Eden's in the shower," Felix explained. "Your woman's sure a feisty one."

"That she is, Felix. Thanks for putting up with her."

They took off for their joint, and Chick entered the trailer. He could hear the shower. No doubt Eden would be happy to sleep the day away after what she'd been through. He set the envelope on the table, but no sooner had he made himself comfortable on the couch when the shower stopped.

Then he could hear her moving around in the tiny cubicle, could imagine her smoothing a towel over her long body. Her long, nude body. Her long, nude, battered and bruised body, he reminded himself. That didn't, however, stifle his immediate and natural reaction to the first image.

The door opened, and she stepped out of the bathroom, a belted, knee-length robe covering her. Water dripped from wet tendrils of hair that contrasted sharply with the white terry.

"Feeling better?" he asked.

"Much."

She was barefoot, natural, her defenses down. She'd never been so appealing. Shoving her hands into the robe's pockets, she approached him. Her leg was already swelling and discoloring where the denim had ripped and left her delicate skin defenseless.

"Did you take care of that scrape?" he asked.

She glanced down at her leg. "This is nothing."

"It looks like it was bleeding."

"It stopped."

"Sit. I'll find some antiseptic. No arguments."

A few minutes later Chick was kneeling on the floor next Eden. He examined her leg—one of the first things about er that had appealed to him. Now every part of her had the ower to arouse him in some way, even her sharp tongue. den made him feel more alive than he'd been since leaving e Hurley-Gurley when his father had finally tracked him own. He'd been twenty years old then—sixteen years ago. e couldn't believe he'd spent half a lifetime without her.

The flesh of her calf was warm and pliant under his hand, d he wished for different circumstances. Someday, he omised himself. Maybe.

Gently he applied hydrogen peroxide to her shin. He was reful, but the flesh had been badly scraped. Eden sucked her breath and pulled a face, but didn't complain. It was er all too quickly. He released her leg.

"Anyplace else need tending?"

She hesitated a fraction too long before saying, "No."

"Where?"

She blinked, her wet, spiked lashes feathering her pale in. "My shoulder. The right one."

Chick sat down next to her on the couch, while Eden pped the cloth down, just far enough to let him get at her her, smaller scrape. She had a beautiful shoulder—or ould have, when the skin healed. He applied the antisep-, felt her wince and wanted to kiss the hurt away. It was onic that his lips would give her more pain, when he anted to give only pleasure.

He suddenly realized that she was staring at him. Her blue es were wide open and vulnerable. She couldn't hide what e was feeling, what she wanted.

Her pulse throbbed in her elegant throat.

He throbbed everywhere.

He replaced the cap on the bottle and set it on the floor, deliberately taking his time. She didn't look away; neither did he. He touched her neck, and her pulse jumped under his fingers. Then he cupped her cheek and brought her face closer.

The kiss was slow, easy, almost casual... but only for a moment. He could feel her heart flutter through the pulse in her throat. Emotion rather than passion prompted Chick to intensify the kiss, to reveal his burgeoning feelings, to convince her that he cared. A few seconds fraught with emotion, because she'd almost been taken from him....

And then she drew back, lowered her gaze, made him feel first foolish and then angry. Even with her defenses down, Eden had drawn an invisible barrier between them before things went too far. The class act couldn't handle what he had to give, couldn't accept her attraction to someone she believed to be from a caste below her own, couldn't see past the fast talk to the man he really was.

Without a word, Chick rose and took the hydrogen peroxide back to the bathroom. Gazing into the mirror, he silently cursed himself. Why didn't he just tell her who he was?

Because she would be relieved.

Because it had become a point of honor.

He'd had to run away to become his own man, to make his own father accept him for who he was and accept what he wanted out of life. He wouldn't take a woman on lesser terms.

When Chick went back into the other room, Eden had composed herself and lay curled in a corner of the couch, her back protected, as if she could thereby guard her own vulnerability.

"What did Zelda want?" she asked. Her voice sounded as unnatural as he was feeling.

"To discuss the robberies," he lied.

"Oh."

He stopped at the kitchen sink, leaned a hip against the counter and stared at her through narrowed eyes. She flushed under his direct scrutiny.

"Do you think what happened to me was really an accident?"

"I don't know what else to call it. Faulty equipment as a result of negligence."

He didn't want to think of the incident as having been planned. He wouldn't frighten her with Zelda's warnings. There was no reason to share the speculations of an elderly woman who might be taking herself too seriously. Chick tried to make himself comfortable with that, even as he remembered the times when Zelda's intuition had been right on the mark. Just in case, he would have to look after Eden every moment—or make sure someone else did.

He wondered what had prompted Eden's question. "Do you really think Sheets tried to hurt you on purpose?"

"I guess not. He made that ride a living hell, and I thought he was trying to get even with me for rebuffing his advances—"

"He may not have liked being rejected," Chick interrupted, "but that's not reason enough to chance going to jail. That's exactly what would happen, if someone could prove he'd rigged the safety bar on purpose. Initiations are meant only to show how tough you are."

Eden grimaced. "I kind of figured that out before I got into the capsule. I knew they were up to something, when Nickles passed on Sheets's invitation."

Chick didn't remember seeing Nickles anywhere around, but then he'd been so concerned with Eden that he'd probably missed the man.

"Well, you came out of the experience alive, and that's what counts. So what else did you do today, other than almost get yourself flattened like a pancake?"

Her lips twitched, but she didn't exactly smile at his teasing. It was too close to the truth to be really funny. "I made a few telephone calls, as you suggested. My boss was disgruntled when I said I might not be in all week." She paused a fraction of a second before adding. "Dennis left a message on my machine."

"And so you called him?" He didn't like the involuntary way he tensed at the thought.

"I didn't have any reason to," she said, allowing him to relax again. "He just wanted me to know that Stanton Barnes was having a political gathering at his home on Friday, and if I wanted to get personal information on the man, that would be the perfect opportunity."

"It just might be," Chick agreed thoughtfully.

"Right. I think we should call old Stanton and ask for an invitation," she said sarcastically. "I'm sure he'd love to see me again."

"Not a bad idea."

"Chick!"

A plan was already forming in his head when he asked, "What about Taffy?"

"I tried to get hold of her." Eden's face gathered into a frown. "No one answered at Hank's place. I guess Taffy could be anywhere."

But she didn't sound convinced.

"It is a weekday," Chick reminded her. "What about where she works?"

"Taffy? She's never had a job in her life. She lives on the interest from a trust fund. I thought maybe she was at her mother's, but no luck there, either."

"That worries you?"

Eden aimed the frown at him as she said, "Of course it does. How do I know that Barnes didn't find her somehow and spirit her off, thinking she could lead him to me?"

"Don't start letting your imagination run wild."

"My imagination couldn't have made me conceive of the situation that brought me here. Reality can be unbelievably creative, when you least expect it."

She had a point. However, he didn't want to see her eaten away by worry for her roommate when she needed her wits about her. "We can try calling again later. I'm sure Taffy is just fine."

Eden nodded. "What about you? Any luck at the Yorke Agency?"

"Some." Chick pushed himself away from the sink. "I found out for sure that Kim Quinlan wasn't independently wealthy. As a matter of fact, she left her country home only last year to come to the big city. The photographer who recommended her to the agency met her at a benefit for Barnes's campaign. Rebecca Yorke thinks a man was keeping her, and Kim kept talking about her ship coming in. Soon."

"I'm impressed."

He picked up the envelope from the table and handed it to her. "I was able to get a few glossies. They might come in handy, if we show them to the right people."

Eden had already opened the package and was spreading the photographs across her lap. Chick had given them a once-over—a couple of close-ups, a torso shot, a couple of product shots. The woman had had such before-the-camera charisma that he wouldn't be surprised if she could have sold an Eskimo a bathing suit in the middle of an Alaskan winter.

"So what do you think?" Chick asked, wondering why Eden's expression was so strange.

When she lifted her head, she seemed surprised. "I think you didn't take a good enough look at these photographs."

"What did I miss?"

She flipped several of the prints around and spread them in one hand like oversize playing cards. Then she rose and brought them closer.

"Take a good look." Her finger tapped the model's throat in each of the photos. "Kim Quinlan is wearing the same piece of jewelry in all of these." Eden's eyes shone with triumph when she announced, "I'd bet this is the same necklace she was wearing the night she was murdered! As a matter of fact, I'd stake my life on it."

"I'M GOING TO LEAVE, but I shouldn't be gone long," Chick said. Morning had found him dressed in another expensive suit that he'd mysteriously obtained from somewhere. He took his briefcase and looked down at Eden, where she sat on her sleep mat, surrounded by pictures of Kim Quinlan. His expression serious, he added, "Stay out of trouble this morning, would you?"

"Look who's talking." Despite her pleading, Chick was set on keeping that appointment with Barnes. The thought that he was putting himself directly into the politician's path drove her crazy, but there was no way she could stop him. "Do you always slap fate in the face?"

"It would be rude to stand Barnes up."

Eden shook her head. She'd tried to keep her mouth shut lest she start an argument, but she couldn't help herself any longer. "I don't know what you think you're going to accomplish. God forbid he should guess the game you're playing with him."

"Sounds like you care what happens to me."

"Of course I care." She avoided his eyes and concentrated on the photographs that she was sliding back into their envelope. "You've been very kind to me."

With what sounded like a growl of frustration, Chick opened the back of the truck and left her alone. Clenching her jaw, she went back to studying the only color close-up of Kim Quinlan. This picture showed off the mystery necklace most clearly.

Suspended from a delicate gold chain around the woman's throat was a distinctive three-dimensional circle and cross—the sign of Venus, or woman. A small but perfect yellow diamond studded the juncture. The piece of jewelry was fairly simple, but undoubtedly as expensive as Eden had guessed, when she'd found the clasp. If only the necklace could talk . . .

But of course it couldn't. Eden rose—slowly. Her "minor" injuries had become major during the night. She'd hardly been able to move when she'd awakened, and she didn't seem to be doing much better now. She was carefully working her way out of the truck to get some fresh air, when Maisie called to her.

"Eden, you gotta visitor."

Her heart began to pound, then she glanced over her shoulder and saw a familiar blond ponytail. "Taffy! I've been trying to reach you." She wanted to jump down and throw herself into her roommate's arms. Instead, she practically fell to the ground with a loud, "Oof." She signaled to Taffy not to say anything just yet.

"You need anything, baby? Chick asked me to keep an eye on you." When Eden gave the good-hearted woman an irritated look, Maisie said, "Oops, I wasn't supposed to say that."

"Thanks, anyway, Maisie."

Eden waited until the other woman disappeared into the silver trailer before she allowed her emotions to surface. "Taffy, I am so glad to see you."

She held out her arms and the two women hugged. Then Taffy pushed her away and stared at her as if she had two heads.

"What happened to you? And what in the world are you wearing?"

Glancing down at her bruised leg, which was exposed below the chartreuse and black miniskirted outfit, Eden said, "I had a little accident yesterday. My jeans were ruined, so I had to borrow this from Maisie."

"Good grief." Taffy's eyes widened. "You mean someone found out where you are?"

"No. This happened on one of the rides."

"Thank goodness! You had me worried for a minute. More worried," she corrected.

"You're not the only one who's been worried. Taffy, where have you been? I've called Hank's place more than a dozen times since yesterday morning."

"I got your messages. I would have returned them, but you didn't exactly leave a phone number," Taffy bantered. "Hank had to go out of town on business, so I've been visiting people on the North Shore, playing detective for you."

Eden groaned. "No! I didn't want you mixed up in this. You're not even supposed to be here."

"Well, if you're not glad to see me, I can always leave." She turned as if to make good on the suggestion.

"No, don't," Eden said, catching her by the arm. "I'm sorry."

"Apology accepted. Now, aren't you going to ask me *why* I'm here?"

Taffy looked as if she would burst if Eden didn't pose the question. "Okay. Why are you here?" she said obligingly.

"Because I'm going to take you for a ride."

"I had my fill of rides yesterday."

"Not a carnival ride. A car ride. Do you remember my godmother's younger sister, Beatrice Hollingsworth?"

Eden stretched her memory back to Taffy's high school graduation party. "I think so. Elegant woman, gorgeous silver hair?"

"That's the one. She lives in Kenilworth. She's always lived in Kenilworth. She went to high school with Rhonda Barnes. And guess what?"

"What?"

"She hates Rhonda's guts."

Taffy beamed at her, but Eden didn't get it. "Go on."

"Don't you see? Beatrice might be able to give you some information that'll help get you out of this mess."

"How? First of all, Rhonda doesn't live in Kenilworth anymore. And second, it's Stanton I'm interested in."

"You're not thinking straight. That ride must have scrambled your brain. Just because they don't live in the same community doesn't mean they don't still know each other. Money sticks with money. You know that. Think about the number of charity functions your parents used to attend. They knew everyone who was anyone in the area."

"You've got a point," Eden said, her enthusiasm for the idea growing. "Beatrice probably knows Stanton, too."

"Exactly. And she's willing to talk. This morning." Taffy checked her watch. "One hour and ten minutes from now."

"You set up an appointment?" Eden had to admit she was impressed. Organizational skills were not something that came naturally to her friend. "What did you tell her?"

"I said you recently started working as a free-lance reporter, and you were looking for the real story behind the loving couple. Beatrice said she'd be glad to help you find it."

"Great. Let me lock up... uh, and change. I don't think Beatrice Hollingsworth would be impressed by a reporter dressed like this."

Taffy followed Eden back into the truck and helped her get ready, although Eden had to admit she was moving more easily now that she'd been up for a while. She was still sore but not as stiff as she had been earlier. A quarter of an hour later, the two women were cutting across the carnival grounds. Eden called out a greeting to Abe and Felix. The owner of the carnival was removing the finish from Madam Zelda's fortune-telling booth, while the dapper carny looked on with a critical eye.

As usual, Taffy had parked her car illegally and had gotten another ticket. Also as usual, she pulled it from the windshield and ripped it up. Eden didn't dare say a word. They'd argued about this before, but her roommate didn't change her habits, just because someone nagged her.

Eden was waiting for Taffy to unlock the fire-engine-red MG when she spotted the dark-haired man. He was sitting in another illegally parked car—a gray Oldsmobile—a hundred feet away from them. Her stomach did a flip-flop, and she looked away quickly. Getting into the sports car, she assured herself she was imagining things. That couldn't possibly be the same man who had followed her to the carnival.

Barnes couldn't possibly know where she was.

Even so, her heart skipped a beat. As Taffy swung the MG away from the curb and headed for Lake Shore Drive, her eyes glued themselves to the side-view mirror—and the man who seemed to be watching them.

Chapter Ten

"I've heard a lot of good things about Lovett Promotions and especially about you," Stanton Barnes said as he pumped Chick's hand. "And people in this town aren't easily impressed."

"I'm glad my reputation has preceded me." Chick didn't believe in modesty when it came to business. People with power respected that. "I won't have to bore you with a verbal résumé."

Barnes indicated a chair as he circled his desk and made himself comfortable. Not too comfortable, Chick noted. Like a hawk, the man was on guard, his expression calculating, his posture ramrod straight as he sat forward in his chair. Deliberately trying to appear casual, Chick crossed one leg over the other.

"Now, what can I do for you, Charles?" Barnes asked, easily slipping first names into the exchange.

"I'm here to discuss what I can do for you... like promoting you right into the governor's mansion."

Barnes raised one silver-slashed brow. "You think I can't get there without you?"

"I think anything's possible, and at the moment, you're looking very good in the polls, but I understand you're a man who leaves nothing to chance."

"It's a little late in the campaign for you to get interested in my chances."

"It's never too late, if I can guarantee you a win," Chick parried.

Leaning back but not losing the hawklike alertness, Barnes asked, "What do you have in mind, Charles?"

"I'd like to go over your current strategy. From that, I can work up some concrete proposals. If you like them, you hire my firm. If not..." Chick held up his hand in a gesture of dismissal.

"Sounds interesting. How soon would you have this prospectus?"

"Give me until Friday night."

"I'm tied up then. I'm having a get-together for some of my political associates."

"I know. A perfect opportunity to test out my concepts."

"How did you know about Friday?"

"Stanton, you can't expect me to reveal my sources. If I did and the word got out, no one would talk to me. And then I would lose my edge."

"I respect a man who guards his edge." Barnes hesitated only a second, then said, "All right. Friday at eight. Bring someone decorative. Now, about my current strategy..."

EDEN FROWNED as she checked the side-view mirror again, shortly after Taffy nosed the sports car north onto Lake Shore Drive. Thank goodness, no gray Olds followed.

Taffy glanced into the rearview mirror. "Something wrong?"

"Just my imagination working overtime. I thought I spotted one of the thugs Barnes sent after me, back near the carnival grounds." Saying that made gooseflesh rise on

Eden's arms under the long sleeves of her electric-blue silk dress.

"Oh, Lord, you mean he's found you despite our precautions? And now he's after us?"

Eden muttered, "I must have been mistaken."

"No harm in taking precautions. Fasten your seat belt."

Taffy eyed the mirror and stepped on the gas. The MG lunged forward smoothly.

"Taffy, you're already ten miles over the speed limit."

"Uh-huh."

Eden wasn't about to argue with a woman who was as reckless behind the wheel as she was with parking tickets. "My belt is fastened—not that I trust it, after what happened to me yesterday."

She shoved her high heels into the carpeting as her roommate catapulted the MG from the right lane to the left, swerving around cars in the two lanes between. Her stomach left somewhere on the road behind, she sank back into the passenger seat and began massaging her sore muscles, which had once more grown tense.

"Taffy, we're not being followed. You can slow down."

"I can, can I?" Taffy returned with a laugh.

Deciding that not answering would work better than insisting, Eden fell silent and stared out at the lake's brilliant blue surface. Along the shoreline, a pair of joggers in brightly colored sweat suits caught her eye. She envied the very normality of their activity. Gradually the MG slowed, and Eden relaxed until Taffy hit her with a question, one she didn't want to think about—and answer even less.

"So how do you feel about this Chick guy?"

"How should I feel? Grateful that he's helping me." Eden squirmed under Taffy's intent scrutiny. "Eyes on the road, Taffy Darling."

"Yes, dear," her roommate said, repeating their old joke. "So that's it, huh?"

"Should there be more?"

"Okeydoke." Taffy used her most aggravating tone. "Then how does this Chick guy feel about you?"

"You'd have to ask him."

"Maybe I'll do that."

"Taffy! You wouldn't!"

Now it was Taffy's turn to fall silent. Eden hoped she choked on the smirk that was turning up the corners of her lips. What a time to ask about her feelings for a man who was totally unsuitable! She kept reminding herself of that fact every time the memory of Chick's kisses intruded. Her body didn't know that he was unsuitable, and neither, she was afraid, did her heart.

Well, she wasn't about to discuss the situation. As much as Eden loved Taffy, her roommate was quite at liberty to follow her impulses, living as she did on a trust fund. She couldn't possibly understand how important it was to Eden that Chick *do* something with his life—something that mattered. And as far as Eden could tell, he was taking the easy way out, existing from day to day rather than channeling the intelligence that she recognized and appreciated in a more productive manner.

Staying on the road that followed the lake, they left the city proper for the north shore suburbs. Evanston. Wilmette. And finally Kenilworth.

Taffy's godmother's younger sister Beatrice resided in the type of house Eden had always disliked. An ostentatious mansion, it was a place that she could only call cold. Perfectly decorated, the enormous interior reminded her of a mausoleum rather than a home in which people really lived. She was more comfortable in the Washingtons' cramped silver trailer.

And she was more relaxed with Maisie and Felix than with Beatrice, who reminded Eden of the life she'd turned her back on. Beatrice was the perfect hostess, in perfect silver lounging pajamas that matched her perfect silver hair. Beatrice made her itchy to get the meeting over and herself as far away from the place as she could run.

The tête-à-tête was oh, so civilized, with tea served by the maid and a yearbook offered for Eden's perusal. Flipping through its pages with one hand and holding her teacup with the other, she listened to the meaningless chatter between Taffy and Beatrice until their hostess finally came to the point.

"I understand you're doing an exposé of the Barnes campaign."

"I'm researching the personal lives of the candidate and his wife," Eden said truthfully.

She'd just gotten to the graduation picture of the young woman in question, under which was printed, "The girl most likely to succeed." And someone—Beatrice, she assumed—had written, "Or to find a man who'll do it for her."

"To think Rhonda Lawrence might actually be the next first lady of this state." Beatrice shivered in a perfectly ladylike manner.

The Rhonda in the picture was wide-eyed, blond and undeniably beautiful. "You don't approve?"

"I never approved of Rhonda Lawrence."

"Would you like to tell me why?" Eden asked, sipping at her tea.

"Once a slut, always a slut."

Eden almost choked, spilling hot tea down the front of her dress and onto the yearbook. She set the cup on its saucer as Taffy handed her a couple of napkins.

"Give me that," she said, taking the book from Eden and wiping the open pages dry.

"Pardon me for shocking you." With a smirk of satisfaction, Beatrice watched Eden mop up her dress. "But I believe in calling a spade a spade. From the time she developed as a woman, Rhonda attracted and was attracted to sleazy young men." She set down her own cup and saucer, then folded her hands in her lap. "But of course Rhonda couldn't leave the nice boys alone, either."

Eden had the distinct feeling that she knew the source of Beatrice's antagonism toward the other woman. Rhonda must have stolen one of her boyfriends.

"There's always one female in the class who gets more attention than the others," Eden commented. "That doesn't make the young woman a bad person."

"Rhonda Lawrence was completely amoral," Beatrice insisted. "She wanted what she wanted—food, clothes, young men—and always took what she wanted, whether or not anyone objected. She had no conscience and thought she could get away with anything."

"And people still liked her?" Taffy asked, sounding a little disbelieving.

"All the males in the class went sniffing after her, but all the girls hated her." Beatrice smoothed the material of her already perfectly smooth satin trousers. "She did get what was coming to her, though."

"And that was?" Eden asked.

"During our junior year she let her greed for gourmet food get out of control. She gained so much weight, she couldn't get a date for the prom. Even though she got back into shape, the boys never saw her in quite the same light."

Tired of ancient gossip, Eden asked, "What about Rhonda Lawrence now? What is the woman like?"

"She still likes boys and food, but not as much as she likes power. She can't resist its sweet taste."

"This is all very interesting, but I need confirmable facts. I can't write a story based on gossip."

Beatrice's smile faded. "Call it what you will, but I've told you nothing but the truth. Now you'll have to excuse me. I have a lunch date."

They were being thrown out—in a perfectly civilized manner, of course. A few minutes later, the two friends were breezing along winding Sheridan Road on the way back toward the city.

"I forgot how snotty Beatrice can be sometimes," Taffy said. "Sorry she wasn't more help."

"That's not your fault. You tried. And I'm sure Beatrice was telling the truth. Her version of it, anyway. How ironic."

"What?"

"That Rhonda Lawrence was a femme fatale in high school, but Rhonda Barnes can't even keep her own husband interested enough to be faithful," Eden said.

"If everything Beatrice said is true, it sounds like Rhonda has gotten some of her own medicine."

Eden was thoughtful. Not only had the trip been a waste of time, it had depressed her to boot. She almost felt sorry for the girl in the yearbook. She had had a certain innocent quality despite her beauty. Maybe a lack of friends, thanks to the other girls' jealousy, had driven her to collecting boys. Who knew?

And why was she concentrating on a detail that seemed so insignificant? Eden felt as if she'd missed something terribly important.

But what?

"WHAT DO YOU MEAN, the Payne woman is still alive?"

Lou Farentino shrugged at the outraged tone, as if it

didn't affect him one way or the other. "Somehow she survived what should have been a fatal ride."

Hostile eyes narrowed on the half-wit. "Now she'll be on guard."

"Nah, I doubt it. Everyone figured it was an accident, including the broad." Farentino shifted uncomfortably. "Chrissakes, it wasn't *my* fault. You took the matter out of my hands."

That was true, but letting Farentino off the hook would be a mistake. He was already too arrogant. He might forget who was giving the orders. "Eden Payne is the only witness not involved in getting a share of the stakes, Lou. And we both know how high they are. I want her taken care of, before she causes irreparable damage."

"I'll see to it personally this time."

"No! We can't take that chance. Stick to our arrangement. Double the ante if necessary, but make sure you give the carny a deadline this time. Friday. Too many important people will be here that night. I don't want to be worrying about some threat hanging over all our heads."

"Got it, boss."

Farentino left the Gold Coast town house, obviously in a disgruntled mood. He'd have to go back to the Hurley-Gurley and expose himself once more. What if someone saw him? Figured out who he was?

That didn't have to be a problem, his boss thought.

Lou Farentino was expendable.

"YOU LOOK like you're ready to bust a gut," Felix observed as he stopped in front of the One-Ball booth.

Chick slammed a milk bottle into place. The carnival was about to open, and Eden hadn't yet returned from the mysterious excursion with Taffy that he'd heard about secondhand from Maisie. "Do you blame me?"

"Women are always unpredictable and delightful creatures. They're what makes life interesting."

"You certainly have a relaxed philosophy."

"And I don't have any ulcers. Take my lead and mellow out, Chick. Your woman will be back. Now I'd better be tending to mine, before Maisie decides she's unhappy with me."

Whistling under his breath, Felix took off, and Chick finished setting up the booth.

His woman. Something Eden Payne would never choose to be. So why was he sick with worry about her? Why did he regret not asking Jud to keep an eye on her as instinct had warned him to? Why did he castigate himself for leaving her at all?

Because he was a fool.

Because he was in love.

And it was love that made him snap at Eden the moment he saw her, looking tall and elegant and incredibly sexy in an electric-blue dress that molded her curves and deepened the color of her eyes. "Where the hell have you been?"

She opened the gate and stepped inside the booth. "Nice to see you, too." Slamming down a small leather bag next to a stuffed hippo, she flashed him a challenging look.

"Don't give me a hard time, Eden. I was doing you a favor this morning, while you were... what?"

Not seeming in the least appreciative of his help, she said stiffly, "Having tea with a friend of Taffy's."

"Tea?" He let loose a string of swear words that made her flush.

"And then we stopped for lunch on the way back," she added. "I had a tossed salad with garlic dressing and a wonderful piece of blackened catfish. Anything else you want to know?''

Noting that they had an audience—Nickles had stopped to watch the show—Chick grabbed Eden by the shoulders and turned her back into a corner. She winced and he let go immediately. He'd forgotten about her injuries, but then, apparently so had she, or she wouldn't have been traipsing around who knew where.

''Don't smart-mouth me, when I'm doing my damnedest to help you,'' he said in a low voice.

''Don't treat me like I'm a lost child,'' she returned.

They looked at each other belligerently for a moment. Sighing, Chick backed down. Acting like some macho idiot wasn't one of his strong suits.

''Look. I'm sorry. I was worried.''

Her expression softened. ''Me, too. The sorry part, I mean.''

From the corner of his eye, Chick could still see the sleazy carny standing in the midway watching them. ''Don't you have something better to do?'' he called to the other man.

Nickles gave him a dark look, wiped his nose on his sleeve and shuffled off.

''So you had tea,'' Chick said, approaching Eden with far more patience than he had the first time.

''Taffy thought I might get something on Barnes by talking to someone who had known his wife since they were in high school.'' She shrugged her shoulders and pulled a face that expressed her disappointment. ''I wasted my time. The woman has a long-standing vendetta against Rhonda Barnes. She had a lot to say, but nothing concrete.''

''Maybe we can get something more concrete on Friday.''

''Barnes invited you to the gathering at his home?''

''Invited us. He told me to bring someone decorative.''

Eden flushed again and muttered, "He'll recognize me."

"As much as I would like to, I can't do this alone, Eden. One of us has to stand guard and act as a distraction, while the other does some prying into corners." He touched her hair, which she'd left loose. It was dark and smooth like a raven's wing. "Different color, different style, the right clothes and makeup, and no one will recognize you. Besides, Barnes would never expect you to be bold enough to walk right into his home. He probably figures you're in hiding, cowering in fear."

"I hope you know what you're getting us into."

"It's our last shot, Eden. Whether we find anything or not, we're going to have to go to the authorities with what we've got."

She seemed agitated at the prospect. "Maybe."

He didn't push; they both knew doing so was inevitable. Chick's only regret was that leaving the case in the hands of the police would end their relationship. Eden wouldn't admit that she wanted him, was maybe developing deeper feelings for him, not even to herself. If she did so after being confronted with his true identity, he would always wonder if she really cared for him, or if she'd allowed herself to do so because he was someone "suitable." He was stubborn enough—stupid enough—to want her unconditional love, no matter what she thought he did for a living.

"So how did you wangle this invitation?" she asked.

"I told Barnes I wanted to promote him into the governor's mansion, and that I would present my ideas at his political gathering."

"And he fell for it?"

Chick couldn't help stiffening at her amazed tone. "We got the invitation, didn't we?"

"What kind of bogus notions are you going to feed him, while I'm doing the snooping? I assume that's how this plan is supposed to work."

"I'll think of something."

"I don't get it." Brow furrowed, Eden crossed her arms over her chest and studied him intently. "Barnes is one smart cookie, or he wouldn't be where he is. We also know he isn't above chicanery. I don't understand how you can misrepresent yourself without his suspecting anything."

That was because she wasn't looking behind the facade to the real man, Chick thought bitterly. He should have his head examined for falling in love with such a nearsighted woman.

"Maybe I'm smarter than he is," Chick finally said, already moving away from her. He slammed out of the joint, calling, "Keep an eye on the place for a while."

Eden stared after him. About to protest, she was stopped by a couple of teenage boys who were obviously playing hooky from school. She took their money and set them up, but when one of them tried to flirt with her while the other was trying to knock down the bottles, she snapped at him. They stalked away, saying they would rather give their money to someone with a better disposition.

No one but Chick Lovett could get her so riled. She reset the two bottles the teenager had knocked down, smacking the bottom one into place with a vengeance. Why did Chick have the power to get under her skin? The answer was obvious, had been obvious for what seemed like forever.

She was head over heels in love with the man.

Eden wedged a hip against the counter and sighed. In love with a shady, if lovable, carny with a silly nickname. Her lips turned up, even as she thought how Chick was wasting himself. Would she really want to change him? He was obviously happy at the Hurley-Gurley. She knew firsthand what it felt like to have family, friends and fiancé trying to tell her how to live her life.

Besides, she'd fallen in love with Chick exactly as he was. How did she even know she would like the man he might become, if he pursued something more challenging than running a joint in a carnival?

What to do?

Nothing, she told herself.

She didn't need another problem now to distract her from the one they were already trying to solve. She would put her feelings on hold for the moment.

But Eden found that more and more difficult as she and Chick took turns running the joint during the afternoon. She hated the combination of antagonism and chemistry that sizzled below the surface every time they crossed paths. And even more she hated the waiting, hated doing nothing to help herself. Friday night seemed a long way away. There had to be something they could do in the meantime, something positive.

On one of her breaks, Eden changed back into the chartreuse and black outfit Maisie had lent her. Somehow it seemed more appropriate than the silk dress. When she went back to the booth, she caught Chick staring at her legs—more specifically, at the injury that he had treated with such gentleness. She softened, he responded, and before she knew it, they were talking again as if their little tiff had never taken place.

The carnival came alive in the early evening hours. Though it was only Wednesday night, customers thronged the midway in droves. Eden got into the spirit of being a carny for a little while longer, taking turns running the joint, enjoying listening to Chick's practiced patter.

He could talk *her* into just about anything, if only he would try....

She remembered Maisie's telling her that Chick had only joined the Hurley-Gurley the week before. She meant to ask him about that revelation, but the opportunity never presented itself as they worked together that evening.

Their easy camaraderie cloaked Eden in a comfortable warmth as darkness blanketed the city and the rides presented a brilliant fantasyland against the night sky. The sounds of people nearby and a rock concert at the festival on the pier were inviting. And when the smell of fresh popcorn assaulted her nostrils, Eden's stomach grumbled.

"Sounds like you're hungry," Chick said.

"Starving," she admitted.

"Let's get something to eat."

"Both of us?" Eden asked.

"You'd rather eat alone?"

"No. But what about the booth?"

"I'll ask Maisie to joint-sit for an hour or so."

A few minutes later, a grinning Maisie watching them, they were walking down the midway, waving to other jointees and ride jocks. At the food tent Chick bought them hot dogs, greasy fries and large beers. They ate at one of the picnic tables under the canvas canopy. At the other end of the open room sat a group of carnies, Abe and Jud among them. Eden waved to the men.

"Why did you let me think you worked for the Hurley-Gurley since you were seventeen?" Eden had only half finished her meal, but she was already slowing down. "Maisie told me you only took over the One-Ball booth last week—after the jointee who ran it quit."

"Carnies move around a lot."

So he meant to be evasive. Munching on her hot dog, Eden wondered why. "Have you worked for many carnivals?"

"You just blobbed mustard on your chin."

He picked up a napkin and wiped it off, getting the corners of her mouth for good measure. Eden felt his fingers through the thin paper and imagined them brushing her more intimately.

"There, that's better." He popped a few fries into his mouth.

Lips tingling, she asked, "Why don't you want to talk about yourself?"

"Lots of other things are more interesting."

"Like what?"

"You."

"Oh, no, you're not going to turn the tables on me."

"Then we'd better find something neutral to discuss," he suggested. "Unless you prefer not talking at all."

Like before, she thought. "No, I hated that."

Their eyes meshed for a moment, and Eden felt a lump grow in her throat. She bit into her hot dog again, chewed quickly and tried to swallow the lump. However the nightmare ended, she was going to miss Chick, and she was already feeling the pain of separation.

So when he suggested, "How about taking a ride on the Ferris wheel before we go back to work?" she didn't object.

Though she was now wary of getting too near anything in the Hurley-Gurley that moved, Eden felt safe in Chick's company. He wouldn't let anything happen to her. Her feeling of security increased as they walked down the midway and he slipped an arm around her shoulders.

And so did the sense of impending loss.

Chick bought a large cotton candy from a vendor, but said she couldn't have any until they were on the ride.

The jock let them onto the Ferris wheel without a ticket or wait. The privilege of being carnies. Despite Chick's very real presence next to her, Eden experienced a small thrill of anxiety when the safety bar was latched. She was in the AstroRocket capsule again. Alone. She felt the webbing give...the bar come loose in her hands. Her stomach churned and her lungs squeezed tight.

As if he could guess at her mounting fear, Chick slid an arm around her and pulled her securely into his side.

"You're not one of those guys who gets a kick making these things rock, are you?" she asked, her laugh sounding unnatural to her own ears.

"Only by request, Toots," he assured her softly. "Cotton candy?"

He offered her the sweet as the Ferris wheel moved a short distance, then stopped to let another couple into the next bucket. Ignoring the mechanical lurch that made her stomach do the same, Eden pulled some of the sticky treat free and popped it into her mouth. The spun sugar instantly changed texture and melted on her tongue.

"Now if you wanted to be really nice, you would pull some of that off for me," Chick said, "since both my hands are occupied."

Not wanting him to remove his arm from her shoulder, she nevertheless teased him. "You could take a big bite."

"And get my face all sticky?" He raised his brows, as if considering. "That wouldn't be so bad, if you promised to lick off anything that didn't find its way into my mouth."

The image made her pulse surge. To cover her reaction, she plucked off a large piece of the cotton candy and fed it to him. Chick ate bit by bit, finishing only after sucking the remains from her fingers. His mouth was so inviting. Eden's anxiety was replaced by a warmth that spread from fingertips to stomach to toes.

The ride continued to fill with new passengers, and Eden went on plucking spun sugar alternately for Chick and herself. And each time his tongue laved her fingers, her longing to get closer to him increased. Finally the Ferris wheel was filled and moving continuously, and both the cotton candy and her apprehension were gone.

All that was left was the feel of the wind on her face and in her hair.... Below them the lights of the city spread out like a blanket of diamonds.... And at her side was Chick.

She couldn't take her eyes from him, nor could he take his from her. She forgot about the inappropriateness of her attraction, the impending separation, the reason they'd been brought together in the first place.

There were only this night and this man, and she knew she wanted them both. Together. Imprinted on her heart, so that she could never forget.

When Chick took her lips, as she knew he would, Eden tried to tell him what she felt with that kiss. It was a single, glorious, time-stopping kiss that filled her both with indescribable happiness and a sense of fulfillment—of belonging—that had been missing from her life for much too long.

A kiss that ended all too soon.

He was breathing hard and staring at her, as if asking a silent question. Her bones seemed to melt in response. Somehow she found the strength to touch his cheek, to tuck her head into the crook of his neck, to run her finger over the small imperfection on his chin.

"How *did* you get this scar?"

"A fight."

"When you were a kid?" She wondered what he'd been like then. What his family had been like.

"Shortly after I joined the Hurley-Gurley." He pressed his chin into her fingers, lowered his head and nipped the pads lightly. "I had a tussle with one of the ride jocks over something stupid. Carnies aren't always the most even-tempered people. Violence is part of the uncertain life, I guess."

Talk of violence intruded on the romantic moment like a splash of cold water. Eden couldn't help remembering why she was there. Suddenly they were no longer alone with the city and the wind. She became aware of the ride stopping, letting off passengers. In a few minutes it would be their turn. She would move out of Chick's embrace and back into the arms of reality, whatever that might be.

When their bucket came to rest on the platform and the ride jock released the safety bar, Eden didn't feel like going directly back to the joint, where she would be with Chick for the remainder of the night. Not right away. Not until she had a few minutes alone. She needed to think rationally, something that was difficult to do around him.

"Listen, I have to stop at the doniker," she said as the cacophony of the carnival seemed to grow louder and louder inside her head.

"Fine. I'll go with you." He started toward the row of portable toilets set up to one side of the carnival.

"No." Eden didn't move. "Go on back to the joint. I'll be there in a few minutes."

"I can wait."

"Don't be silly." She smiled uncertainly. "Maisie's been so nice, we shouldn't take advantage of her."

Chick gave her a long look before agreeing. "See you in a few minutes, then."

When he strode down the midway, she escaped in the other direction, toward the back lot. She really did need to make that pit stop, but in privacy. She didn't want an audience for her emotions, but as she passed the Ferris wheel, she had the sensation of being watched. Chick must be staring after her, she thought.

Turning to face him, Eden was confused when she realized Chick was already out of sight. As her gaze swept the area, she noticed Nickles a short distance away, talking to one of the other jointees. Nickles glanced at her, his demeanor almost furtive. When he realized she was watching him, he turned away quickly—guilty, no doubt, about having talked her into the ride on the AstroRocket.

She shook off a sense of discomfort and went on, away from the loud mechanical noises and music and into the silent back lot. Away from the fake brilliance of the carnival into the natural cloak of the night skies. She knew her way well enough, even in the dark. Ahead, surrounded by a clump of bushes and trees opposite the sprawl of trucks and trailers, two portable toilets had been set up for the carnies' use. One was marked Jake Doniker, the other Jill Doniker.

Carnies not only had a language of their own, but a weird sense of humor, as well.

About to press down the handle on the toilet door, Eden heard a noise nearby. Sort of a shuffle. A footfall. She glanced around, but though her eyes had adjusted to the night, the moon hid behind a bank of clouds, and the streetlights were far away. She couldn't distinguish any human form in the shadows.

Maybe someone was on break and looking for solitude, just as she was, Eden told herself as she entered the small cubicle and latched the door behind her. Or maybe her imagination was playing tricks again. Hadn't she thought the guy in the Olds was one of Barnes's men? She was spooking herself for no good reason.

Even so, anxious to get out of the claustrophobic space, she hurried.

Her mind hurried as well, drawing pictures she didn't want to see. Kim Quinlan being dumped into the storage space; the earth coming at her fast as her fingers began to slip on the cage door of the capsule. What was wrong with her? There couldn't possibly be any connection between the two events.

So why did she jump when she heard another noise, directly outside the enclosure, and why did her hands refuse to cooperate in adjusting the miniskirt?

A scrabbling sound at the door made her eyes widen and the breath catch in her throat. Someone was trying to get in.

"Who's out there?" she called, hoping against hope that one of the other women would respond.

No answer.

"Come on, I know someone is there. Don't joke around. Who is it?"

Light footsteps moved around the doniker, but the person didn't say a word. Eden tried not to panic. Someone was trying to scare her, that was all. Another initiation. Well, it wasn't going to work. Without making another sound, she placed one hand on the door handle, the other on the latch. She was going to unlock and open the door and bolt out of the cubicle so fast that it would make the other person's head spin.

She took a deep breath, threw the latch and jerked the handle. Nothing. It didn't budge. She tried again. And again. She kept trying until the truth hit her. Whoever was out there hadn't wanted in. The prankster had made sure she couldn't get out by somehow jamming the handle from the outside.

The walls seemed to be closing in on her as she yelled, "Unlock this door! You're not funny!"

The person didn't answer, but merely moved about, making sounds she couldn't identify, brushing high against the molded walls. What the hell was going on? She began banging at the door and yelling.

"Someone help me! Help! I'm locked in the doniker!"

She only heard the weird sound behind her because she stopped to take a deep breath to yell even louder. The sound of liquid dripping from above and behind her made Eden fly around.

She couldn't see in the dark, but she could smell. Something sharp. Toxic. Dripping down the back wall, permeating the air of the small space. Trying not to breathe, she began banging at the door again, but she'd never been good at holding her breath for long periods of time.

"Help!" she yelled once more, before sucking in the noxious fumes.

Dizziness and a feeling of faintness made her pause to get her bearings, but she wasn't so far gone that she didn't realize the truth.

This was no rite of initiation.

Someone meant to kill her.

Chapter Eleven

"Hey, pal . . . doin' there?"

The muffled male voice barely broke through the fog in Eden's mind as she fought to stay on her feet. Her palm met the door in a weak imitation of a blow. She couldn't speak. Couldn't breathe. Her nose and throat were raw, lungs burned, all seared by the fumes that multiplied their effect each time she sought oxygen.

And behind her came the steady drip of toxic liquid. . . .

Help!

She screamed the word inside her head as she clawed at the unyielding door. Her cheek lay against its cold, hard surface. Someone other than her attacker was there. At least she didn't think she was imagining things. If only she could make herself heard.

She could barely distinguish more sounds outside . . . a short scuffle . . . a sharp crack.

Then Eden's knees gave way. She hugged the door, clung to the handle. But that didn't stop her from slipping. Down . . . down . . . down she went. She could see Chick's image inside her mind. She held onto it, too, for as long as she could.

Then everything slipped away. . . .

CHICK HAD ALMOST REACHED the One-Ball joint when he turned and doubled back to where he'd seen Nickles with Frank, one of the jointees who'd been robbed. Chick had been too angry with Eden at the time, but now that he thought about it, he wanted to talk to the man who'd lured her onto the ride that had almost killed her. He wasn't certain that it had been just an accident, and wanted to see if he could wring the truth out of the shifty-eyed carny.

But Nickles wasn't where he'd seen him.

"Hey, Frank," Chick called. "Where's Nickles?"

"Don't know. Said he had something important to do."

"Which way did he go?"

Frank shrugged. "Back lot, I guess. I had a customer."

"Thanks."

Chick took off at a lope. He passed the Ferris wheel and, calling out to the man, exited the carnival grounds.

"Nickles. It's Chick. I want a powwow. Nickles?"

If he had indeed come this way, Nickles was intent on avoiding company. He didn't answer. Chick stopped in the middle of the lot, disgusted that he'd gone on a wild-goose chase. About to leave, he froze when he heard a muffled sound coming from the direction of the donikers. Was the little weasel hiding there?

"Nickles?" he called again into the dark. When he got no reply, he added, "Is *anyone* around?"

Still no answer.

Digging out the high-powered flashlight he'd been keeping in his jeans pocket, Chick snapped it on and swept the area with the beam. No one. He strode to the Jake and banged on the door, after which he tried the handle. It gave, and the door swung open. The light illuminated the compartment. Empty.

Then what in the world had he heard?

And what was that smell?

Potent fumes reached him. The Jill. He crossed the couple of yards separating the two portable toilets and tried the handle. This one didn't give.

"Is anyone in there?" he called, giving the handle another jerk. Something came free and pinged against the plastic molding as it fell to the ground. Someone had jammed the handle...and Eden had said she was going to the doniker. "Eden?" He ripped the door open; her body flopped to the ground at his feet. "Eden, can you hear me?" he asked, suspecting that she couldn't.

He fell to his knees, scooped her into his arms and felt for a pulse. She was alive; who had tried to kill her?

"Hey, what's going on?"

Flashlight in hand, Chick twisted toward the male voice. "Sheets. Get help. It's Eden."

"What? Holy...! Be right back!"

Chick had already refocused his attention on the inert woman in his arms. With some difficulty, he lifted her and moved away from the area that was now permeated with the escaping fumes. If he'd arrived even moments later....

"O-o-h-h."

The faint sound passed her lips as he set her down on a stretch of grass near the Hurleys' trailer. Chick placed the flashlight near her head, so that he could have full use of both his hands. Her face contorted into a grimace.

"Eden." He stroked her cheek in a gentle effort to arouse her. "Can you hear me?"

Her chest heaved, and she groaned with the effort to suck in air. When her eyes opened, their expression seemed unnatural, clouded with confusion and filled with such pain that she was forced to squeeze them shut again.

"Wh-what...happened?"

Her breathing was still ragged, and she was trying to wet her lips with her tongue. Chick continued to stroke her cheek in a gesture of comfort.

"Do you remember anything?"

"The smell...choking me...couldn't breathe." Her eyes opened again and she lifted a trembling hand to her forehead. "Oh, my head."

"I know. The pain must be unbearable." He was hurting just from looking at her. "Lie still. I sent for help. We'll get you to an emergency room."

The fact that she didn't argue made Chick realize how close he'd come to losing her. But who had done it? Nickles? Why would he want to hurt Eden? Before Chick could reason it out, Sheets returned, carrying a power-operated lamp. Abe and Jud followed.

"Is she all right?" Abe asked, his voice trembling. Looking helpless, he knelt beside Eden.

Chick tried to reassure the elderly man. And himself. "I think so."

"I'm alive," Eden whispered. "But the way my head feels..."

"Don't even say it," Chick ordered. He addressed the men. "We have to get her to a hospital. Someone locked her in the doniker and put something toxic in there. She passed out from the fumes."

"You can use my van, but it wouldn't be a bad idea to see if we can figure out what kind of chemicals the bastard used first," Jud said. "Let's go look."

Sheets followed with the lantern.

"I don't like this," Abe muttered. "An accident yesterday, and now this. I didn't want to face it, but maybe the safety on the AstroRocket coming apart was no accident."

"I was thinking the same thing," Chick admitted.

"Me, three," Eden croaked. She was rubbing her forehead and temples with all ten fingers. "Got any extra-strength aspirin?"

"In the trailer." Abe rose to his feet. "I'll get a couple and some water."

Chick put a hand out to stop him. "I think a doctor should make that decision."

Groaning, Eden pushed herself to a sitting position, and Chick was afraid she was about to object. But she merely leaned forward and held her head. Frustrated that he could do nothing to ease her pain, he glanced toward the portable toilet, where Jud seemed to be attacking the back wall. A tearing noise was followed by a couple of clunks.

"Well, look at this," Jud said.

Sheets swore softly. "Hell!"

"What did you find?" Chick asked as the two men headed back toward them.

Jud held a gallon can with a narrow tube running from its mouth. "The vents were covered with duct tape, and this was rigged to pour down the inside wall a little at a time. Lacquer thinner. Good thing Eden doesn't smoke."

"That stuff doesn't need a match to be deadly," Chick retorted.

Silence ensued.

Ready to help Eden up, to get her to that hospital, Chick realized that Abe was staring at the object in Jud's hand.

"Th-that can. It's mine. I was using it to work on Zelda's booth this morning."

"Don't go blaming yourself," Chick told him. "Anyone could have known where you kept it."

"Maybe, but Felix said he'd lock all that stuff up someplace safe. He's the one who put it away."

Chick frowned. "Let's speculate later." He bent and helped Eden to her feet. "In the meantime, I appreciate the offer of your van, Jud."

The patch took a key ring out of his pocket. "Want me to drive?"

"Thanks, but I can manage." Chick caught Jud's keys and slipped them into his pocket. "How about letting me carry you, Toots?"

"And have you blame me for a hernia? Keep your arm . . . right there."

"I can take her other side," Abe offered. "I'm coming with you." He turned to the other two men. "Will one of you tell Zelda about this?"

Jud nodded. "Sure thing."

Chick and Abe escorted Eden the short distance to the vehicle and helped her get into the back, where she could lie on an upholstered bench seat. Chick cleared his mind of anger and speculation and concentrated on getting her to Northwestern's emergency room as quickly as possible.

Barely five minutes later, he turned Eden over to the hospital staff. She concocted a story—saying she'd been careless about ventilation while stripping furniture—and Chick relaxed a little. She had to be okay, if she had the presence of mind to lie so blatantly to the nurse.

Then the wait began. Thank God, he wasn't alone, Chick thought.

Sitting next to him in the half-empty room, Abe patted his arm. "She'll be all right now. The doctors will fix her up fine."

"But who fixed her up so we had to bring her here in the first place?"

"Like I said, Felix was supposed to have put the lacquer thinner away."

"What reason would he have to harm Eden?" Chick asked, unable to conceive of the polite, dapper man as some kind of ruthless villain.

"What reason would anyone have?" Abe asked. "Zelda told me about helping you get into Lake Point Towers. Why'd you have to get into that apartment?"

Chick took a deep breath. If he didn't talk to someone openly, he'd go crazy. And whom better to trust than his old friend? Eden wouldn't like sharing her secret, but he didn't like what had happened to her. Maybe Abe could help him make sense of the thing.

So he began with Eden's unexpected appearance at the carnival, and didn't stop until he'd told the older man everything he knew.

When Chick finished, Abe shook his head. "Whew. I've heard a lot of wild stories in my years as a carny, but this beats all."

"This isn't just any carny story. I haven't exaggerated. It's the honest-to-God truth."

"I thought my troubles were big ones. My business may be teetering, but at least no one's trying to kill me."

"If one of Barnes's men was around, waiting for an opportunity to get rid of Eden, we would know it," Chick said, trying to sort things out. "Marks don't exactly blend in. Barnes must have gotten to someone at the Hurley-Gurley, someone who could openly watch Eden and make his opportunity, someone who's desperate for money."

"Someone who's been robbing the other carnies?"

"That would make sense," Chick agreed. "Now all we have to do is figure out who."

"Felix?" Abe asked.

"Felix and Maisie have been so nice to Eden," Chick observed. He hated suspecting them of having ulterior motives.

"And they've gotten almost as close to her as you have," Abe said. "None of the other carnies know her habits as well."

"I don't believe it. No, the guilty one has to be someone more threatening. Nickles, for instance."

"Ah, he talks tough, but he's harmless."

Before Chick could pursue the argument, a man in a lab coat called him.

"Mr. Lovett, I'm Dr. Knudson."

"How is Eden?"

"Resting and hooked up to an IV."

When Chick jumped to his feet and said, "I want to see her," the doctor held out his hand.

"Now, don't get all worked up. We're merely taking precautions. We don't have the results of the blood test yet, but from Miss Payne's apparent rapid recovery, and knowing she was only out for a few minutes, I would say she'll be fine. Her respiratory system will be irritated, and she'll have a doozer of a hangover, but I hope that's it."

"Thank God." He felt as if he, too, could breathe again. "When can I get her out of here?"

"We would like to keep her under observation until morning, but I suspect she'll be able to go home then. You might as well get out of here and get some rest."

"Can't I see her first?"

Dr. Knudson smiled. "Sure you can, but just for a minute. Come with me."

"I'll time myself," Chick promised. He was quick to assure Abe that he would be right back. The elderly man waved him on, and the doctor led him into an inner room, where he indicated a curtained-off area.

"Remember, keep it brief."

Chick slipped into Eden's small sanctuary, which had been thrown into semidarkness. Her eyes were closed, and a tube had been inserted into her outstretched left arm. As if she sensed his presence, she opened her eyes and smiled.

"Hi."

The single word set his insides rolling.

"Hi, yourself. You don't have to talk. I just wanted to see that you were all right with my own eyes."

"But I haven't thanked you for saving my life."

"No problem, Toots. I expect I'll think of some way you can show your appreciation, once you're out of here."

The smile widened. "I bet you will."

"I'm not supposed to stay long, but before I go, I wondered if you had any idea of who tried to—" he couldn't even say it "—who did this to you."

"Not really. I heard someone, but I couldn't see who it was." She frowned. "But before I left the carnival grounds, I felt someone watching me. It was Nickles, and when he realized I'd caught him at it, he got kind of nervous."

"I was wondering about Nickles myself. I intend to have a little chat with him when I get back to the Hurley-Gurley."

"Chick, there's something else...." She paused, as if it hurt her to speak. "This morning when Taffy and I went to her car, I thought I saw one of the guys who worked for Barnes."

"Why didn't you tell me?"

"I figured I was imagining things. And then I just forgot. Maybe he was the one." She shuddered.

Chick's mind was already assimilating the new information. He doubted that her imagination had been playing tricks on her. Barnes must have gotten to one of the carnies—Nickles?—just as he'd figured.

"You're safe here, so you get some sleep. I'll be back in the morning."

Eden nodded. Chick leaned over to kiss her on the cheek, but she moved her head, and their lips connected. It was one of the sweetest kisses he'd ever tasted. He had to force himself away from the hospital bed.

"In the morning," he repeated.

On the way back to the carnival, he shared what Eden had told him with Abe. The elderly man sat in silence, his once-straight shoulders stooped, as if this were all too much for him. Chick remembered a time when the carnival owner had been able to handle anything.

Zelda and a small group of carnies, including Jud, were waiting for them when they pulled into the lot. Chick put his arm around the rattled-looking Zelda and assured them all that Eden would be fine.

"Abe can answer any questions. Right now I want to have a little talk with Nickles. I think he can tell us what we want to know about the attack."

"Good luck," Jud said. "No one can find Nickles. He went on break long before you found Eden—and he hasn't been back to his joint. His relief has been bellyaching about it for the last hour."

Chick couldn't help jumping to conclusions. "Anyone checked his quarters?" Nickles, Sheets and two other single guys shared the back of a truck.

"He wasn't there a half hour ago," Zelda said.

If Nickles wasn't there and wasn't at his joint, the reason was pretty obvious. He'd made a run for it. "I think I'll check again, anyway."

Chick, Jud and a man nicknamed Moon joined forces, while Abe stayed with Zelda and the others returned to work. The truck's interior was empty as Chick had suspected, but when he declared his intention of going through the carny's things, neither of the other men objected.

It was Moon who found the coin in the bedding. "Hey, look at this," he said, holding it up for Chick's inspection.

"A silver dollar. What's your point?"

"This is *Frank's* lucky silver dollar. See the worn spot here. That's where Frank used to rub it every day. He always kept it in his cash box, including the night he was robbed."

"Let's do a more thorough search," Jud said.

Searching every nook and cranny, the three men tore the place apart. This time Chick struck pay dirt. Buried in one of Nickles's boxes under a load of cheap prizes, he found a shaving kit that held bills—twenties and fifties, even some hundreds. Odd that Nickles hadn't hid his cache more carefully. Then again, maybe he'd wanted the money where he could get at it fast.

"Almost eight thousand dollars' worth," Chick said when he finished counting.

"No way did Nickles make that kind of money," Moon insisted.

"You're right. Maybe we should have Abe deposit this in his safe, until we can ask Nickles about it."

The other two men agreed.

But Nickles didn't show that night. Not that Chick had expected him to.

When the carnival shut down, and every employee gathered in front of the Hurleys' trailer to discuss the situation, they came to a single conclusion. Eden must have seen or found something having to do with the thefts, and Nickles had been desperate to make sure she didn't talk. Now he was on the lam, and good riddance. They could all breathe easier.

Chick let them believe what they liked. Why not? They'd formulated a good story, so he didn't have to make up another to cover Eden's real predicament. He only wished he could get his hands on the shifty-eyed little bastard. He'd drag Nickles to a cop shop and make him sing. And if that were impossible...

No, he wasn't prepared to tell the man good riddance, after what he'd done to Eden.

BY THE TIME Chick got back to the hospital with her clothes, Eden had had hours to think about what had happened the night before. Her memory had blanks, big ones. Those fumes had obviously gotten hold of her brain.

If only she could remember more. Eden was sure she'd missed something vital. Even so, she wasn't surprised when Chick told her Nickles was the guilty party, that he'd done a disappearing act, and that they'd discovered a great deal of cash in his possession. The man obviously had been willing to do anything for money.

"It makes sense." The words came easily, but her voice had lowered a notch. Sitting on the edge of her hospital bed, she stared down at the scrape on her leg. "Nickles was so insistent about my getting on the AstroRocket. Later I kept wondering if the safety bar coming loose on the ride really was an accident."

"Me, too." Chick was pacing back and forth, wearing down the shine on the hospital tile. "Nickles spent so much time with Sheets, he probably was familiar with every little detail of the ride. And he's always seemed sneaky—enough to have thought of last night's incident."

Remembering made Eden shudder. "He must be convinced that I know he was responsible...and terrified of coming back to face your wrath."

"I only wish I could get my hands on his scrawny neck."

Chick was so serious, so deeply disturbed by what had happened to her. While Eden appreciated his concern, she couldn't let it get to her. She'd been terrified; she'd come close to death. But she was alive and more determined than ever to see Stanton Barnes and his partners in crime behind bars. She was reluctant to say anything more to upset Chick until she could reassure him that her sore throat and lungs were already on the mend, and that she could deal with the headache that still lingered. According to the doctor who'd seen her that morning, other than those side effects, she had a clean slate.

"I think I'll get dressed," she said, carefully rising from the bed.

While hospital technology had made leaps and bounds in the past few years, hospital gowns hadn't. With one hand she held together the edges of the opening behind her; with the other she picked up the clothing bag that Chick had brought. Even if Maisie's things hadn't been filthy, Eden would never be inclined to wear them again. The chartreuse and black outfit would always remind her of how close she'd come to the afterlife.

"We can finish this conversation when I get out of this place," she said, trying to warn him that she had ideas of her own as to how the day should proceed.

"Take your time. You could get dizzy or something," Chick said, sitting down on a visitor's chair. "Yell if you need help."

"I promise."

Once inside the bathroom, she momentarily forgot about Chick. As she pulled on one of her own dresses, a sweeping cream silk georgette Oscar de la Renta that swirled around her calves, her plan for the morning clicked into place inside her head. Designer clothes with pricey tags from exclusive shops...why hadn't she thought of it before, when they'd searched the Quinlan woman's apartment?

Eden brushed her damp hair into a simple style and applied some makeup. After the gaudy colors she'd been wearing lately, she looked pale. Or maybe her face reflected the terrible trauma she'd been through. When she rejoined Chick, she was delighted when his lips softened into a lazy grin. Now was the time to tell him her scheme. She twirled in front of him and stopped just inside the V of his knees.

"I hope you have the stamina to spend the next few hours shopping."

"What are you talking about?" Chick asked. "I'm taking you to the police."

"You certainly are not. Is that why you wore the suit? So you would look respectable for once?" she asked, choosing to make a comment that was sure to rile him...and distract him from his purpose.

His reaction was immediate. He scowled. Eden resisted the temptation to kiss his furrowed brow and merely played with his lapel instead. She was learning from him, turning his own tricks against him. He seemed slightly off balance.

"Damn it, Eden, I'm not going to be worried about your safety."

"You won't have to. The biggest danger that lurks on Michigan Avenue is the temptation to spend too much money. You don't have to come along if you don't want to."

"Be reasonable."

"I am. I refuse to go to the police until I have a chance to search the Barnes's home tomorrow night," Eden insisted. "And in the meantime, I refuse to sit idly around when I have a great idea."

"Shopping is a great idea?"

"If we go to the right stores." Amused by his exasperated expression, she laughed away some of her building tension. "The ones where Kim Quinlan might have bought her clothes. Those designer labels are found in a few expensive stores and exclusive boutiques in this area. Chances are our model didn't shop alone. I hope you have those professional photographs of her in your briefcase. I can show them to the saleswomen, while I look for something to wear Friday night."

"I happen to have everything I've saved about this case in here, but forget about shopping and forget about Friday night." Chick's face wore a no-nonsense expression. "You're not going."

Eden clenched her jaw and took a ragged breath. "Try to stop me. As you yourself said, new clothes and a change of hairstyle and color, and no one will recognize me."

The instant she waltzed away, he was on his feet. He grabbed her arm. Gently. He was always gentle with her, even when he was at his most threatening.

"Eden, be sensible. This game has gone on far too long, as it is. It almost got you killed last night."

Firmly resisting the sincerity of his tone, she pulled herself free. "This isn't a game, Chick, and I'm aware of the stakes. If Nickles had been caught, I would feel differently. I doubt it would have taken much to make him squeal. But there's no one to back up my story, and I don't have real proof—just bits and pieces. If I go to the police and they don't believe me, then what? Barnes would get away with murder, and everything I've gone through would be for nothing."

"But then he wouldn't be able to touch you, without the authorities knowing you were telling the truth."

Eden laughed. "Small consolation, if I'm dead. Oh, I'm sure he would make it look like an accident. Barnes isn't stupid." She restated her position. "Unless I have something more substantial to give them, I'm not going to the police."

"And what if we don't learn anything new today and don't find anything in Barnes's home tomorrow night?" he asked. "Then what?"

She couldn't face that possibility. "We'll find something. We have to."

A nurses' aide chose that moment to enter the room, wheeling a chair in front of her. "Transportation out of here," she announced. "Ready to get going?"

Eden was more than ready, not to mention being weary of arguing. Her throat felt raw, and her head had begun to pound again. Docilely she got into the chair, while Chick collected the garment bag and the shoes she'd been wearing the night before. He carried them in one hand, his briefcase in the other.

A short while later they were out on the street, and Eden was gearing herself up to go another round. To her surprise, Chick didn't challenge her.

Instead he indicated her garment bag and shoes. "So what am I supposed to do with these things, while we shop until you drop?"

"Trash them." She indicated a nearby wire can bearing the legend Keep Our City Clean.

Chick did as she suggested, and they began the short trek to Michigan Avenue in silence.

By noon they'd been to Saks, Neiman Marcus, I. Magnin and Bloomingdale's. Eden had neither found a new outfit for Friday night, nor had she gotten useful information about the dead woman.

A saleslady in Bloomingdale's had recognized the photo Eden had shown her of Kim Quinlan, but she'd been wary and closemouthed. Eden hoped to learn whether a man had accompanied Quinlan on her shopping excursions—or even better, obtain confirmation of who had paid the bills. She didn't get that far. She never had a chance to take out the newspaper clipping Chick had saved—the picture of Barnes and his supporters at the fund-raiser. The saleslady merely suggested that Eden talk to the department manager, who happened to be out to lunch.

"I shouldn't have used the picture," Eden admitted later, as she and Chick wandered through the Avenue Atrium, glancing into boutique windows as they made their way to ground level.

"Maybe we should talk to restaurant staffs—"

"I doubt Stanton Barnes would be so indiscreet as to take his mistress to a place where his wife or political adversaries might dine."

"You're right. The same probably goes for the stores."

"No, I'm sure that saleswoman knew something."

"You have a zealous gleam in your eyes," Chick said as they descended another level on an escalator. "I'm sure you intend to hit every store in the area before we're through, and I'm already starving. Why don't you pick a nice restaurant, where we can relax and have a leisurely lunch?"

Eden had the distinct feeling that he was trying to sidetrack her. But she was hungry, as well. "I think we'd better settle on a fast-food place."

"Why?"

"Because restaurants around here are incredibly expensive. What are you planning to use for money? My credit cards?"

"If you insist," Chick said, giving her an arch look. "Unless, of course, you think I might embarrass you by using the wrong fork."

"At least you know that there *is* more than one fork to choose from," she returned sarcastically. Why did she always get the feeling he thought her a snob?

She compromised by leading him to a place in the basement of the Michigan Avenue building. Hoppers had a dining-car atmosphere, and a toy train circled the restaurant. Luckily they were able to get a table without a wait.

Chick gave his order to the waitress, who obviously found him attractive. Eden studied him intently. She couldn't figure out how he could move so smoothly between two different worlds. She didn't have long to wonder, however, because Chick expressed concern for her health. Eden dutifully took the pills she'd brought from the hospital and listened to his well-meaning argument to give up and leave the case to the pros.

An hour later, over Chick's protests, they were sleuthing once more.

This time, however, Eden planned on checking out a couple of boutiques on Oak Street. She remembered seeing price tags complete with store names on several articles of clothing in the Quinlan woman's apartment. And this time she wasn't going to flash around a photograph that would raise suspicions, although she put both it and the newspaper clipping into her purse, in case her idea didn't work.

Leading Chick into Maxie's, Eden made him help her pick out several incredibly expensive outfits under the watchful eyes of an eager young saleswoman. Then, leaving him to stew out front, she tried on each of them at a leisurely pace, checking herself with a critical eye in the floor-length mirrors of the luxurious dressing room. The saleswoman fluttered around and told her each outfit looked better on her than the last.

Eden *was* pleased with the indigo jumpsuit and jacket, its sleeves trimmed in yellow and indigo sequins to match the *bustier* top.

"That outfit was made for you," the saleswoman assured her.

Eden considered. A week ago she would never have chosen something so bright, so daring. But wearing Maisie's garish clothing had made her face a side of herself she hadn't been aware of. She enjoyed being colorful once in a while.

"I do love it," she admitted as she put her plan to work. "Kim told me Maxie's had the most wonderful designs, and she wasn't exaggerating one bit."

"Kim?" the young woman asked, puzzled.

"Yes, Kim Quinlan. Surely you remember her. Model-type. Masses of gorgeous auburn hair. Always wears a special necklace—a circle and cross with a yellow diamond."

The saleswoman brightened. "Oh, yes. I know who you're talking about. The name didn't register, because I haven't worked here all that long. But I remember your friend was in, oh, maybe two weeks ago."

"Lucky girl." Eden pretended to admire herself in the mirror while she watched the saleswoman. "Kim told me Stanton was going to take her shopping again."

"She *was* with a man," the saleswoman agreed.

"Was he tall and distinguished?" Eden asked, trying not to betray her excitement. "Dark hair with silver wings at the temples?"

The saleswoman frowned. "I can't say that I remember."

"Really." Eden tried not to let her disappointment show. She hesitated only a second before opening her purse and pulling out the clipping. "Do you recognize him now?" she asked.

After studying the newspaper photo for a second, the saleswoman nodded, though she gave Eden a peculiar look. "Yes, of course. This is the man."

Eden's eyes widened as she realized that the woman was pointing not to Stanton Barnes, but to Wylie Decker.

Chapter Twelve

Eden waited until they were out on the street and walking toward Michigan Avenue to tell Chick about her conversation with the saleswoman. He didn't seem too surprised.

"Decker's name was on the lease of Kim Quinlan's apartment," he reminded her, taking the package with the indigo and yellow outfit from her hands.

"What if we've come to the wrong conclusion? What if she was Decker's mistress?"

"That's possible, but it's more likely that Decker played nursemaid for his boss. Why would Barnes involve himself with dumping the body, if she belonged to his manager?"

"Okay, just assume for the moment that she was Decker's woman, and he was the one who killed her. A death connected to anyone in Barnes's campaign would have spelled disaster, once the press got hold of it. Or maybe she found out something about Barnes that made her dangerous. Either way, he would have been protecting his own interests." Realizing they had arrived at the intersection, she said, "Let's grab a taxi."

Chick signaled an empty cab, which pulled over to the curb. He opened the door for Eden and climbed in beside her.

"Where to?" the driver asked.

"Navy Pier," Eden said.

"What?" Chick lowered his voice. "Eden, I'm not letting you go back there. It's not safe." He leaned forward. "Driver, Marriott Hotel."

"Don't listen to him," Eden insisted. "Navy Pier." She tried reasoning with Chick. "I'll be fine for the moment. Since Nickles took off, he's no longer a threat."

"What if he's still around, merely in hiding for the moment? Nothing's to say he won't be back to try again. Or what if...our friend...sends someone else to finish the job? Marriott Hotel," he repeated firmly.

If Nickles did return, Eden wanted to be there. She was sure that carnies had their own code of justice. And after what Nickles had tried to do to her the night before, she was ready to take on the skinny little man herself. Then they could deliver him to the police. Nickles was her main reason, she assured herself, though others presented themselves, whether she wanted to face them or not.

"Navy Pier," she insisted. "We'll talk about it when we get there."

The vehicle slowed with a screech of tires. The driver pulled his taxi to the curb and turned to face them. "You folks just settle where you want to go, okay? Remember the meter's runnin'."

"I know where I'm going," Eden stubbornly maintained.

The look on Chick's face told her he would accept defeat, but he didn't like it one bit.

"Navy Pier," he echoed.

Muttering to himself under his breath, the driver turned the vehicle back into traffic.

A few minutes later they left the taxi at the back lot. Several people were around to greet them, ask about Eden's recovery and wish her well. While all appeared surprised by their unusual clothing, no one commented. Chick dragged Eden back to the truck, telling the others she needed to rest.

"I meant that," he said as he helped her inside.

"I am tired. Maybe I'll lie down for a bit after I change."

"But first let's have that talk about why you wouldn't go to a hotel."

She grabbed Maisie's purple and yellow outfit and stepped behind a pile of boxes that she'd been using as a dressing screen. At that moment it would protect her from Chick's disturbing gaze.

"Maybe I just didn't want to be alone," she finally admitted.

That was only part of the truth. Actually, Eden didn't want to leave Chick any sooner than necessary. The mere thought of separation made her head throb and her throat feel scratchy.

"Who said you had to be alone? Maybe I was planning on staying."

The teasing half promise made her heart beat faster, but she didn't turn to face him. She reached for the zipper and began undoing it. She could hear him disrobing, as well. Tempted to turn around and look over the top of the boxes, she stopped herself.

"Come on, Chick, I know you have to make a living. After everything else you've done for me, I wouldn't want you to be out of money as well."

"And you wanted to be here, if Nickles showed his ratty little face. Admit it."

"That, too."

"Eden, promise me you're not going to do anything foolish."

"Like what?" she asked, dropping the dress to her waist.

"Like walking around alone at night. Promise me that you'll let me make sure you're safe. If I can't be with you every moment, then I'll see that someone else is."

"It sounds as if you care," she said softly, remembering he'd said the same to her.

As the dress puddled around her feet, she turned to face Chick, and found him staring at her. He'd walked around the boxes. She was wearing only a wispy camisole and high-rise hip huggers trimmed with lace. Even though they were both half-shadowed by the gloom, she could tell his eyes were dark and smoldering; the knowledge lighted something inside her that burned with equal intensity.

"I do care," Chick returned. "Very much."

He didn't reach for her, as she thought he might. He was so close and yet so distant, as if he were looking at a work of art, something to admire, yet not to touch. As if he were afraid to touch her.

She should pick up the blouse and put it on, before he got the idea that she wanted more than his eyes on her. But she didn't move a muscle, merely staring at him in return. His feet and chest were bare. He'd slipped on his jeans, but hadn't yet zipped them up. Hair crinkled within the soft V of the material, making her think he wasn't wearing underwear. Or maybe he was wearing that leopard print bikini again. Her breath caught in her throat at the memory.

"Tell me to finish getting dressed and I will," he said.

But Eden didn't say a word. She met his gaze, silently challenging him to tell her what he wanted. Without hearing the words, she knew. She wanted the same.

She'd wanted him since the first time they'd kissed.

Desire clouded issues such as potential and whether or not they were right for each other...at least for the moment. Desire made her unable to think of a single reason why she shouldn't be with the man who had helped her so selflessly, the man who had saved her life, the man about whom she cared more than she wanted to admit.

How could she be certain that they would ever have another opportunity to be together?

Chick spoke with action rather than words. Moving closer, he reached out and stroked her hair away from her face. He brushed his mouth across her lips; his hand moved down the slope of her shoulder and across her chest to settle on her silk-covered breast. His fingers curled around one nipple. Eden's insides uncurled and blossomed.

He kissed her temples, making even that a sensual experience. "How's your head?" he whispered.

"I wasn't thinking about my head." She rubbed her cheek against his and felt the beginnings of beard stubble. The rough texture excited her. She could imagine his cheek scraping across her breasts. Over her belly. "Other things need to be soothed more."

His heat laved her, even though his chest wasn't quite touching her. The space between them grew as he backed away. Eden was startled and disappointed, until he found her hand and drew her with him, around the boxes to the makeshift mattress on the floor. He slid out of his jeans and kicked them to the side, then pulled her onto the bedding.

The surroundings intruded for a moment, reminding Eden of why she was in the back of a carnival truck. But she quickly banished them to a darkened corner of her soul. She wouldn't let thoughts of a murderer or a dead woman come between them, and spoil what might be the only chance she had to show Chick how much she loved him.

CHICK WATCHED Eden sleep for a while, but he couldn't stand doing so for any length of time. He would get too depressed. Dressing, he reluctantly left the truck to phone his father. But first he would make sure that the woman he loved was protected. He spotted the Hurleys, relaxing on portable patio chairs in front of their trailer. Their backs were to him, and they were deep in conversation.

As if she sensed his presence, Zelda looked around at him before he'd gotten halfway across the lot. Her gray eyes lighted with a knowing smile.

"Chick, come sit with us for a spell. Abe, get him another chair."

"No, that's all right." Chick placed a restraining hand on her husband's shoulder, before Abe could rise. "I have a favor I would like to ask of you."

Zelda's brows raised. "Eden?"

"Is there anything you don't know?"

"There's much in the universe that I don't know," the fortune-teller stated matter-of-factly. "But I still know *you* well enough, and when it comes to a certain woman, you're an open book."

Hearing the satisfaction in her tone, not pleased that his emotions were quite so easy to read, Chick grimaced. He might feel differently, if Eden were as open. But even while they'd made love, she hadn't done more than murmur phrases that heated his blood to boiling point. Even with encouragement, even during her most vulnerable moment, she hadn't been able—or hadn't seen fit—to express her feelings.

Then again, who was to say she was more than sexually attracted to him?

Chuckling, Abe reached for his wife's hand. "Zelda's a die-hard romantic."

Not wanting the elderly couple to feel sorry for him, Chick didn't comment. But, as if she knew what he was thinking, the smile faded from Zelda's eyes.

"What's wrong?"

He couldn't tell her what was really bugging him—that he was certain Eden had given in to desire in a moment of weakness, that he was afraid that once she awakened, she would regret having made love with him.

Instead he said, "I was hoping you wouldn't mind helping me keep an eye on Eden."

Abe was visibly alarmed. "You don't think there'll be more trouble?"

"I hope not, but I would rather be safe than sorry. Eden is sleeping, and I have to make a phone call," Chick explained. "And then I have to open the joint."

"You don't need to work undercover anymore," Abe told him. "You got our man, and we haven't even properly thanked you yet."

"No thanks are necessary. And I didn't really get your man. If Nickles hadn't attacked Eden—"

"Stop fussing," Zelda interrupted. "You don't know how much your caring means to us."

"The caring is mutual."

No, for the Hurleys he didn't have to pretend to be a carny anymore, Chick thought; only for himself. Running the joint would keep him distracted, would keep him from wondering how much longer he had, before Eden was out of his life for good.

"I might as well finish out the week," he said, trying to sound casual. "You don't have another jointee to replace me, do you?"

"No one could replace you." Abe pushed himself up out of the chair and clapped Chick's shoulder. "And you know we would do anything to help you."

"You're family," Zelda added, "the child we never had. We were lucky that fate brought you to us when you ran away from home."

Chick stooped to hug her. "I'm the lucky one. I have two sets of parents, when most people only have one. So you won't mind keeping an eye on the truck entrance until Eden wakens?"

"For as long as necessary," she promised gravely. "We'll take turns if we have to, but we won't leave her alone."

"No one would dare try anything with one of us around."

With Abe's reassurance, Chick set off for the pay phone at the bus stop. There he placed a call to Lovett Promotions and asked his father's secretary to put him right through.

"Well, son, I didn't expect to hear from you until Monday," Samuel Lovett said in greeting. "Tired of playing at being a teenager already?"

Chick forced down his irritation. While he and his father had mended their fences, Samuel had never quite forgotten his son's defection, nor his choice of life-style. Two weeks before, when Chick had explained how he was going to spend his time off, he'd been afraid his father would suffer a stroke.

"I haven't been playing at anything," Chick said patiently. "As a matter of fact, I've run into a little trouble, and I need your help."

"Trouble?" Samuel thundered. "I knew it! Should I contact Matthew?"

"No lawyer. Not yet, anyway. I need information." Chick looked around, but no one was within hearing distance. "Get me everything you can on a man named Wylie Decker. He's Stanton Barnes's campaign manager."

"I've heard of Decker, but what does he have to do with you? What in tarnation is going on?"

"I can't explain now. You'll have to trust me until I can see you in person. This may be important, a matter of life or death."

"What do you want me to find out?"

"Anything you can about the man, about his past. Especially anything negative. I want to know if Wylie Decker's clean, and I want to know tonight."

"Tonight? These things take time."

But his father had even more contacts than he did, including a friend in the public relations department of the city police. And Wylie Decker was in promotions himself, if in a different area.

"If anyone can do it, you can."

"Think you can soften the old man with a little flattery?" Samuel demanded.

"I don't know. Is it working?"

"It's working. I'll clear my calendar and see what I can do."

"Thanks. I knew I could count on you. And, Father..." Chick felt the warmth of embarrassment creep up his neck. "If I haven't told you lately...I love you."

A worried silence was followed by a gruff, "You watch your back, son. Call me at home at ten. And if you get your mother, don't you go frightening her."

"I'll be okay. I'll talk to you later."

Chick hung up, hoping he wasn't alarming his father for nothing. He couldn't be sure that Wylie Decker was guilty of anything, but it wouldn't hurt to delve into the campaign manager's past.

She was locked in the doniker... banging on the door and breathing in deadly fumes... choking and dizzy. Someone was out there...someone trying to kill her...someone trying to help. Help! Someone open this door, please! *She was unable to hold on....*

THE NIGHTMARE startled Eden out of sleep into a claustrophobic darkness. Her heart was beating like mad, and her hands were shaking and sweaty. As she tried to see, she came more fully awake and remembered that she was inside the truck.

Perspiration beaded her skin under the sheet. Skin? She was nude, she'd made love with Chick. She grew calmer. Tender memories chased away the remnants of the bad dream. She remembered every detail of their lovemaking—all glorious. If she still had any reservations about committing herself to the man, she was determined to ignore them.

Where was he, anyway?

And why was she in the dark, alone?

Eden groped around until she found the battery-operated clock near the bedding. She'd been sleeping for hours. Other than sensing a lingering shadow of unease, she was refreshed, vital, almost as good as new.

And she wanted to see Chick as soon as possible.

She scrambled to her knees and turned on the lamp. Finding her underwear was a more difficult task. Chick had thrown the camisole in one direction, the hip huggers in another. It took her a while to find them.

After slipping into her undergarments, Eden dressed in the purple and yellow outfit as she'd set out to do earlier. Within minutes she was ready to leave the truck. When she opened the back, she wasn't surprised that dusk was about to give way to night. What did surprise her was that Madam Zelda was sitting a few yards away like some exotic guard. She was wearing a long red dress, and an embroidered black shawl cradled her plump shoulders.

"Hi, what are you doing here?" Eden eased herself to the ground and locked the back of the truck.

"Chick asked Abe and me to help keep you safe."

Eden squirmed under the woman's unnerving scrutiny. "Thanks. Normally I wouldn't agree that I needed guarding, but after last night..." She let her words trail off, as fragments of the dream intruded once more. And then she noticed that Madam Zelda was looking at her with a disturbing intensity. "I'm going to go find Chick. Thanks again."

"Wait!" Madam Zelda rose before she could get away. "I'll walk with you. I might as well open up the fortune-telling booth, though business will be slow tonight."

"Tomorrow's Friday. You'll have plenty of business then," Eden assured her. Knowing what little money carnies made, she felt guilty at depriving Madam Zelda of a night's pay. But if she offered to make restitution, she was sure the elderly woman would be insulted.

Keeping her thoughts to herself, Eden went on, Madam Zelda gliding next to her like a silent shadow. They were approaching the Ferris wheel when the elderly woman grasped her arm, the hold light yet firm. Eden stopped. The moving colored lights of the ride flickered over Zelda's serious features which, as usual, were distorted by too much makeup.

"Eden, you are still in jeopardy."

That sense of unease whispered through her again. "You've seen Nickles?" Was that why she'd had the dream—was her subconscious warning her? Eden looked around as if to spot him. "Where?"

"No. I haven't seen Nickles. I feel...a great threat." Muttering to herself, the fortune-teller held out flattened hands and ran her palms around Eden's body without touching her. "Danger surrounds you and tries to penetrate your aura. You must be very careful."

Trying not to be alarmed, Eden insisted, "I am being careful."

Even as she told herself that the older woman was merely being overdramatic, as was befitting to her carnival guise, Eden couldn't stop the rapid pounding of her heart. She had to confront a truth. She'd thought she wanted to come face-to-face with the shifty-eyed man, but she'd been wrong. The very idea frightened her.

"I sense you are afraid... and yet... you do not believe me," Madam Zelda said in a tone that made the hair crawl on the back of Eden's neck. "Free yourself from conventional reasoning, loosen your imagination and listen to your instincts. You have it within you to find the solution you need to save yourself."

Her heart pounding even more rapidly, Eden forced a smile. "Sure. I'll do that."

Madam Zelda shook her head and moved forward. "You are anxious to see Chick."

Eden started, then realized the woman didn't have to read fortunes to know that. Any fool could see that she was in love with the man.

Any fool but Chick himself.

She followed Madam Zelda to the One-Ball joint with a sense of anticipation. Then her feelings were tempered by Chick's pleasant if distant attitude. At first she assumed he was tired, but gradually Eden came to realize that he was purposely withdrawn, as if her presence somehow made him uncomfortable. And when he did talk to her about something personal, she was even less pleased.

"I've had second thoughts about tomorrow."

"What kind of second thoughts?" Eden asked.

"I'll go to the political gathering at Barnes's home... alone."

"Like hell you will. You can't search the place and watch your own back."

"Look," Chick said, his tone reasonable—and impersonal. "I thought about it and decided I don't need you."

Eden stared at Chick, trying to read meaning into his words. Was he saying that he didn't need her to help to search Barnes's home—or that he didn't need *her*, period? Hurt blossomed in her, making her defiant.

"If you don't take me, I'll find a way to get in myself." She was bluffing, but Chick couldn't know that. "Maybe Dennis was invited."

She could tell he was instantly angry and ready for an argument, but a whole family stopped at the booth and wanted to play. So the battle was postponed for the time being. Then customer followed customer, keeping Chick marginally occupied and giving Eden too much time to think.

Only a few hours ago, she'd been secure in his arms; now she only felt awkward.

She was glad when Maisie dropped by to chat.

"Hey, baby, looking good. But you shouldn't let that man of yours put you to work so soon."

Chick—her man? Was he? Eden wasn't sure of anything at the moment. "I've just been hanging around."

"You look tired."

Actually she was still upset, something she couldn't tell her friend. "Well, it's getting late. We'll pack it in soon."

The guy who'd been trying his hand at the booth finally gave up, and Chick checked his watch. "Good timing, Maisie. I have to make an important phone call. Would you mind staying with Eden until I get back?"

"No problem."

"Who are you calling at this time of night?" Eden whispered as Chick passed her.

"My father," was his only explanation; he left the booth without looking back.

Eden stared after him, anger adding to her hurt.

"That man is acting mighty peculiar," Maisie noted. "You two have a fight or something?"

"If we did, I was unconscious when it happened."

As her anger mounted, Eden determined to get to the bottom of Chick's peculiar behavior the moment she got him alone.

CHICK CARRIED guilt on his shoulders like a burden as he strode away from the One-Ball joint. He was sure that Eden had no idea that he himself was upset—not by anything she had done, but by his own doubts about having a future together. If only she could have told him she loved him... Then he wanted to protect her, wanted to stop her from putting herself into further danger, and so had made up his mind that he would go to the Barnes's home alone. She hadn't taken the news well, and Chick castigated himself for not explaining. Eden was feeling rejected, and he couldn't blame her.

The carnival crowd was already beginning to thin, and people were getting onto buses when he arrived at the pay phone. He slipped a quarter into the slot and dialed his parents' number. His father answered.

"It's me," Chick said. "What did you find out?"

"Is that any way to greet your father? No hello. No amenities."

"Sorry," Chick said, trying not to let impatience creep into his voice. He had enough on his mind and didn't need a hassle with his father on top of everything else. "Like I said, this is important, and I appreciate your help."

"Mmm. You wouldn't want to tell me what's going on?"

"I told you I couldn't. Not now. So what did you get on Wylie Decker?"

Chick thought that his father was going to press him, but Samuel did a surprising turnabout.

"This is not common knowledge, but Decker was a kid from the slums. Seems he had a short temper—and a reputation as a disturbing influence in the classroom. He was thrown out of high school three times for fighting. He broke one kid's arm, loosened another's teeth. Somehow he made it through to graduation and eventually through college."

"He liked to fight when he was a teenager? That's it?"

"Not quite. Decker got himself in hot water early in his career, but I couldn't get the specifics on such short notice. All I know is that fraud of some kind was involved. Sorry I couldn't do better."

"You did great. Thanks."

Chick's mind was already spinning ahead. So Decker had a violent temper and had been caught in a fraud of some kind. Maybe Eden had been on to something.

"Son, when am I going to hear from you again?" Samuel asked, interrupting his thoughts.

"Soon. A couple of days."

"I'll be worrying until I hear from you."

The men closed the conversation without undue sentimentality, and Chick started back across the carnival grounds. He didn't see Frank until the other man stepped directly in front of him and grabbed his arm.

"Chick, you've got to come with me right now. You won't believe this!"

"Believe what?"

But Frank was already running down the midway toward the back lot. Alarmed, Chick jogged to keep up. Several carnies awaited them around the donikers. Had they found something more to do with the attempt on Eden's life? Chick slowed as he realized they were clustered in front of the Jake. The door was open.

Sheets stepped forward and handed him a flashlight. "Inside."

Chick swept the interior of the small room, but didn't see anything but a few spiders. "What?"

Frank pressed down Chick's hand, so that the light shone into the tank below. "In there."

The sight that met his eyes made Chick's gorge rise.

It couldn't be . . . but it was.

Now what the hell was he supposed to tell Eden?

Chapter Thirteen

"How long can a phone call take?" Eden muttered, more to herself than to Maisie. The longer she waited, the more resentful she grew. After what they'd shared, she'd expected Chick to be more considerate and tender with her than he'd been in the past week. Instead he'd begun by making her angry and now was doing a first-rate job of avoiding her. "Holding you up like this is ridiculous."

Maisie gave her a worried look. "No hurry. Felix can mind the store without me."

"But he shouldn't have to." She decided to close the joint, even though the carnival had another hour to run. It was a slow night, anyway. If Chick complained about losing money, she'd be happy to make restitution out of her own pocket. "I'm locking up."

"Gonna make a bad situation worse, huh?"

"Chick Lovett is going to get a piece of my mind, no matter what." Eden threw milk bottles and balls into a box. "I'm just taking charge of my own life."

"Ooh, you got it bad, don't you?"

"Got what?"

"Lovesickness."

"It's a sickness, all right," Eden agreed sarcastically, setting another empty box on the counter. "One I can do without."

"Uh-uh. None of us can do without it. God saw to that. Why'd you think he had Noah gather up pairs of animals for the Ark?"

"So the humans could be entertained?" Despite herself, Eden smiled. She began packing the stuffed animals. "That's what I'll do when this is over—I'll get myself a pair of Dobermans and train them to keep Chick Lovett away from me."

"Baby, you got me confused. When *what* is over?"

"Nothing," Eden muttered, avoiding her friend's inquisitive gaze. The way Chick was acting, she probably wouldn't need the Dobermans.

"Don't 'nothing' me. I kept my questions to myself, ever since you showed up looking like something the cat dragged in, but I got bad feelings. What happened last night—that wasn't over no carny money, was it?"

"I don't know what you're talking about." Heat crept up Eden's neck, and she avoided looking directly at Maisie as she put the last stuffed toy into its box. "There. Now I can leave, and Chick can get the merchandise back to the truck himself. Assuming he ever shows."

No sooner had Eden exited the booth, than Ginger walked up to Maisie and herself.

"Eden, gotta message for you from your old man." The orange-haired woman took a long drag on her ever-present cigarette and began hacking. "Damn things ain't worth the paper they're rolled in."

"What does Chick want?" Eden asked.

"Meet him over on the north walkway of the pier. Alone. Something important."

"Is that it?"

Ginger's eyes glinted with hostility. "Hey, I'm just passing on the message. You're supposed to know what it means."

"Yeah, thanks."

As she walked away, Ginger hacked some more. "Damn cigarettes."

Eden was puzzled. The last she knew, Chick had gone to make an important phone call to his father. But what did that have to do with her situation? Although she was tempted to ignore him, to let him see how indifference felt, she couldn't. She had to know what he'd learned...and she could give him that piece of her mind!

"Listen, Maisie, thanks for keeping me company."

"Maybe I better come with you."

"He said alone. I'll see you later."

Before Maisie could argue, Eden took off, walking as fast as she could manage. Still angry with Chick, she left the carnival grounds and crossed the street to Navy Pier, all the while trying to figure out what she was going to say to him. Fighting the pedestrian traffic kept her distracted. She was the only person going toward the pier. Everyone else was headed for home. While the carnival was merely winding down, the other features of Septemberfest had already closed. The sound stages had emptied, as had the exhibition halls.

At the entrance to Navy Pier, she veered toward the north walk. It was deserted. She wondered what Chick could have found, and tried to decide if she should let him tell her before or after she gave him what-for.

The moonless night was black but for the glowing skyline, silent but for the sound of water lapping against the pier. The walkway was unlit. All she could see was shadows...none human. The click of her heels softly echoed off the north pier wall, reminding her just how vulnerable she was. A thrill of uncertainty washed through her. Maybe she should have listened to Maisie. But Chick had said to come alone. Odd, when he'd made it clear earlier that he wanted her to be with someone at all times.

Then again, who knew where his head was, considering the way he'd been acting...?

Barely a fourth of the way down the mile-long pier, Eden stopped. How far was she supposed to go? And why had Chick wanted to meet her here? She hadn't been thinking straight herself.

"Chick?" she called uneasily.

No answer.

She stood for a moment, trying to decide what to do. Her pulse surged, and her mouth went dry. Madam Zelda's warning insinuated itself into her thoughts. Danger trying to penetrate her aura—could it be possible that the woman had foreseen the events of this night?

The fortune-teller had told her to free herself from conventional reasoning, to loosen her imagination and listen to her instincts.

Instinct told Eden she'd done a very foolish thing, and her imagination drew graphic and frightening pictures of what could happen to her. She wasn't stupid, but upset as she'd been by Chick's erratic behavior and eager for any crumb of knowledge that would help indict Barnes, she clearly hadn't been thinking when she'd set off alone.

Keeping her back to the lakeside rail, listening for any strange sound, watching the shadows for the slightest movement, she retraced her steps as silently as possible.

What had she let herself in for?

Had a trap been set? Had Nickles returned?

Nickles? She remembered the dream...the voice... someone trying to help....

Eden concentrated. She'd heard the voice before, while she'd been trying to keep from passing out in the doniker. A voice that challenged. A voice that belonged to the shifty-eyed carny. Startled by the memory, Eden realized that Nickles had been trying to save her, not kill her.

Then why had he disappeared?

No sooner had she asked herself the question than she heard a muffled footfall. The furtive sound whispered along the semienclosed corridor and scraped up Eden's spine. Not knowing from which direction the sound came, she turned and ran, unable to miss the immediate slap of leather soles on concrete, a sound that seemed to surround her.

If not Nickles, then who?

The last thing Eden thought about, before strong fingers laced themselves around her arm and jerked her to a teeth-jarring stop, was that Ginger Tresnick had given her a counterfeit message.

CHICK FILLED IN the Hurleys on the situation before calling the police. The charade would be over within the hour. The body would be recovered from the doniker, and then Eden would have to come clean. Everything would be in the hands of the authorities, and he could only pray that they would believe her story and offer the kind of protection he couldn't. Dreading the upcoming scene he was sure to have with her, he returned to the joint—to find it closed and Eden gone.

"What the hell?"

Unpleasantly surprised, he stood and stared for a moment, then reasoned that she was probably at the Washingtons' joint with Maisie. He set off to find her, but his relief was short-lived.

Maisie was handing a prize to a customer; the woman he loved was nowhere to be seen.

"Where's Eden?" he asked.

"You tell me. She went to meet you outside the North Pier." Her face expressed her concern. "I thought you wanted her to be with someone at all times, after what happened last night."

"I did—do." He had a bad feeling about this. "Why did she want to meet me at the pier?"

Maisie's eyes grew round. "I don't understand. Ginger said she had a message from you—and that you wanted Eden to meet you there. Alone."

"I didn't send Eden any message."

The feeling of being out of control intensified.

"What's going on?" she demanded.

But Chick was already jogging across the carnival grounds, which were still alive with light and sound. He slowed as he passed Ginger and Gator's joint. Unlike the others surrounding it, their booth was locked. He raced out the gate and across the street, his mind moving as quickly as his legs.

Why would Ginger have told Eden to meet him? Because Gator had put her up to it?

If he'd been wrong about Nickles being the one trying to kill her, he might have been wrong about the thefts, as well. The money could have been planted to throw them off the track, so that they would relax and let down their guard. He remembered that Eden had seen Gator around the truck, the day his cash box had been emptied.

But why the hell would Eden have been foolish enough to believe he wanted her to set off alone, when he'd been so concerned about her safety?

Chick didn't have time to contemplate the answer; a woman's scream pierced the air.

FROM THE SIZE of him, Eden knew her attacker couldn't possibly be Gator. One of Barnes's men, then? She couldn't be certain, pinned as she was against his broad chest, her neck caught in a muscular vise. Her single scream was effectively cut off. She was barely able to breathe... but that was undoubtedly the point.

Why didn't he get it over with?

His mistake.

It took Eden's entire reserve of internal strength not to panic. Keeping her head, she harnessed the adrenaline that coursed through her body to the power of her anger. She focused on her right side, on the knee she raised, on the quadriceps that jerked downward and propelled her slim high heel with such force that it would have gone right through his instep, if he'd been barefoot.

"Aa-ghhh!"

The damage done through the material of his shoe was enough to make him loosen his hold. Eden used the momentary slack to effect her next move. Even as she thought she heard a noise down the pier, she dug her sharp nails into the bare arm that was pinned under her breasts, dug until she felt a wet warmth ooze over her fingertips.

"You witch!"

Her heart pounding with fear and hope, Eden elbowed her captor in the stomach, pulled free and ran for her life. More curses flew from his mouth. He was mere yards behind her and limping. Their pounding footsteps resonated along the walkway almost in tandem, countered by an echo that made it sound as if another person were running toward them.

Eden looked at the rail, wondered if she had enough leeway to vault over the thing and dive into the lake to escape her attacker. Knowing she had nothing to lose, she slowed and reached for the barrier. Her pursuer was closer than she'd hoped. Lunging for her and grabbing her arm again, he didn't give her the opportunity to make the attempt.

She spun around, fingers clawing at his face.

"Oh, no, you don't."

He caught her free wrist and squeezed, making her cry out and unclench her fingers.

Eden's eyes had adjusted to the dark; with the aid of the city's glow behind her, she could just make him out. What was more important, she recognized her attacker's voice. This was not one of the thugs who worked for Barnes. This was someone Eden would never have suspected... someone she had trusted.

"Jud Nystrom!"

The patch, the born peacemaker, was the one intent on killing her!

"Why make this harder on yourself, Eden? I like you. I don't want to see you suffer. Stop struggling!"

"Don't hold your breath." She spoke through gritted teeth. She was trying to free her mind from pain as she did her best to free her body from his hold. Fighting him was getting her nothing but more bruises, yet she refused to let up. "You fixed the safety in the AstroRocket and then tried to poison me in the doniker. And you killed Nickles, didn't you? That's why he just disappeared."

"He should have kept his nose to himself."

As Eden tried to stomp him a second time, he twisted away and threatened her.

"You try that again, and I'm going to break your leg before I put you out of your misery."

"Don't think I'm going to make your murdering me easy, so you can just get it over with and walk away before your conscience interferes."

"He doesn't have a conscience," said another voice nearby that was at once fierce and slightly winded.

"Chick!" Eden cried out.

Jud whipped her around, so that he could face his approaching adversary.

"Don't come any closer, Chickie—"

"Or what, Jud? You're planning on killing Eden anyway, aren't you? So what do I have to lose? You can't get us both at the same time."

Sensing Jud's predicament, Eden took advantage of the situation. "You're having enough trouble with me, a mere woman," she taunted, renewing her physical battle with him so that his attention was divided. "Do you actually think you'll get by Chick?"

"She's right, you know," Chick said. His voice was even closer now. "I can't let you go, anyway. Nickles might have been a poor excuse for a human being, but he didn't deserve to die. You're not going to get away with his murder."

Startled by the accusation, Eden stopped fighting Jud and glanced over her shoulder, but she couldn't see more than Chick's silhouette, and not even that, when he flipped on a light that dazed her.

As if he were also blinded, her captor shifted to one side. He hesitated, then let Eden go and made a run for it. Chick flew by her and within seconds connected with Jud's back. He threw the bigger man off balance. As they both went down and rolled over the walkway, so did the flashlight.

Eden made a dive for it, but the light rolled under the rail and into the lake with a splash. Now she couldn't even look for a weapon.

But she still had her heels!

As Jud's greater bulk and strength won out, and he landed on top of Chick, she removed her shoes and gripped them tightly, one in each hand. Fury guiding her, she whacked the golden-haired giant on the head, just as he was about to deliver his first punch. The crack of heel on skull echoed around them.

"A-a-ah. What the hell?"

Jud whipped an arm out at her, but Eden danced out of reach. "Face it, Jud, you're no match for us both."

He ignored her, and the struggle on the ground continued; punches were thrown and were followed by groans of pain. The men went rolling again, depriving Eden of the opportunity to strike another blow without the risk of hitting Chick. Anxiety made her heart pound and her ears ring, so she did the only thing that was left to her.

She screamed—loudly—at the top of her lungs.

"Fire! Help! Fire!"

She kept on screaming, praying that someone would hear.

Before she knew what was happening, the fight on the ground broke up and a large bulk headed toward her. Jud. He grazed her with his shoulder and sent her flying into the wall before he took off. All the breath either screamed or temporarily knocked out of her, she sat on the ground, dazed.

"Eden, are you all right?"

"Uh-huh." She shook her head to clear it.

"Fire?" Chick asked as he gripped her behind the elbows and helped her to her feet.

"That's what they say to yell...if you want someone to respond." She was simultaneously gulping air and putting on her shoes. "Go after him. I'll be right...behind you." When she felt him hesitate, she pushed at him and yelled, "Go!"

Chick took off like a shot, while Eden jogged after him at a slower pace. She took deep breaths and called up reserves she hadn't known she possessed. She was going to see this through. Jud wasn't going to get away, not when he could put the finger on Kim Quinlan's murderer.

CHICK CHASED Jud back to the carnival, which was winding down but still open. Keeping the golden head in sight was easy; it rose above all the others, many of which were heading away from the rides toward the exit. He dodged a large family that spread across the midway, and for a moment almost lost his quarry, as the patch zigzagged between rides and booths.

"What's going on?" Sheets called as Chick passed the AstroRocket.

"Jud murdered Nickles and tried to kill Eden."

He ran on relentlessly, unwilling to stop for anything. He couldn't let the man who'd almost killed Eden get away.

As they neared the Ferris wheel, he closed the gap when Jud was stopped, trying to get through a line of tightly knit couples. Probably under the impression that he was trying to butt in, several of the guys pushed at him. Not caring about giving a murderer a fair chance, Chick clenched his two fists together and brought them down savagely on the back of Jud's neck. The larger man dropped to his knees and shook his head.

"Hey, what's going on?" a teenage girl asked.

One of the guys added, "Why'd you do that?"

But Chick was too busy avoiding Jud's backhanded swing to answer. Then he kicked out at the other man's side, hoping to wind him, but Jud whipped around, caught him by the ankle and twisted. Chick went down hard, the other man flew to his feet and headed for the narrow passageway between the ticket booth and the Ferris wheel itself.

Chick scrambled after him with energy born of desperation. Should the patch get to his van on the back lot, that would be the last they'd see of him. Then as if out of nowhere, a handful of angry-looking carnies appeared, headed by Sheets and blocking Jud's escape route.

He reversed direction...right into Chick's closed fist. The patch stumbled backward toward the ride but caught himself before he fell. Chick advanced, avoided Jud's right and struck out again, successfully connecting with the larger man's jaw. Jud stumbled, and this time fell back against the Ferris wheel, which had been stopped to let on new passengers.

"Give up, you bastard!" Chick yelled. He pointed to the other carnies, who had closed in menacingly. "They all know you murdered Nickles and tried to kill Eden, as well. You're done for."

"Give up yourself!"

Jud tried to rush forward. When his limbs flailed, but he didn't budge, his horrified expression was almost comical. The Ferris wheel began to turn, Jud with it. His clothes were caught on a moving part. He grabbed at a steel girder to steady himself as the wheel lifted his feet from the ground. Chick made a single attempt to pull him free, but Jud kicked him in the chest. Stunned and winded from the impact, he stood back and watched the ride make its circle, Jud dangling from the spoke like a puppet gone out of control.

An excited murmur spread through the crowd, and the numbers grew around the ride.

"Want me to stop him at the top and let the guy sweat it out?" yelled the jock at the controls.

"Yeah!" Gator yelled back. "In memory of Nickles Vogel."

"It would serve him right, after what he did to Eden on my AstroRocket," Sheets added.

One part of Chick agreed, while another—his conscience—couldn't let the man risk taking a fall that would kill him. No matter what his crime, Jud's fate was for a judge and jury to decide.

"Keep it moving and let him down," Chick said. "He's not going to get away from us." Not with all the carnies hot for revenge, he thought.

Besides, if Jud were dead, he couldn't point a finger at *another* murderer—the one who'd killed Kim Quinlan.

Before the wheel peaked, the patch got a toehold and managed to rip his clothing free. He steadied himself, then began scrambling along a spoke that took him toward a bucket holding three kids.

"Hey, what's he doing?" someone asked, as the wheel continued to turn, bringing Jud earthward.

"That bastard is going to take one of those kids hostage," Sheets said. "Count on it."

"Oh, no, he isn't." Intent on going after the man himself, Chick started forward, intending to mount the ride. He was caught from behind and held fast by a couple of the carnies.

"You ain't goin' nowhere, Chick. He ain't hurtin' no more innocent people."

"We'll do this our way."

The last words came from the jock, who manipulated the controls so that the ride stopped and started with a jerk. Jud lost his balance and grabbed at the girder as his feet went out from under him. More than halfway to the ground, he tried to find another foothold, but the jock repeated the trick.

With a bellow, Jud came flying down.

Chapter Fourteen

The crowd's screams reverberating in her head, Eden watched Jud fall from the ride, bounce off the roof of the ticket booth with a loud crack and hit the ground. The patch lay still, his limbs twisted grotesquely like those of a shattered puppet. She squeezed her eyes shut so that she wouldn't have to look, but Eden could still see him in her mind.

Three dead. Kim Quinlan, Nickles Vogel, and now Jud Nystrom.

She should be glad about Jud, she supposed, but she wasn't. She couldn't celebrate a man's death. Only someone's idea of a perverse joke had kept her alive this long. Did fate have something worse in store for her? God help her, she was going to be sick.

Trying to force her way out of the crowd, she was stopped by people who were closing ranks to get a better look. Police sirens wailed nearby. Her head suddenly felt light, and she fought a rising panic.

She was certain she was hearing things when Chick called out, "He's not dead."

"Are you sure?" someone asked.

"Positive. I've got a pulse—a weak one."

Taking a deep breath, Eden whipped around and stepped forward to see for herself. She didn't stop until she was standing between Ginger and Frank, close enough to see the slight rise and fall of Jud's massive chest. Her eyes met Chick's. Hesitantly she smiled at him. He rose from his position beside the patch's head and stepped across the prone form to take her into his arms.

"Thanks for coming to the rescue," she said.

"Why in the world did you go out there alone in the first place?"

"Ginger said you wanted me to meet you."

They both looked at the orange-haired woman, whose defenses were already up. "Jud asked me to pass along your message because he had something to do." She hugged her thin body. "How was I supposed to know he was lying? I didn't mean no harm."

"I believe you," Eden said. "And I wasn't thinking straight." She felt the same uncertainty about Chick that she'd experienced earlier. "But I'm thinking straight now." She moved out of his embrace and tugged at his arm. "Let's get out of here while we can."

"We can't . . . the police have already arrived."

Eden could hear them clearing a path through the crowd. "That's exactly why we have to go," she whispered. "They can't find us here."

Chick grabbed her wrist and held on with a gentle firmness. "We're not going anywhere. Too much has happened. We found Nickles tonight—floating in the tank below the Jake."

Her stomach turned over once more, and Eden fought the wave of nausea again. She knew that staying was the right thing to do, but Jud wasn't in any condition to talk, and nothing guaranteed that he would do so, even if he fully recovered. She was afraid the police wouldn't believe her story, and that by warning Barnes through them, she'd be giving up her last chance to connect the murder to him. Chick wanted her to tell them everything, to leave the investigation to the authorities. She could sense it. Her love and gratitude were tempered with disappointment.

"Listen, Toots, before the police get involved, I want you to know I was sorry about being short with you earlier." He stroked her cheek, and his eyes meshed with hers. "This afternoon meant a lot to me, but I've got to face facts, don't I? I'm not the kind of man you need in your life. I was already regretting losing you, I guess."

His heartfelt speech touched her, even as he said what she'd been fearing. He didn't think they stood a chance together. They *were* from two different worlds, Eden reminded herself. He was more realistic than she. He saw how impossible a relationship between them would be.

"I wish..."

But Eden's thoughts were cut off by the arrival of the police, who'd finally broken through the crowd.

Chick handled the situation. He told them about Nickles and about the multiple attempts on Eden's life. But when their questions began, he called a halt and said they would be glad to answer everything—but only to the officer in charge of the investigation.

His name was Isaac Jackson. They didn't have the opportunity to be alone with him until they'd been in the hospital waiting room for more than two hours. Jud still hadn't regained consciousness by the time Lieutenant Jackson escorted them to a private conference room that he'd arranged for their use.

While she and Chick sat at a long table, Jackson stood, a speedy metabolism keeping the slight man pacing and beads of sweat popping out on his dark forehead.

"You have me alone," Jackson said. "So start talking."

Chick squeezed Eden's hand before speaking. "We'd like some assurance that what we say doesn't go outside this room, not until we're ready."

Jackson stopped at the other end of the conference table and leaned on his hands. "Mr. Lovett, you are not operating from a position of power here. I could lock you up for obstructing justice."

"Not if we can't give you facts, Lieutenant," Eden said, hoping she wasn't kidding herself. "I could tell you Jud was trying to kill me because he thought I knew he was ripping off the other carnies. I doubt that a judge would hold us responsible for keeping any other rumors and speculations to ourselves."

"Speculations? You wanted to see me alone to present some cockamamy theory?"

"Something like that."

Jackson made as if he were about to leave but stopped in his tracks when Chick said, "But a theory that could earn you some gold stars, if we're correct."

He turned back toward them and perched on the corner of the table. "All right. I'm listening."

Now that the time had come, Eden had to choke out the words. "What if someone was walking home from work—say a week ago—and thought she saw a body being dumped onto a boat in the Chicago River?"

"This someone is a woman?"

"Theoretically," she said quickly.

"Yes, of course. Go on."

"So this theoretical witness recognizes one of the men—a very famous person—and is spotted in return." Eden's pulse was picking up. Jackson's dark, staring eyes were unnerving. "What if she runs, tries to call the police to report what she's seen, but is treated like a crank? And what if she goes into hiding and tries to make a connection between the dead woman and the man she recognized? Would the police be receptive to her continuing her own investigation?"

"Of course not. As a good citizen and *smart woman*, she should turn over any information she has and let the police handle the case."

"But what if there have been three murder attempts on her already, and the well-known man in question may have the police—some of them," she amended, "in his pocket?"

"That's a strong and very disturbing allegation, Miss Payne. I hope you can back it up."

"We're talking theory, Lieutenant Jackson, remember?"

Their eyes met. Eden lifted her chin and was unable to conceal her growing hostility. She had nothing to hide. She was a victim, not a criminal.

"A theory," he echoed. "You wouldn't be able to attach a name to the dead woman, would you?"

"Kim Quinlan."

His closed features remained set. "Now why am I not surprised? And what about giving a name to this famous man? Theoretically speaking, that is."

Eden hesitated and looked at Chick. He was leaving the decision to her, but he indicated his support. His expression encouraging, he took both of her hands in his.

"Stanton Barnes." The words flew from her lips, almost before she had time to think them.

Jackson popped off the table. "Are you out of your mind, accusing the attorney general of murder?"

"But I saw him, and he sent his bodyguards after me...."

Realizing that the admission had been a mistake, Eden shrank back into her seat. Her heart threatened to pound right through her chest. The lieutenant was staring at her as if he were trying to decide whether or not to believe her.

So when he asked, "Have you found any proof, anything substantial?" she sagged in relief.

Eden took a deep breath and started from the beginning. Anything she left out, Chick added, including some information about Wylie Decker's not so pure background that Chick said he'd only learned hours before. When they finished, Jackson spoke thoughtfully.

"I should arrest you. Breaking and entering, concealing evidence..."

"A man like Stanton Barnes can't be allowed to take the governor's seat," Chick insisted. "Even if he's innocent of killing the Quinlan woman himself, he's an accessory, guilty of a cover-up to protect his campaign. That's what's important here."

"We're so close," Eden added. She shifted under Jackson's unreadable stare. Did he believe them or not? She had to take a chance that he wouldn't let a killer go free. "There must be some kind of physical evidence linking Barnes directly to the woman. That's why we have to carry through with our plan for tomorrow night. Chick got an invitation to Barnes's home."

"But it's out of the question, Miss Payne. As a deputized officer of the law, I cannot condone—"

"You have no choice," Chick interrupted. "Not unless you plan to arrest us for spinning tall tales."

Jackson's jaw clenched at Chick's challenge. But there was also a gleam of admiration in his dark eyes. Eden could tell he was warring with himself—human being versus cop.

"Well, the past half hour has been quite interesting," the lieutenant finally said, circling the end of the table where they sat. "Too bad you couldn't give me anything concrete to explain why Jud Nystrom tried to kill you, or I would have to include those facts in my report."

She was almost afraid to ask. "Then we're free to go?"

Jackson shrugged his shoulders and pulled a face. "I don't have any reason to hold you. But don't be surprised if we run into each other in the very near future."

Like tomorrow night, Eden thought. "Thank you."

He nodded. "You say that now. I hope you won't have reason to curse me before this is over."

Chick stood and helped Eden out of her chair. He offered the detective his hand. "You won't regret this, Lieutenant."

Jackson shook his head and stared as intently at Chick as he had at Eden earlier. "I sincerely hope not, Mr. Lovett. See that I don't have reason to."

As they left the room, a thrill shot through Eden. They had one more chance to nail Barnes. She didn't want to think about the consequences if they didn't succeed.

THE HOURS after their meeting with Isaac Jackson had been divided between the hospital—Jud still hadn't come around by the time they left—and a room in one of the lovely small Gold Coast hotels.

As Eden sat in a salon chair the next afternoon and distractedly studied a mirrored wall while her hair was cut, colored and waved into a more radical if fashionable style than she usually wore, she had plenty of time to think.

She thought about Chick. He'd left her in that room alone while he went back to the Hurley-Gurley to make a report to the others and to pick up their things. He'd chosen not to waken her when he returned, but had slept in the second bed instead. And he'd disappeared while she'd been in the shower this morning.

Chick had left a note—he had to prepare for their final performance, and she was to stay out of trouble until he returned—but the message hadn't made up for his absence. It had merely aggravated her feelings of loneliness and resentment.

"What do you think?" the hair designer asked, offering Eden a hand mirror so that she could check all angles.

The stylish redhead that stared back at Eden looked only vaguely familiar. A bit awed that she didn't feel the least bit uncomfortable with the new look, she touched the left side of her hair, which was waved close to her head, whereas the right side curled dramatically around her face from forehead to chin. She'd even had her eyebrows dyed to match.

"Very chic. You've transformed me from a career woman into something of a bombshell."

"We try to please."

Eden smiled up at the hair designer, but inside she felt brittle. She was losing Chick and she didn't know what to do about it. No matter how many times she reminded herself that even he'd admitted they weren't meant to be together, something inside her protested that they were both wrong.

"I guess I'm ready for that manicure and face make-over. You're sure this Valentina is the best?"

"Even your boyfriend won't recognize you."

What would be the difference? That morning, Chick had looked right through her.

Aloud, Eden said, "Good." Maybe she was wrong. Maybe he would sit up and take notice.

When she walked out of the salon an hour later onto Michigan Avenue, Eden was sure her own parents wouldn't recognize her if they came face-to-face. Pencil and shadow had widened and rounded her eyes, blush had defined cheekbones she hadn't known she possessed, and liner and lipstick had given a sensual fullness to her mouth. Her purse contained samples of everything that would allow her to freshen the makeup job later.

In the meantime she had no desire to go back to the hotel and stare at the television set or out the window, until it was time to leave for the gathering. So instead she wandered along the Avenue and window-shopped, sometimes stopping in a store and making a purchase that she couldn't really afford on her salary. Anything to keep her mind off Chick.

Glancing through racks of designer clothing reminded her of Kim Quinlan's apartment, however, and the jumble she'd found there. Clothing that didn't go together. Furniture that didn't go together. All chosen by a farm girl who'd come to the big city...for what purpose? To be a model? No, that photographer Paco Jones had given Kim the idea. To find a rich lover? How had she chosen Stanton Barnes or Wylie Decker?

The more she thought about it, the more Eden became involved in trying to figure out Kim Quinlan herself—who she was, what had made her tick, why she'd been killed. The dead woman was still the key to the mystery.

What if she'd come from the farm with a specific goal in mind? To make a better life for herself? With some commodity other than her looks that she could count on?

Blackmail?

Had Kim Quinlan come to Chicago possessing the knowledge that had led to her death?

Knowledge about what? About whom? Decker? Barnes? His wife Rhonda? If only she could grasp whatever it was she'd missed during the meeting with Beatrice Hollingsworth, but that scrap of knowledge still eluded her. The thoughts went round and round in her head until Eden could no longer sort them out.

When the store she was in closed for the evening, she strolled back to her hotel. Chick would probably be waiting. Anxious. Ready to pop his cork. She was rather looking forward to him losing his cool. So she was disappointed when she entered the room and realized that he was in the shower.

Throwing her purchases onto the bed, Eden made her way to the closet where she stripped off her dress, took the indigo and yellow outfit from its hanger and stepped into the jumpsuit. The shower stopped, and she could hear Chick moving around. She laid the jacket over a chair and searched the packages for the earrings she'd just bought. When the bathroom door opened, she glanced over her shoulder and tried not to look at the hard male body that was concealed only by a towel tucked low on the hips.

"Just in time," she said, trying not to let the sight affect her. "I need your help."

"So I can see." His voice was husky, his eyes glued to the expanse of her back that was exposed by the open garment.

"I'm not used to the longer nails yet." She straightened and waved the crimson tips at him.

His brows shot up as he took in the make-over. A low whistle escaped him, and he moved closer. "The nails aren't all that's different. Barnes will never even guess who he's entertaining."

"I'm surprised you noticed." Tossing her copper curls, Eden turned her back on Chick and steeled herself against his touch; he straightened the material along her spine before zipping it. "You hardly looked at me this morning."

"Maybe that's because I got my fill watching you while you slept."

"You didn't."

"Okay, I didn't."

She whipped around. "Stop that."

"What? I thought you wanted me to zip you."

"The pretended indifference. You said you cared...."

Sliding his palm along her cheek, he wrapped his fingers in the curls and pulled her closer. "I do."

Her sequin-covered breasts were pressed against his naked chest, and her heart was beating in double time. "So why do you keep trying to hide it? What are you afraid of?"

"For a smart woman you can be awfully dumb sometimes," he said. He was perfectly serious.

Eden was certain that Chick was about to kiss her. He was staring at her lips as if they were a gourmet meal and he a starving man. Her breathing grew short and shallow, and excitement spiraled within her.

Then he let her go, and the excitement plummeted. "We'd better get ready. We don't want to keep our number one suspect waiting... whoever he may be."

Chick moved toward the bathroom. Disappointment making her want to scream at his back, Eden stared after him until he whipped the towel from his hips to dry his hair. One flash of his naked tush, and she was searching her packages for the damn earrings. How could he do this to her? Why wasn't he reassuring her that they would work things out? They couldn't just go their separate ways as if nothing had ever happened between them.

One thing at a time.

Eden focused on the evening ahead. If she let him get to her, Chick would drive her crazy, and she needed all of her faculties to survive the most important—and undoubtedly most dangerous—night of her life.

EDEN WAS driving him crazy. With her sexy disguise distracting him, Chick was having a difficult time keeping his mind on the purpose of the charade. As they were about to enter the Barnes mansion, she draped herself over his shoulder and whispered, "I don't care if we are from two different worlds. I'm in love with you, and you're not going to get rid of me when this is over."

Chick was ready to choke her.

A fine time to tell him. He'd been waiting to hear those words for days, and now, when he couldn't do a thing about it, she'd finally made her declaration. He followed her inside and introduced her as his assistant Edie to Stanton Barnes, who in turn presented his wife Rhonda and campaign manager Wylie Decker, as well as several other guests.

"My husband tells me you're eager to help him win this campaign," Rhonda said, resplendent in a bronze cocktail dress, clearly cut low to show off not only her full breasts, but a topaz and diamond necklace that trailed between them.

"I have a few ideas to impress you," Chick told her without false modesty. "Your husband agreed tonight would be the perfect time to pitch them."

The still-lovely blonde glanced up at her spouse. "How clever of you, my pet, but could that wait a bit? It would seem rude to ignore our guests too early in the evening."

"Of course." Barnes nodded to Chick, but his eyes were on Eden when he said, "Later?"

Chick realized that Rhonda was staring at Eden, as well. From her intense expression, he thought the blonde might be afraid of the competition for her husband's favors. He wrapped an arm firmly around Eden's shoulders.

"Business can wait a while longer," he agreed, and dragged Eden away to the buffet table.

"Did you see the way his wife was glaring at me?" Eden whispered as she dipped a spoon into the bowl of caviar and spread it onto a cracker. "And the way Barnes himself gave me the once-over was creepy." She shuddered within the half circle of Chick's arm and popped the cracker into her mouth.

"You need a drink to steady you."

"I didn't eat all day. A drink will make me tipsy."

"A sip then. Just think of this as a prop." He swiped two glasses of champagne from the tray of a passing waiter and handed her one. "To tonight."

"Whatever it might bring," Eden added, and Chick thought that the words somehow held promise above and beyond their present exercise in madness.

As he sipped from his glass, he looked around, trying to spot any ringers. If Isaac Jackson had a plant in the crowd, the undercover cop was a good one. Chick could have sworn they were on their own. According to their plan, he and Eden worked the party, investigated every corner of the open rooms on the first floor and played their roles of political allies to the hilt. By ten, the place was bursting at the seams with people.

"Don't you think we should get down to business?" Eden suggested quietly as they wandered from one room to another.

"I'll see what I can do to create that diversion."

Chick reluctantly left her side and shouldered his way through the mob toward Stanton Barnes, who stood in the parlor, the center of a small group of men that included his campaign manager.

Chick glanced back at Eden and tried to quell the worry that had made him consider ditching the plan. Nothing was going to happen to her with all these people around. She'd wandered into the hallway and was picking up a drink from a tray on a table. With seeming innocence, she looked around as if trying to spot a friend, when in reality he knew she was making sure that she wasn't being observed.

"Stanton," Chick called out heartily to make sure all straying eyes would alight on him. "Why don't we go over those ideas I prepared for you?"

"Good timing," Barnes responded. "You can bounce them off my associates and see what they think."

Chick joined the group and drew on the strategies he'd carefully spent the afternoon planning. The associates seemed receptive—all but one. Wylie Decker studied him silently without comment. A few minutes later Decker stalked off to the kitchen, giving Chick the opportunity to glance surreptitiously toward the stairs.

Eden had disappeared.

WITH THE EXCUSE of looking for an empty powder room in mind in case she got caught, Eden crossed the landing and entered the upstairs hall as casually as she could. Her pulse was racing, and the resulting sensation was a mixture of anticipation and dread. She checked three doors before she found the master bedroom. Once inside, she realized that she was in a three-room suite.

She remembered thinking it ironic that as a teenager, Rhonda had been a femme fatale, but as a woman she couldn't keep her husband's interest. Separate bedrooms—here was proof of sorts. Now, if only she could find the kind of proof she needed to make the charade she'd gone through worthwhile.

Eden searched Barnes's room—every drawer, every shelf, every nook and cranny. Nothing. Not a clue that he'd ever known Kim Quinlan existed. She went through the bathroom, checking everything down to the names on the prescription bottles in the medicine cabinet. No luck. Now what? People were milling through every downstairs room, including the study. She couldn't exactly ask them to leave so that she could conduct a search.

Might Barnes have an upstairs office, as well? Or did Wylie Decker have some kind of quarters in the place?

About to leave the suite to find out, she hesitated. She hadn't yet checked Rhonda's bedroom.

Figuring that it was really a waste of time, Eden entered the softly appointed and luxurious room. A sense of sadness washed through her as she remembered the girl in the high school yearbook who'd had an innocent quality about her. That innocent had turned into the savvy, somewhat bloodless woman she'd met downstairs. What had happened to change Rhonda Lawrence? Men? Or women like Beatrice Hollingsworth?

She went through Rhonda's things with little enthusiasm. Poking through another woman's underwear was abhorrent to her. Maybe it would be to anyone, Eden thought, remembering the scene with Chick after he'd searched her wallet—he'd said it wasn't as if he'd gone through her underwear drawers. Knowing that she shouldn't be thinking about Chick now, she shoved a silk teddy back into its pile and concentrated on her search.

None of the other drawers were any more revealing, not even the one laden with expensive costume jewelry. Undoubtedly Rhonda kept her real jewels in a safe. Where? In the closet? Eden opened the louvered doors. Inside, every garment was encased in a zipped plastic bag. Every pair of shoes lay in a separate compartment. All neat, nothing out of place, nothing startling, she was thinking as she made a cursory search through the shelves of sweaters.

Then she felt something long, thin and hard in the folds of a beaded cream-colored angora....

Eden's hand trembled as she pulled a jeweler's case free of the garment.

Why wasn't it in the drawer with Rhonda's costume jewelry? Or, judging from the richness of the deep gold velvet covering, in the safe? Her artificial nails looking like splashes of blood against the velvet, Eden lifted the lid.

There against a rich brown background lay the symbol for woman, molded in heavy gold. A yellow diamond winked up at her from its setting at the juncture of circle and cross. The heavy chain was broken, the clasp missing.

The missing link.

"It's beautiful, isn't it, Edie? Or would you prefer to be called Eden?"

Turning to face Rhonda Barnes, Eden slipped out of the closet as the older woman shut the bedroom door.

"Yes, beautiful." It was all coming together now. Eden held up the box. "You were wearing this necklace in your high school yearbook photo. And Kim Quinlan wore it in all her professional photos." She paused only a beat, then asked, "You're not denying you know her, are you?"

Something like panic filled Rhonda's eyes, yet she sounded very cool when she answered. "No, denying it would be foolish."

"And you don't seem like a foolish woman. I've been assuming Kim Quinlan was your husband's mistress. Then I had doubts and wondered if Wylie Decker hadn't been the man in her life. But your giving her that necklace under either circumstance would be unbelievable." Eden was certain she was on the right track when she said, "You're the connection, Rhonda."

"You're bluffing. You don't know anything."

"Ah, but you just admitted it." Eden lifted the necklace from its case and took a few steps toward the foot of the bed. "Now why would a woman give a twenty-five-year-old necklace to another woman...unless they were related?" Eyes wide, she stopped and intently studied Rhonda's face. Was it possible? "Kim was your daughter, wasn't she?"

Eden knew she'd hit home, but Rhonda quickly covered her vulnerable expression.

"Yes, Kim was my daughter. Her father gave that necklace to me for my sixteenth birthday, when we made love." Staring at the necklace, Rhonda frowned. "No, I must be honest. Had sex. He never loved me. He told everyone and never wanted to be with me again."

"When you gained weight in your junior year, it wasn't from overeating. I'm surprised the gossip mongers didn't know all about your pregnancy."

"That's because I was sent off to Wisconsin for the summer to have my child." Rhonda's eyes met Eden's with a touch of sadness. "My father wouldn't let me keep Kim. He gave her away to the Quinlans, the couple who took care of me during those last few months. They were rewarded well, given the deed to our summer home, a dairy farm, in return for which they vowed to keep my secret."

"But Kim found out."

"She found scrapbooks with newspaper articles and pictures of me and her real grandparents in the attic. Kim had my mother's hair and eyes...and my necklace. I visited her only once, on her first birthday. That's when I left it with her."

"So Kim came to Chicago to find you."

"To get what she considered was her due," Rhonda corrected, her laugh harsh, bitter. "Not that she put it that way, not at first. To think I felt something for her, even after all those years. I was a fool."

"Your daughter blackmailed you?"

"Not exactly. She played on my guilt, convinced me that she had been deprived of her rightful place in the world, deprived of parents who really loved her. She said she could never claim to be a Lawrence, but she wanted to be near me."

"And she took you for everything she could get," Eden said. The strange mixture they'd found in Kim's apartment now made sense. The young woman had cared nothing for taste or style, only for how much compensation she could squeeze out of her natural mother.

"Ironic, isn't it, how genes tell?" Rhonda murmured. "Kim was every bit as power hungry and determined as I am."

"Is that a reason to kill your own daughter?"

Eyes welling with unshed tears, Rhonda said, "It was an accident. She wasn't supposed to come to the fund-raiser. People were already asking questions. But Kim did exactly as she pleased. I pulled her into an emergency stairwell to talk sense into her. All her resentment—no, hatred—came pouring out. She said I owed her, that I had abandoned her and that I would never stop paying. She was horrid to me. I was sorry I ever gave her anything, starting with the necklacc."

"So you took it back."

The woman nodded. "Kim lost her balance and fell. By the time I got to her, she was dead, her neck broken from connecting with a step edge, I imagine. Stanton and Wylie covered for me—for the campaign," she amended "—by disposing of the body, while I covered for them at the party."

"If it was an accident, why didn't you just make out a police report?"

Rhonda glanced at the nightstand. Eden thought the other woman was looking for a tissue, until she reached for the drawer handle. Reacting immediately, Eden tried to stop her, but she wasn't fast enough. The glint of blue metal looked deadly in the other woman's hand.

"Stay right there, Eden." Rhonda trained the gun on her. "Reporting Kim's unfortunate death would have ruined everything. Stanton's chances at the governor's seat, possibly at the White House. I worked too hard to let her ruin that for me. And no one outside of our small circle knew. No one but you," she said, her demeanor bloodless once more. "I had to fix things. Stanton and Wylie had some fool idea that you could be bought. But I was afraid the price for your silence would be too high."

"*You're* the one who hired Jud Nystrom to kill me?" Eden had been hoping that Rhonda wasn't quite as amoral and ruthless as Beatrice Hollingsworth had claimed.

"Not personally," Rhonda answered, "although that might have been interesting. I hear the young man in question is quite good-looking. No, my dear, Lou Farentino, one of our bodyguards, takes care of...many things for me. He hired Nystrom."

Wondering if she could distract Rhonda long enough to get the gun away from her, Eden asked, "Why did you keep the necklace, when it could connect you to the dead woman?"

The older woman lifted the talisman from its box. "I take it out every day to remind myself what a fool I was to think that maternal love could equal the desire for power." She opened the door and jerked the gun toward the hallway. "Now it's time to tidy up the mess I made."

To free her hands, Eden tossed the box onto the bed. "Where are we going?"

"The attic. Distance, added to the noise of the party downstairs, should muffle the sound of a gunshot...."

Hoping someone would be in the hall, Eden was disappointed. She was on her own. But Rhonda was too close, the shot too easy even for someone who had never handled a weapon before, and Eden figured Rhonda had.

She kept moving, kept waiting for her opportunity. One didn't seem to be forthcoming. And she couldn't expect help, if Chick didn't realize she was in trouble. Rhonda must have slipped from the party by a back way. At the bottom of the attic stairs, she hesitated. An unyielding hardness in the small of her back prodded her forward.

Eden went cold at the touch; her legs moved as if of their own volition.

They were almost at the top of the stairs before she grew desperate enough to try anything. Once in the attic, she was a dead woman. Gathering her courage, she pretended to trip and cried out as she went down onto her knees.

"Get up!" Rhonda commanded.

"I can't... my leg..."

"You won't have to worry about your leg much longer."

Eden thought her ploy had been for naught, until Rhonda took a handful of her yellow jacket and tried to force her to move.

The gun was no longer touching her.

Realizing that this was her chance, Eden swung around and went for Rhonda's right hand. The gun discharged, but the older woman refused to let go. And then her gun hand was whipped right out of Eden's grip as both shifted and Eden fell against Rhonda, making her lose her balance.

Her voice shrill with terror, her expression a mask of shock, her gun hand leading backward, Rhonda Barnes went sailing down the stairs.

The gun discharged again, and distant screams sounded from below. Feet trampled the stairs from first floor to second, and Rhonda landed in a heap, her limbs twisted, her head cocked at a grotesque angle. Shaking, Eden descended the attic stairs one at a time, her eyes glued to the woman who was not moving and did not seem to be breathing.

Stanton Barnes got to his wife first. Chick was directly behind. Another man, one she didn't recognize, pushed them both out of the way. As Chick drew her down the last few steps and wrapped a comforting arm around her, the stranger felt for Rhonda's pulse.

"She's dead. Her neck's been broken."

And in her open palm lay a chain and talisman, a symbol that had followed Rhonda Lawrence Barnes not only through her life, but to her death as well.

MORNING FOUND EDEN in a fit of pique as she sat in the passenger seat of her roommate's car. In the back was her largest suitcase filled with jeans, T-shirts and sweaters.

"I don't blame you for being mad," Taffy said as they breezed down Grand Avenue. "Just when you need the guy, he ups and disappears. I'd kill him before I kissed him."

"I'll take that under consideration."

She could hardly blame Chick for disappearing from the police station the way he had. No doubt she'd scared him off with her unexpected declaration the night before. Either that, or he figured he was being noble.

Taffy ran a red light, saying, "I still can't believe something so weird and dangerous happened to someone I know."

"Well, it's over now."

Not only was Rhonda dead, but Barnes, Decker and the two bodyguards were in custody and would be prosecuted as accessories to a crime. Jud had finally come around and was willing to talk to cut a deal, so that his sentence would be lightened. Eden knew that she would learn to deal with Rhonda's death in time, just as she would the other bad memories. She wasn't going to blame herself for something that had started twenty-five years ago.

"Pat yourself on the back for bringing me to see Beatrice."

"A stroke of genius," the little blonde admitted without false modesty. She swerved around the corner and pulled up to the curb along the back lot of the carnival. Hugging Eden, she asked, "How long will you be gone?"

"Until the Hurley-Gurley goes to the barn for winter... I hope."

"Well, if it doesn't work out..."

Sharing one last hug, Eden jumped out of the car, grabbed her suitcase and took off. She wriggled through an opening in the snow fence and headed straight for the Hurleys' trailer, where half the carnies were gathered, Chick in their midst.

Eden shoved her way in until she was face-to-face with the man she loved. She couldn't read his expression. Ignoring the impulse to kill him first as Taffy had suggested, she threw down the suitcase, wrapped her arms around Chick's neck and kissed him for all she was worth. He seemed startled for a moment, then kissed her back, until she was breathless and the jointees and jocks surrounding them were laughing and shouting encouragement.

When Chick lifted his head, he wore a silly grin. "I love you, too."

"Good, because you're stuck with me," she said, indicating the suitcase. "I've run away from home to join the carnival."

"Gee, that's too bad, because I was just saying goodbye to everyone."

"What do you mean?" Eden looked around in confusion, but saw the truth of his statement written on the carnies' faces. "Are you sure you would be happy in a sucker job?"

"It is rough sometimes," he admitted.

"Is?" She peered at him suspiciously and wondered exactly how dumb she was about to feel. "You already have a sucker job, right? And you've had one for a long time, until last week, when you decided to play detective for the Hurleys."

"When I took a little vacation from the family business," he added.

"Just what is this family business?'

Chick pulled a face, but Abe clapped him on the shoulder and said, "Tell her, son. Might as well get it over with as quick as possible."

"Lovett Promotions," Chick said. "Father and I have been full partners for the past several years."

"You've what?" Eden's eyes grew wide in shock. "But you told me you ran away from home rather than go into the family business."

"I did. I never said I didn't change my mind. If my father hadn't pushed so hard, I might have made this decision years sooner."

Even though Eden had suspected that there was more to Chick than he'd been letting on, she hadn't been prepared for this. Feeling equally foolish and angry, she shoved at his chest, but to no avail.

"Let me go, you liar!"

Chick refused to free her. "Now, wait a minute, I never lied to you—"

"You just conveniently forgot to tell me anything current about yourself, right? Even though I asked. Anytime I got too close, you changed the subject. *I'm* the one who had reason to keep secrets, not you."

"He had his reasons, as well," Zelda said in Chick's defense.

"He was doing it for Zelda and me," Abe added. "We were afraid we'd lose the Hurley-Gurley, if someone didn't help us catch the thief. He had to pretend to be a carny again."

"So you see," Chick said reasonably, still holding her fast, "I couldn't tell you who and what I was without betraying the Hurleys' trust."

"That's an excuse," Eden retorted, though her initial anger was wearing off. "I wouldn't have repeated anything you told me in confidence."

"Besides, I wanted a woman who loved *me*, not an image," Chick continued. "You were so bothered by what you thought I did for a living that you didn't see the real man."

She gave him another ineffectual push. "Well, I thought I'd found him until a few minutes ago."

"You have found him. And that means I've found what I wanted, too."

Eden narrowed her eyes.

"C'mon, baby, tell the man you love him," Maisie said from the shelter of Felix's arm.

"Yeah, tell me you love me, like you did last night."

Eden's lips twitched. As much as she wanted to give him a hard time, she couldn't help herself. "I love you." Grabbing his shirtfront, she pulled herself closer and whispered, "Hey, Chickie-Loves-It . . . want to be my old man?"

"You bet, Toots."

This time Chick initiated the kissing—to a round of applause. Eden vaguely heard Zelda saying something about their auras merging and multiplying. . . .